THE

INDIGO

PRESS

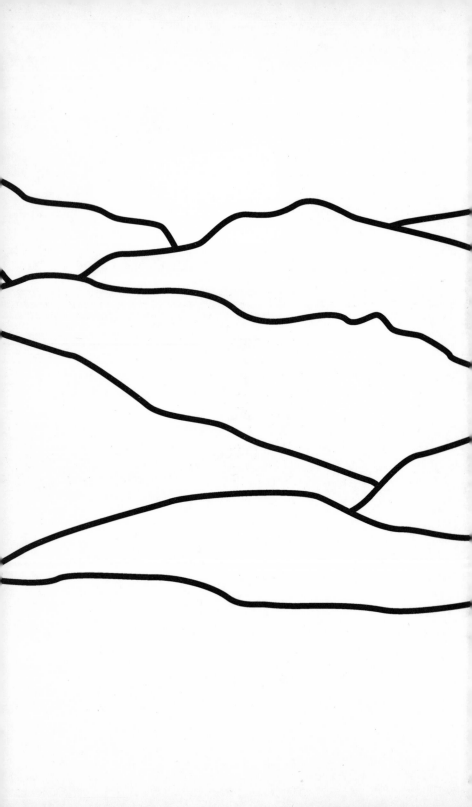

THE CLOTHESLINE
SWING

THE

INDIGO

PRESS

THE CLOTHESLINE SWING

AHMAD DANNY RAMADAN

THE

INDIGO

PRESS

THE INDIGO PRESS
50 Albemarle Street
London W1S 4BD
www.theindigopress.com

The Indigo Press Publishing Limited Reg. No. 10995574
Registered Office: Wellesley House, Duke of Wellington Avenue
Royal Arsenal, London SE18 6SS

This is a work of fiction. Names, characters, places, and incidents are
products of the author's imagination or are used fictitiously and are not to be
construed as real. Any resemblance to actual events, locales, organizations,
or persons, living or dead, is entirely coincidental.

ISBN 978-1-9996833-6-8
eBook ISBN 978-1-911648-01-7

Design by www.salu.io
Typeset in Goudy Old Style by www.beyondwhitespace.com
Printed and bound in Great Britain
by TJ International, Padstow

MIX
Paper from
responsible sources
FSC® C013056

To the children of Damascus,
This is what I did with my heartache . . .
What about yours?

He sank into the rocking chair, the same one in which Rebecca had sat during the early days of the house to give embroidery lessons, and in which Amaranta had played Chinese checkers with Colonel Gerineldo Márquez, and in which Amaranta Ursula had sewn the tiny clothing for the child, and in that flash of lucidity he became aware that he was unable to bear in his soul the crushing weight of so much past.

Gabriel García Márquez

PROLOGUE

The sweetest kisses are the ones we share in forbidden places. The kiss I stole from you in the back of a dark cab roaming Damascus, while the driver was cursing at checkpoints and wars; the time I pulled you back into the changing room in H&M in Beirut and printed my lips upon yours; the one you gave me as we hid in the depth of tall grass on Vancouver's Wreck Beach.

For us, most places were forbidden. We met in war-torn Damascus and moved in together in sectarian Beirut before we finally arrived in Canada. For us, foreplay wasn't sweet touches and soft kisses; it was finding a place where no police officers, angry parents or nosy neighbours would find us. It was closing the curtains tight and hushing each other's gasps of pleasure, giving us a false feeling of privacy and security that did not last long.

If I had to pick, the sweetest of all of our kisses was our very first. I cherish that kiss, for it was the first blossom in a garden of forbidden fruits we planted together. It was the spurt that broke through the soil of our mundane lives and taught all the other flowers how to grow.

I can see us as we stood on top of Mount Qasioun on a late spring evening in 2011, gazing silently over Damascus. The labyrinth of streets beneath us was slowly becoming lined with the lights of evening street lamps; the thousand mosques were garnished with green fluorescent lights. The evening stars built up their momentum and started to shine through the blanket of the dark sky; we were engulfed in an immortal scene of dancing light.

'No matter what happens to this city, this will remain,' you said, your eyes reflecting the lights of the city, as if a universe was built within their dark. 'No war can end the beauty of Damascus.'

You pointed out the Umayyad Mosque to our left and guided me through the streets near it until I could pinpoint your family home, a tiny house with grape leaves covering its walls. I vaguely waved my hand in the direction of the dark home that used to be my family's, singled out like a sore tooth just a few blocks away from yours.

I was shivering; my nose felt like a cube of ice melting on my face, my eyes were teary. You pulled me closer, placed your arm around my shoulder and broke a shy smile. 'I had a good day,' I whispered. You hummed in agreement.

There, close to the peak of that mountain, deep in the darkness of its shadows, we kissed. My lips locked upon yours for a mere second; you pulled my upper lip between your teeth and I felt the warmth of your face tingling my icy nose. Suddenly you weren't a stranger any more. You weren't an unknown entity I was equally enchanted and terrified by.

You became someone familiar, safe, welcoming and warm.

Wary that soldiers or passersby might find our hiding place, the kiss didn't last long. With a final stroke to my hair, you pulled your face away from mine. You smiled your crooked, shy smile and you sighed. 'We should do this again,' I said. You laughed.

The day that ended with us on top of the mountain started in the depth of Damascus's old town, when I waited for you nervously in Pages Café. The café, tucked away in the corner of a narrow street next to a historical school building, had a cozy, dark feeling to it, and became a gathering space for liberals, free thinkers and intellectual rebels in Damascus before they were arrested or killed, or became refugees.

On the wall, abstract posters and paintings were hung. Some promised a revolution to come, others imagined a utopian Damascus that would return to its sixties' glory. The smell of Turkish coffee and freshly baked Syrian delights filled the café with a homey feel. Somehow it masked the smell of sweat produced heavily by the plainclothes secret policemen who were tucked away between the rebels, eavesdropping on our conversations, bringing mud from their boots to the black-and-white tiled floors, waiting to report free thinkers or arrest activists as they left the café.

'Have I got a story for you,' I told you, as you sat down at the corner table by the old piano, the sun hitting the school next door, shining upon its walls and its windows, reflecting through the tall, narrow windows of the café. You smiled, and your beard, black and well-trimmed, shone with your teeth. It was the very first time I met you – I saw you as you walked through the glass door, and I knew it was you. I remembered your photos from the dating website. As you stepped into the shadowy café, the sun drew an angelic light around you.

You looked surprised, almost baffled. I learned later on that you wondered what kind of a fool you were to come on a date with this stranger. You seemed uncomfortable, almost frightened, that I didn't rely on the traditional hellos and how-are-yous. You've always been blurry outside of your comfort zone.

'Sure, you can tell me a story,' you replied tactfully, counting the steps you would need to escape through the door.

'The earliest memory I have,' I said, 'I remember, was of me sitting in my grandmother's lap. She was tickling me and producing these god-awful noises with her mouth. I must have been three, but I remember laughing from the bottom of my heart.'

For a second you had the *Are-you-fucking-serious?* look on your face. You weren't sure how to respond to that. You weren't sure what would come next. You looked at your mobile screen, hoping for a phone call that would save your afternoon from this freak.

'You see, I tell you this because I'm a storyteller,' I said. 'I'm a fabulist, a writer, a hakawati.'

You took a second. You looked me in the eye, and you smiled, and you said, 'Tell me a story, then.'

That smile, that beautiful, deep, unbearably sweet smile that breaks through layers upon layers of protective iron around your soul, that smile is what made me ask you to come with me to Mount Qasioun, what made me kiss you, what made me fall in love with you while we navigated a city engulfed by war.

For the rest of our time in Damascus, you stayed over in my apartment twice a week, fabricating stories to your mother about your whereabouts. You slipped into my pajama pants and they fitted you perfectly. We played cards with my roommate, and stayed up too late. When you reached your limit on social interactions, you always had that look in your eyes, which I picked up on easily. I pulled your arm, and walked with you to my bedroom. My roommate giggled, making assumptions about our desire for privacy. Instead we cuddled most of the night, having fallen asleep mid-conversation.

Our morning coffees on my balcony were frequently interrupted by the shouts and screams of army officers and the police, running after another person to arrest. They would pull on the prisoner's shirt and drag him to the ground while the women in his family wailed in agony from their windows, tightening their white scarves upon their heads. The prisoner would be pushed into the trunk of the car under the eyes of gazers, among them you and me, before they locked the trunk on him and drove away. The first time we saw that scene, our hearts bounced and we hid in my bedroom for two hours. After a couple of arrests, we got used to the screaming and the wailing and we would just return to our morning coffee and turn the radio back on.

I lost count of how many times we woke up at three a.m. to the sound of distant explosions coming from the other side of the city. The calm in the streets carried the sounds of war swiftly to our ears and woke us up, frightened and lonely. You whined one night, half-asleep, pulled out of your land of dreams, worrying that the explosions were too close to us. I brushed your hair with my fingers, calming you down. 'It's fireworks, it's just the sound of fireworks,' I whispered, and you went back to sleep.

One night, the explosion was too close; it shook the apartment and woke us both up. We heard the explosion and thought it might have happened right outside our building. It was followed by the sound of machine guns rushing through the streets.

We crawled on all fours as we escaped the exposed bedroom to the windowless bathroom. I lay down in the bathroom tub and you rested your body upon mine. Your eyes were open wide, like small white dishes. You shivered and started to bite your lips. 'My back hurts,' you said, pointing to the small burn on your upper back ribs. 'I got you,' I whispered, and hugged you closer until the sound of machine guns morphed into an unrecognizable noise.

That night in the tub, I made love to you as if I were reciting poetry about the beauty of Damascus. I woke your senses with opening lines and flirtatious gestures, sneaking into your world like the first drops of sun rays on the mountains of Damascus. I coloured your face with the shades of sunrise as I pulled on your earlobes with my teeth. I roamed the corners of your body like a lost traveller exploring the old sleepy streets of the city, knocking on the doors of your soul with the tips of my fingers like a shy delivery boy knocking on the wooden doors of old homes in Sarouja carrying warm bread and baladi cheese. I turned your body around and tickled your feet, and you laughed like a child riding the dowikha in al-Jallaa amusement park. I murmured whimpers of pleasure in your ears, like the sighs of an old wooden bridge aching under the pressure of the souls it carries. I joined my body with yours and we moved as if we were slipping up and down the hills of the waving roads of al-Muhajireen. I printed breathless kisses on your forehead while I let your body slip away from mine, covered in my bite marks and glorious sweat.

That night, you made love to me as if you were an invading army in a sudden war. You exposed my body with steady hands and planted your head between my ribs. You covered my mouth with your palm, fearing the thin walls and eavesdropping neighbours. I surrendered to your hands like a frightened teenager taken away into an abyss of pain. Through struggles, fights and tight teeth on my skin, you could finally give a glorious bloody birth to your soul for me to see and touch. You moaned then restricted your own moans, like a resilient prisoner who doesn't want to see the look of victory in the eyes of his capturers and torturers. As you entered my body I felt speechless, as if all of my body had given up on living. I tightened my arms around you as if I were drowning, clutching your body. You finally left my side with apologizing eyes and deep regrets that you'll never share. I caught my breath as I returned from a journey into your inner thoughts.

By the time we opened the bathroom door and returned to bed, the sound of machine gun fire was long gone.

Those moments were the only times we could be ourselves completely, naked in each other's arms, almost unaware of the world around us. Outside of my bedroom, we had to calculate every step and every gesture, fearing the war, fearing our own families, fearing everything other than the two of us.

'Hakawati, don't go,' you told me as I got dressed a couple of mornings later. You were topless in my bed and we could hear the voices of our friends as they were waking up. What was it? Was it a birthday party we had thrown the night before, and everyone stayed too late, so it became too dangerous to go back to their homes across Damascus? I can't remember. We ended up spending the night playing cards and drinking cheap vodka. 'We are eight people in my house, and I don't have any food for breakfast,' I said as I searched for a clean T-shirt. 'I'll be back in ten minutes, I'm just running down to the shop across the street.'

'I'll go with you,' you told me, and I smiled. You reached out with your hand and I reached with mine. Our fingers touched for one second. From afar, we heard the sound of a small explosion, but we didn't care. It's Damascus. You grabbed my hand and pulled me back to bed, I laughed, I called your name in denial, then I gave in, you unzipped my pants, I reached down yours. Our fingers were crossing paths along our backs. Your lips were locked with mine and our bodies collapsed into bed.

'It's getting hot here,' I told you, and you reached for the window. At first I thought you had dragged the windowpane too fast and broken it. In the corner of my eye, I saw the flames expanding across the street, like a rose of fire suddenly bursting to life. The thunder-like sound resonated in my ear, and pieces of glass and wood rained on me. I grabbed your body and we rolled to the floor, the glass piercing our backs. I screamed, but I couldn't hear myself screaming.

Then, like the calm following a storm, the explosion stopped and it was suddenly quiet again.

'Are you okay?' I asked you, your eyes wide open. 'Yes. You?' I stared at your face for a second and then I stood up. Dazzled, I walked to the broken window. I looked out for a second, turned around to you and said, 'It's a car bomb, right across the street. Right outside the shop.'

But all of this is a distant memory now. These memories are my only solace as I lie here on this bed, on the second floor of our heritage home in a calm, quiet corner of Vancouver's West End, an old man of nearly eighty, trying to forget the days of terror back in Syria without losing the memories of love we built together.

I have spent endless nights, sleepless, counting your breaths as you cling to the last bits of life left inside you. Your beautiful chest, covered in white hair, rhythmically moves up and down like the waves upon the shore of Beirut, where you saved my life once. Your chest hair was black then, a masterpiece of masculinity on your muscles. You looked at me from afar, and you smiled. I allowed my eyes to wander about your body, remembering your curves and the touch of your skin, before I smiled back.

I was the weak one for thirty-seven years; I'm the one who always gets sick, crawling into bed and cursing the mere touch of anyone. I'm the one who cries when he hits his toe on the leg of that damned table. I'm the one with broken bones and a dislocated shoulder. Yet you outrun me to death? I feel cheated, betrayed even. It's not like I didn't do my best! I promised you on that beach that I would quit smoking and slow down on the whisky. Look at me now, an old, grumpy man wandering around with a glass in hand and a cigarette on the lips, while you are in your final sickbed.

You had to say that damned Syrian pun so many million times, didn't you? 'Tou'borni enshallah.' May you dig my grave. You say it jokingly, and I respond with 'Beed el-shar.' May evil remain away. How did our grandfathers, and their grandfathers before them, find this endearing? Gambling with death has consequences, and Death, it seems, has a wicked sense of humour.

I can see the surprise on your face as well. You're wondering the same things. *Why me*, you must be asking, *why would Death pick me?* Death is an act of randomness in its own right. A woman with children died once outside our home here in the West End. A car hit her. You said you could see her spirit escaping from her body as people gathered around her. I couldn't see her soul, which you claimed to be glowing like a thousand suns. I blamed this whole version of reality on your medications; they were pushing you deeper down the rabbit hole.

It has been almost forty years since we left Syria in 2012. We grew up in a city we weren't born in. We breathed air that wasn't meant for us. We pushed and pulled each other through a life we did not anticipate. We held deep within us the memories of Syria as we watched each other lose hair, grow wrinkles and become an agitated version of our young, restless selves. We had a simple life here in Canada; almost uneventful, as if all our lived experiences gathered in the first four decades of our existence. We spent our final thirty-something years mesmerized by our earlier adult life, and we forgot to live our new life to the maximum. Now, we're two old men sitting on the edge of the forgotten, ready to jump into the abyss of what's gone.

Waiting for your final moment has me drifting through my own final moments in life: I feel like I'm floating on my back in the middle of a calm sea, the sun in my eyes charming me into relaxing into the waves – wave after wave carrying me to the unknown. I can't see the sands on the horizon, but I accept the cool waters; they invite me to the dark depths of the sea. 'You belong with the creatures of the cold,' say the voices. Like a burn victim, my nerve ends are exposed to the world, and the waters are my salvation. 'But I can't leave yet,' I whisper back, my voice shallow and weak. 'He still needs me.' The voices insist, and it feels like the right thing to do, just surrender to the cold. Just allow your tired self to disappear into the final abyss. I argue and the waves get angry, they carry me high, and leave me trembling for air on the sand.

The treatment lately has put you on edge; you rarely talk to me, you rarely sleep and you demand attention all the time. The only relief you find is in my stories. You ignored my stories all through your life with me; you thought I included too many details, you discarded them and you interrupted many of them. Now, in the wee hours of the night, you wake up, slowly lifting your body, turning the light on, and you wake me up. 'I can't sleep. Tell me a story,' you say. 'I always loved your stories.'

You become my Shahryar, and I'm your Scheherazade. Death is the swordsman at our door; he will behead me if I allow my sleepy brain cells to disobey your orders for entertainment. We're the reincarnation of three characters we know so well. I somehow feel that, just like Scheherazade spared her own life by keeping the king curious for tomorrow's tale, you're also keeping your soul from departing your body, waiting for the story to be over. Like a TV-show addict, you are waiting for the series finale.

When I was a boy, I used to write stories to save my own life; now I'm telling you those same stories in hopes of saving yours. You open your eyes; you're awake. You lift your body, you turn on the light and you look at me. 'Tell me a story,' you say.

1

THE HAKAWATI'S TALE
OF HIMSELF

There are tremors around us; it's like an unwritten piece of music. That hidden melody is creating a routine for us. Every action we take in our lives is like a gentle touch on the strings of a violin. We create a symphony of traditions and daily practices that mimic life; yet it's not life, it's a motion across the musical scale. The sound of your steps as you leave the bed in the late morning hours, heading to the bathroom; the whistle of the electronic water heater as I prepare your coffee; the sounds of pain I make as I walk up the stairs to our room – they all join together with the endless sounds coming from across our old house. They create a life that we can feel within us even when we're not paying attention to the noise.

I have grown attuned to this music, and now I cannot imagine my life without it. It's a secret joy of mine to allow my mind to wander around, drawing pictures of your heavy white-haired eyebrows in my head as you look in the mirror for an old, beautiful self that you've lost. Even when I'm sitting in the garden with the dogs, I can see you trying to slowly take another step on the stairs, the fifth stair always creaking a bit; I have to find time to fix it.

Our garden is vast, with greedy trees and bushes growing around it like a bracelet surrounding a wrist. In the numbered sunny days of

Vancouver, it turns green, with flowers eyeing each other, preparing for another mating season. During the rainy days of winter that last too long and bind us to the house, it gets muddy, with small pools of water gathering in its corners. The heavy rain adds to the symphony, producing a rhythm of endless drums when it hits the ponds around our garden.

Our house used to be white when we bought it twenty-something years ago. We painted it red back then. We thought it looked lively and sweet, and then decided to turn it green. The colour reminded you of your family's home back in Damascus. Finally, as we got older, we abandoned the happy colours and resigned ourselves to a dark shade of grey for the walls, the same colour I see in your eyes in the early morning hours as you wake, asking for your medicine and your breakfast.

The wind used to hit the southern side of the house, opening windows and cracking doors. It freaked the dogs out and woke us up in the middle of the night. The wind whistled like an amused stranger catcalling us. It brought in the smells of English Bay and Sunset Beach. It carried the flavours of the doughnuts from the nearby Tim Hortons and made you desire them almost every morning.

We don't feel the wind hitting the house any more, taking away one of our symphony's main instruments. Tall skyscrapers ganged up around our little two-storey home and surrounded it slowly but aggressively over the years.

You used to fill the house with paintings, mosaic pieces and traditional seating areas, like your own family home back in Damascus. You used to spend weeks moving furniture around, then standing in a corner, silently making calculations in your head for all the possible social gatherings that we never held. You would wonder if your grandfather's black-and-white framed photo should be centred on one wall or tucked away in a small corner of your den. You suggested a blue carpet for the living room, then replaced it with a dark-yellow one, which you regretted days after you bought it. You used to work in the garden and enjoyed watering the plants.

You don't wonder any more. You don't garden. You haven't moved a single piece of furniture in five years. The living room has no carpet and your grandfather's photo is collecting dust, where you left it in an abandoned corner of our storage room.

At night the sounds of our lives disappear, opening the air for sounds of the unknown, which escape through the windows into our home. At night you sleep and I stay awake, listening to their voices and trying to decode their messages. Will they tell me a story for you? Sometimes they do, sometimes they don't. Your rhythmic inhale and exhale keeps me awake, and I wonder. Are you dreaming of your own paradise?

When you were just a boy, you expected the world to be yours for the picking. You opened your heart with laughter and cracked jokes. You showed me an old video of yours, recorded on a camera borrowed from a wedding planner your father knew. You were standing there, listening silently to the beat of a reggae song that got too famous in Syria in the early nineties. You were wearing a white jacket and a red bow-tie. You suddenly started to dance, unaware of the people around you, unhinged by the laughter of your father. You started imitating the movements of the dancers in the music video, swaying left and right to the song, repeating its chorus loudly. You moved your feet as fast as you could and shook your head to the beat.

That, you've told me, is your heaven. That was the time you were still yourself, before you escaped the reality of life and imprisoned your thoughts inside your skull. As you grew older, you left behind the laughter and the dancing and embraced a sarcastic sense of humour that you only share with yourself, and a desire for a personal space, and a need to be left alone to your thoughts.

Your inhale gets heavier and for a second, my heart jumps in fear. I finally see you opening your eyes. You smile to me. 'Will I get to tell you the ending this time?' I ask while I pull you closer to my chest; you rest your tired brain, filled to the brim with medication, there on my chest. I hear the little crack my broken rib produces as it aches under the weight of your head. I ignore it like I have for the past sixty years. You hear the crack too.

'I don't want to bother you,' you say, adjusting your head. 'You never healed that broken rib of yours.'

I pull you closer. 'Don't worry about it. I rarely feel it any more.' I scratch my chest right on the corner where my broken rib rests.

In my early twenties, I lived in Cairo for a while. I told you this story once, years ago, but I've never repeated it. I don't enjoy telling old stories of broken ribs and painful experiences. They don't feel like stories of mine; these are the stories of the other men who lived them instead of me. Every stage of my life feels like a story of a different man, each one a man I don't know well. A man I don't understand any more. This story is of a man who lived in Egypt in his early twenties. He was the one who escaped his family in Syria and moved to a country he only knew through mummy films and young adult books. Why did that man make those decisions? What made him ignore all the signs and walk down that empty, dark road on the outskirts of Cairo, alone and innocent?

That stranger man was outed as a homosexual to a group of Egyptian friends. You know how this story goes: he got a phone call one afternoon from one of these friends. He was asked to come to a mall, and he went there. In a food court, right next to the smelly meals of McDonald's, that stranger sat with his friends.

'We hear stories about you,' one of them said. He was a tall, dark-skinned man with a heavy moustache and the belly of Santa Claus. 'We want you to know that we support you, we will carry you, we will stand behind you.'

'What are you? Are you a top or a bottom?' said Fady, who the stranger man had a crush on. 'I mean, if you're a top, just get married to a girl and do with her as you please.' The stranger didn't want to reply to their inquiries; he felt cheated and cornered. He wanted to leave the table and never look back. He wanted to escape into his own fantasies. Inside his head, he was holding Fady's hands, and Fady understood, even welcomed his emotional advances. The two shared a kiss, a touch and a whisper.

The group, all eight of them, were still discussing the matter of this man's sexual life; they were all attempting to agree on a plan to salvage what was left of his soul. 'We might each be able to afford to contribute a small amount of money for him,' Fady said, referring to that man who used to be me. 'And we can prepare him for marriage.'

The stranger man finally found a reaction within himself.

'I never asked for your approval or for your understanding,' he said. He spoke to them about the endless nights all of them had spent in his house, the many times all of them shared the same bed with him and spoke of love and loss as the wee hours of the night came to a close. He felt that all these moments, which he held dear, were becoming meaningless. 'You slept next to me.' He pointed to Santa Claus, whose face was now red. 'Did I touch you? Did I bother you? Did I even remotely make you feel uncomfortable?' Everyone was lost for words.

The stranger man escaped the table; he jumped the escalator and found himself standing in front of the cinema. He gazed at the posters and decided to watch V for Vendetta. On his way into the cinema hall, he found himself starting a conversation with a clerk. The clerk was a handsome, dark-haired young man around his age. They exchanged short sentences as the man waited in the line for the door of the cinema hall to open. The stranger man wondered if they were flirting, and as the conversation continued, he realized that they were. 'I've seen this movie a couple of times before,' the clerk said, playing with the small flashlight he carried in his hand. 'It's a great one.'

The clerk explained how the movie had touched him. 'V is a lone wolf,' he said, gazing into the man's features with his wide dark eyes. 'He is abandoned by society and rejected by his peers simply for who he is.' By that time, the man only wanted to grab the clerk's side, and dip him into a deep kiss.

'But he managed to change his society to accept him for who he is,' the clerk added softly. His lips were attractive, his skin was glowing with warmth. 'It was an act of revolution.'

'I have no idea how they missed it,' the clerk whispered to the stranger, 'but there are two women kissing in the movie and the censorship gods of Egypt didn't remove it from their final cut.'

As the stranger walked through the hall toward his seat, the clerk followed him with his eyes; in the darkness of the cinema, deep between the scenes of the movie, the clerk slipped into the empty seat next to the stranger man. He whispered a quick hello and then sat there, watching the movie.

Moments passed, and the clerk's hand found its way to touch the tips of the stranger's fingers. The stranger man pulled the hand toward him and grabbed it with his own. The two hands clinched into each other as the two women on the screen shared a sweet kiss. Their fingers played a game of hide-and-seek while V and Evey danced to the beats of their own hearts at the start of the third act. Silently, the two of them heard V whisper, 'A revolution without dancing is a revolution not worth having.'

As everyone started to leave the hall, and light returned, their hands unclenched. They looked at each other and smiled. 'Can I have your phone number?' the clerk said shyly, and the stranger man smiled. They both shared their contact information as they felt blood streaming to their faces. They departed on the promise of a meeting.

The cold desert wind broke into the stranger's clothes; he shivered as he walked the empty roads back home, unable to find a taxi. He felt safe, high on the promise of a date with a cute clerk with soft hands. He could hear footsteps behind him. The sounds of the night invited him to a slow dance. He walked, drunk with the cool breeze.

That was the night I was born from that stranger man's body; I fractured from within him. That innocent man-child was alive as he left the cinema, and he was dead when I woke up in the hospital the next day with that dislocated shoulder, with those broken ribs.

When that stranger and I – still in one body – turned around, we saw them coming. They came fast. They were seven. Fady wasn't among them. Their familiar faces were holding unfamiliar expressions. The first kick came right between the legs. 'Khawal,' one of them said. 'Faggot!'

The stranger man and I didn't argue; we just stood there, trying to protect our faces. There was a blow to the chest, followed by a sharp pain in the lungs. There was a kick to the knee that dropped us to the ground. Then the many kicks came. 'I'm doing it for you,' Santa Claus said. 'You should know who you truly are.'

The stranger's hands were weakened. He couldn't protect his face any more. Slowly, they slipped to his sides. His chest took a kick from the sole of a shoe. He heard the crack echoing in his head, as his fractured rib gave up and broke completely. I heard it too. His mind was racing, his thoughts interrupted. Their kicks mangled his insides every time they connected. He tried to take a deep breath. He tried to speak. The words died on his tongue. He tried to beg for forgiveness to a sin he didn't believe in. He heard his own breaths. He gasped, but couldn't get the air inside his body. He felt suffocated. He wished for them to stop. He wished for them to hear the cracks of his bones. He wished for mercy.

In his mind, he saw their smiling faces when they gathered in his little apartment on weekends; someone would bring the shisha, another would buy enough kushari or sunflower seeds for everyone to enjoy. They played Red Alert together, sometimes online, sometimes on two computers they assembled in his apartment. He would make them tea. They would borrow his books and read his short stories.

His pain started to fade away from his body. He couldn't feel it any more. I became his hurt locker; I became his vessel of sorrow. He started to lose his grip on reality. While I remained behind, taking blows, he slipped into his fantasies. In his mind, he would call and the clerk would pick up the phone. They would meet again for a coffee somewhere over by the banks of the Nile. He would buy the clerk a rose from a flower girl wearing a dirty scarf. The clerk would take it and press it inside a graphic novel he had bought weeks before. The book would forever smell of flowers, and the rose would become immortal like a rose made of glass.

Every weekend they would go together to the movies and watch a comedy or a drama. They would argue over superhero movies and hold hands in the darkness of the cinema. When they went home, they would kiss goodnight. They would grow old together and one day, while asleep in his lover's arms, in a bedroom covered in movie posters, he would peacefully slip into his final slumber.

With a final kick that landed on his face, he returned to the dark alleyway. He coughed blood, spat it to the side. 'Bas,' he begged, 'enough, please.' His cracked rib must have punctured his lung; I felt it root itself there. It grew like a tree within his lung, with parched branches that carried no leaves. It reached the corner of his heart and scratched the inside of his ribcage. He was finally dying. 'Bas,' he whispered, but his gasp came out as a hiss, coated with blood.

That night was my first encounter with Death.

He came swiftly, a smile on his skeleton face. He waved his fingers and the world stopped; a drop of blood from the corner of my eye froze on my face, like a red tear that I didn't cry. The faces became masks of anger; the feet were suspended millimetres from my body. 'You can let go now,' Death said. 'Just announce yourself gone, and you will be gone.'

Death was wearing a black cartoonish hood; his fingers, touching my face softly, were sticks of ice. He showed me everything that night: he showed me the future I would have, the stories I would tell and the men I would meet. He showed me you, my love, and I saw you. 'This is your life,' he told me. 'You will be sitting at the bedside of your loved one as he dies, and slowly, you will tell him stories, trying to keep him away from my final touch.'

He asked me, while darkness was coming over me, if I was ready to let all of this go and disappear with him into the unknown. I wasn't. 'You're not telling the stories to keep him alive,' he told me. 'You are telling the stories because you don't want to face life without him. It will be a selfish, sad act of self-preservation.' Scheherazade did not love the sultan. She didn't want to fix him. She murmured her stories to keep her neck away from the hands of the swordsman.

The world around me was dark and I only saw the light in Death's eyes. I reached with my palm, and I grabbed Death's face in my hands. I printed a bloody kiss on his white teeth and begged him to let me stay.

That was when Death skinned me from that innocent man. It was a painful moment; it felt as if part of my soul were being removed. Death smiled at me, and from within me, he took a ghostly figure, a man-child who I used to be, and now he is a stranger to me.

That man visits me sometimes, while I'm lying here in bed with you. He reminds me of stories long gone. He whispers poems in my ear as I wait for you to wake up so I'll know you're still alive.

'Tell me a story,' you say now. Death peeks his head from behind the cracked door; within his robes, I see that stranger man. He looks happy. He has poured his pain into me and left this world for an innocent heaven. His pain within me cannot be silenced. It rises every now and again. It becomes louder within my own bones. It feels like the scream of a child abandoned by his mother. Sometimes it echoes in my mind. It slams against my broken ribs and bounces against my dislocated shoulder. It pulls me away from you and slips me into dark places I don't like, yet I keep it to myself.

I smile to you, my love, and I start telling you a story. 'Once upon a time, a man told his lover a story called "The Most Beautiful Suicide", about a woman called Evelyn McHale.'

Evelyn McHale was long gone before she even hit the car. In her calm descent, falling from the eighty-sixth floor of the Empire State Building, her soul departed from her body, swiftly moving upwards, following her white scarf – the one she dropped off the edge of the building before she jumped.

I guess ghosts haunt in flocks. As I tell you the story of Evelyn, another ghost escapes the grasp of Death. She stands in the corner of our bedroom, eavesdropping on my story about a woman who, like her, abandoned the world.

I know the smell of her clothes; I know the deep look in her eyes. The ghost of my mother stands there silently. I hear her voice echoing from under the bed, hiding there like a monster. 'I carried you for nine months within my body,' the voice repeats, yet the ghost remains still. 'You're a part of me.'

I was born in Damascus, a lonely child. I was called evil-eyed since even before the day I was born. On one of her good days, my mother told me that when she felt my first kick, an old maiden aunt of mine touched her belly. 'He will grow and be a strong boy,' she said, her eyes sparkling with green envy. 'You should take good care of him.' Since that day, my mother's final months of pregnancy were troubled. When I was born, her milk was dry and salty. I grew up weak, easily picked on, lonely.

She looks at me with accusing eyes and I shiver. I remember you far too well, Mother. You steal me away from my listening lover, away from my bed, and you throw me into the icy hole of memory. I see you sitting there in the corner of our dusty living room, waiting for my return from school, holding your knitting kit and working on a blue-and-yellow winter sweater. The sweater is ugly as fuck. Yet, I will have to wear it. The living room is dimly lit, the dust is everywhere and the TV is playing some nonsense Syrian soap opera. I hate the dust, I hate the soap opera, I hate the sweater and most of all, I hate you.

The air has its thickness; the wooden-framed windows haven't been opened in months and I feel suffocated the moment I walk in the door, carrying my heavy school bag. You look at me from afar, you see the darkness behind my eyes and you know how much I'm afraid of you. You start smiling; your smile cracks into a laugh, as if you're enjoying all the fear you're pouring into my insides. Your laugh echoes throughout the house. It hits the schoolbooks in my room, my old tapes and the photos I hide from you.

'Hello, Mother,' I tell you.

'Fuck you!' you say.

She didn't hear the loud noise her body made when it hit the Cadillac limousine parked in front of the building; she didn't see the people gathering around her dead body. She didn't see herself, arranged in her usual elegant demeanour, her legs crossed at the ankles, her pearls neatly placed around her neck, her white gloves clean and sparkling. She didn't feel the metal of the car, folded around her like a cloud in a child's imagination; she didn't mourn the loss of her high heels, gone midway through her flight.

Like a green moray eel, you sneak into my room in the middle of the night. Your clothes are dishevelled. There is no elegance to your love. One hand twists the doorknob slowly, while the other holds onto a kitchen knife. My trained senses wake me up, my eyes adjust to the dark in a second and I see you. You're standing there on top of me, like a statue of poison and piss.

'Your eyes glow in the dark like a demon,' you tell me, and I jump out of bed, pushing you away. You fall down, taking with you two shelves of my books, my only friends in the world, and I dive for an escape. Barefoot and in my underwear, I rush to the door.

'Come back here, you little shit!' I jump down the staircase three steps at a time. My fourteen-year-old heart is pumping blood across my young body. My muscles tense in fear, and tears on my face feel like rivers. I'm fearful, scared. You're a goddess in your child's eyes and a goddess is capable of anything. You're a dictator bathing in my blood, and I'm weak, powerless and incapable of defending myself in the face of your knife stabs.

I can still hear your noise as you roam the house like a tiger in a cage, roaring with your loneliness. I rush in front of the closed shops, heading to my favourite hiding place behind the dumpsters at the corner of the streets, where a public staircase protects me from the eyes of passersby and the cold wind of the night. I pass the time counting cars and stars, waiting for your latest episode to be over.

Tucked away there, I break into a loud cry. I feel like I'm locked in a freefall, pushed from an edge into a hungry abyss. You're a goddess, and I'm betrayed by my faith. Your heart was supposed to produce love for your children, the way your breasts were supposed to produce milk for them.

Between the buildings on both sides of our narrow street, leaning on each other like old friends, I must have fallen asleep. It wouldn't have been the first time. In the morning, I gather myself and walk back home, avoiding the eyes of curious neighbours and shop owners. I bring my tired body up the stairs. I eavesdrop at our gate, hoping to hear your snores filling up the house. When I'm assured you're fast asleep, I slip through the door to my bedroom.

I remind your ghost, as you stand there in the corner of my bedroom, stealing my fleeting moments and final nights with my lover, that it wasn't the last time I took that walk of shame.

Like a moon rising from the darkness she appears in front of me, in a photo taken four minutes after she met her end. I try to ignore Evelyn McHale, but she is haunting me. She lies there like the daughter of a goddess who sacrificed herself for the sins of others. 'Tell my father,' she said in her suicide note, 'I have too many of my mother's tendencies.' She feared for her lover and her own offspring, and she atoned with a blood sacrifice. She calls my name, wondering if I needed a hug, a kiss or a bedtime story. Her closed eyelids, her hair, her dress, which I assume is the colour of red wine, are all printed on my brain cells; they glow, leaving a negative of her image in the back of my mind.

Like the men gathering around the dead body of McHale, I'm alert. I can smell the smoke coming from outside my room in the late morning hours. *What now?* I ask myself and I open the door, only fearing that my well-studied exit route might be blocked with fire. I slowly walk into the house, sniffing air through my nose, trying to find the direction of the fire. I go to the kitchen. Maybe you forgot another failed attempt at cooking in the oven. The kitchen is deserted, the sink is filled to the brim with eggshells I left there alongside dirty dishes from an endless number of omelettes I made for myself. A rotten banana cluster is in the corner with flies roaming around it, and the potatoes in the plastic basket grew long, twisty roots. The smell of burning oil fills the ceiling. The fridge's door is forgotten open, but the fridge is empty.

My heart beats faster. I wonder if you're burning the front door. The thought of death suffocates me like ash.

The smoke is coming from the balcony. You stand in a corner, in front of you a huge tank; I see flames of fire reaching out from within it. The flames reflect in your eyes; they never blink. On your face, a smile grows; you're amused, like a child repeatedly hitting his sister's doll on the wall, smashing its face in.

I decide to investigate. I move closer. I take a step toward you and cough loudly, hoping to break you out of your trance. You don't acknowledge my existence. I finally cross the door and I join you on the dusty old balcony. I always imagined this balcony as an escape; I wished it was wide enough for me to build a swing.

Deep within the fire, dozens of photos are burning slowly. I gasp as I realize that those are my photos: photos I took at camp when I was twelve; a school photo I looked utterly sick in; a photo of you, a rose in your hair, the sea glowing behind you; a photo of me and my cousins in our Eid clothes; a photo of me laughing my heart out while playing a game of jump rope with another boy. My little face in that photo is burning. The fire is eating the sides of the photo, burning the rope, destroying the features of the other boy, reaching my body, burning off my arms, my ears, my hair, my forehead and my eyes, and finally reaching my laughing mouth, hushing a painful scream.

Across the narrow street, from the balcony of an old building, a neighbour is curiously gazing at us as we stand quietly for an hour. The fire takes you into a land within your own imagination; your eyes are following its flames. There goes #ThrowBackThursday and the endearing photos of my childhood.

Fuck it, I'm not giving you a reason to slap me across the face. I will remain silent; you can burn down the house for all I care. At least the smoke masked the rotten smell of our kitchen.

The neighbour, however, isn't as wise as me. 'Is there a problem?' he asks from his balcony across the street. Two people look up from the street and wonder. You don't respond. You calmly go back inside and pick a book from my room – the Arabic translation of A *Portrait of the Artist as a Young Man*. I'm happy that I've already read it.

You aim and throw the book across the street; your weak hand doesn't help you, but the theatrical act scares the neighbour into minding his own business. 'Fuck off,' you whisper to yourself. The book hits the building across two floors down, and then continues its descent to the street, waving its pages like a frightened bird.

'All photos are haram, they are all sinful,' you say. 'They are gateways to hell and will bring ghosts and demons across.' I stare for a second at my book, all the way down in the street. A man steps on it, another kicks it, until it disappears.

Jumping off the Empire State Building immortalized her forever. She jumped to be forgotten. Her final portrait tells only of her struggle, her relief to end a longing to belong. She looks as if she has been walking a long walk in a jungle of hay and decided to rest on the grass, kicking her high heels away and enjoying the sunlight with closed eyes, touching her chin lightly with a daisy she picked on her long journey. Except the grass is a bed of metal, the body is dead and the daisy is a sharp piece of glass.

When did I decide to run away? I honestly can't remember. It came like an unexpected spring after a long winter. The idea got hotter like the heat of the sun in April, breaking through the storms of your screams. It shone into the dark haze of your abandonment and isolation.

That final moment, with its urgency, will forever travel around with me. You tell me that you're leaving for a walk. You go for a long walk every day; you disappear for hours. No one knows where, and no one seems to care.

You put on your makeup, bright green mists of colour across your eyes, a touch of red on the lips and a white scarf, and you walk down the stairs step by step, your high heels knocking on the floor, creating a hypnotic rhythm. As soon as it disappears, I rush to the balcony; I see you walking down the road, your famous blue jacket, your favourite stockings, your white handbag. My nose is filled with the smell of my burned memories, their ashes still resting in the bottom of that barrel. You take your steady steps down our street and you're gone. My sun is shining. I'm leaving.

My books are disposable. I only keep my favourite. My clothes are not many; I only pick the ones without a stain of blood or a stain of memory. The bag, which used to be my school bag, is filling up fast with my stuff. In my pocket, there is money. My shoes are waiting for me by the door.

I take a final look at my room with its single bed, the blue mattress, my wooden windows, my shelves of books – some broken, some intact. The small white sofa and the small fireplace. I say my goodbyes, and I never see them again.

As a final joke, I close the outside door behind me and I turn the key, breaking it inside the lock. I smile wickedly.

Ten years have passed since I saw you last, Mother. I avoided you at every corner of my life; my escape continues for what seems to be an eternity. How to escape your own DNA? How do you look back and think to yourself, 'fuck this shit!', and move on?

At the top of three steps leading to a small restaurant in a corner of Damascus, I was reunited with you on an early spring day in the late 2000s. I wondered if you would walk down to me, or if I should come up to you. Conscious of my surroundings like a street cat, in the back of my head, I couldn't stop myself from studying the area around me looking for possible escape routes.

You hugged me and I shivered. You asked me about me, about my journeys around the world. You smiled, you laughed and you seemed calm and balanced. I felt claustrophobic, and I longed for a breath of air. You spoke about how you felt lonely. Alone you would sit in your old house, after you drove away everyone around you. Cornered in a war zone you didn't understand and left to fend for yourself. I don't know what bothered me more: the fact that you seemed to assume you were still my problem, or the fact that you seemed to have forgotten every moment you abandoned me, every slap on the face I got when I asked for dinner. I felt a shake murmuring through my body, like the whisper of a child in my ear. I felt weak in the knees, as if I were still a young boy, crying for your attention, dying for your approval, hiding behind dumpsters.

An hour later I said my goodbyes and you asked me where I would go next. I answered, honestly, 'I don't know.'

Did she scream? I ask myself. The story I tell my lover feels weak, unprepared. My fantasy stretches through time and place; I see Evelyn falling off the Empire State Building. In my mind's eye she doesn't. She relaxes her body, allowing the wind to carry her, closes her eyes and moves on to the next life. Did she scream? I doubt it. But there must have been a second of a gasp. That moment of uncertainty before she accepted the coming death, a moment when all the logic in the world crumbled and she produced sounds like a squeezed lemon, bitter, ugly sounds, before she calmed down, allowing the wind to carry her softly. Only then the pain stopped, the heart stopped pumping and death came, quick, inviting and final.

For twenty years, my mother was stuck in the first moments of the most beautiful suicide, insanely trying to change the outcome of her decisions, screaming, hitting the air with her fists, angry at the world. Now, as she accepts her unchangeable fate, she clings to the memory of an elegance that was never hers; she adjusts herself, allowing her final portrait to show what she considers her real self: pearls around her neck, perfect hairdo, disregarded high heels and the smile of acceptance on her face. But I won't be part of your descent, Mother. I'll meet you at the limousine.

'I feel sad,' you tell me, as I finish the story. The sounds around us are filling the air again; it's a new morning at last. Once more, I managed to keep you alive for another night; I can now sleep in peace. This Scheherazade needs her beauty sleep.

'I'm sorry I made you feel sad,' I respond as I click a button and the curtains slowly close, like the curtains of an old theatre after a well-acted play.

'This story is about your mother, isn't it.' You state the question like a fact; you don't wait for a response and you turn your body around, giving me your back. On your back, I see the small burnt bird tattoo.

I smile and I pull the covers toward me. 'You're always a puller,' I say, 'leaving me with no covers.'

As I slowly allow my body to welcome the smaller death, enjoying the last waking moments of the day before I let myself depart this world and enter the world of dreams, I whisper a song to Death, still standing at the door. He smiles at me; under his robes I see her face. She looks at me, sometimes with guilty eyes. Sometimes she blames me for abandoning her back in Damascus as I travelled with you across the world.

'Give me some space,' Death tells me, as he makes his entrance slowly into the room. I hear him, but you don't. I see him walking there toward our bed, but you're blinded to his presence. He mirrors your movements sometimes, mocks you while you look him straight in the eyes but can't see him. He smiles at me like an old friend; he is my own private torturer. He is my constant reminder that you're soon to be gone. I welcome him to our bed. Like every night since I can remember, he joins us, sleeping in between you and me.

2

THE TALE OF THE LOVER
WHO BELIEVED HIMSELF AN
ADVENTURER

'There isn't much time left,' you tell me; in your voice, there is a sense of urgency. 'It's okay. You did your best. We all know we're going to die.'

I stare blankly into your eyes as I beat eggs in a little white bowl and watch the mix as it fuzzes. I always add a teaspoon or two of flour into my omelette. It makes it lovely and fluffy. The sun is coming softly from outside, the sweet, warming late-summer sun of Vancouver. The teapot is boiling on the stove, and I have already placed two tea bags in the dog-themed black-and-white mugs.

'Ah. I forgot to add salt to the eggs,' I respond. These conversations of impending death and doom excite you; they give you the feeling that you have a purpose. *I am taking the final steps of my journey toward death,* you must be thinking. *Might as well enjoy the ride.*

You rarely break our silent routine except to announce one of your gloomy remarks. You've always been a master of keeping your thoughts to yourself. You guard them protectively, like a dragon defending her eggs from the hands of the hungry Sinbad. You build walls of one-word answers, head shakes and dirty looks, and leave me to interpret them.

Am I in love with you, or with the voyage of discovering you? Am I addicted to the emotional puzzle you place before my heart? Have I filled all the missing pieces with accurate representations of you, or was I painting the missing colours from my own canvas? I guess I won't have time to find out. I'm annoyed, and you are aware of it. 'Fuck,' you say, 'you've lost your sense of humour.' You've always been the funny one.

'No. I just do not appreciate conversations about death while I'm preparing breakfast,' I say while pointing the spoon behind my back, where our constant guest sits at the table in his black cloak, wiggling his fork like a child, waiting for his share of the toast.

The older you got, the shorter our conversations got. We used to talk about gods and kings, songs and beautiful springs, and now we discuss breakfast items and pending deaths. As you got older, your emotional mess became overwhelming for you, as if you were a glass filled to the brim with drop after drop of vile water; now it's pouring over the sides, slipping onto your tongue, and you spit it on me whenever it devastates you.

You weren't always this locked in. You were the joy of your family, the youngest of your brothers, the last grape of the cluster. Everyone stood by you, surrounded you with love and attention. Your father would ask your brothers to share their candy with you, and your mother would favour you with the last piece of cake. I wonder sometimes why you rarely talk to me the way you speak to your brothers and sisters; am I a disappointment to you? Would I be able to make you cake the way your mother did? Did I ever make you feel as special as your family did?

'It smells good,' you say from your side of the table, and I know you're lying; you lost your sense of smell three years ago. 'Back in my days in the Syrian army, freshly cooked eggs were so hard to come by. We would spend weeks, maybe months, before we got any eggs. Have I told you about that officer who investigated an egg theft incident in my unit?' I smile; my back is to you as I lean on the kitchen table, but you know I'm smiling.

'Oh, here we go again with those stories,' I say. 'Yes. I even remember the punchline: *We calculate everything in the Syrian Arabian Army, my comrades.*' I imitate a deeper voice. *'If you eat more than one egg per day, you will shit the second one.'* We both laugh, then you cough; I look to see if you're all right and then return to the eggs.

'The worst part was when the officer came by our post,' you say, returning to the story. 'We were stationed on the Syrian–Jordanian border, you see, and we would get frequent visits from high-ranking officers. They came around hunting rabbits with military rifles while pretending to investigate smugglers. I was once in my underwear, sitting in the heated bunker room making tea when the officer just emerged through the door.'

'That sounds like the beginning of typical military-themed porn,' I say.

'Fuck you. The guy was an ugly sixty-eight-year-old fat man; I was nineteen.'

'Wow. You certainly have a type,' I say. It takes a second for you to figure out what I mean. You stand up, grabbing the back of a chair, walk slowly toward me, and while I'm elbow-deep in egg mix, olive oil and labneh, you place your hands around me and you print a kiss on the back of my T-shirt. 'For me, you will be forever young,' you say.

You toy with my emotions. You take me into your darkness with a swift sentence, then pull me to your sunny light with a gesture. Like a fool, I follow. I'm hopelessly attached to your enigmatic love. The fact that I was your first lover remains a sign of danger that glows red in the corner of my mind – even now, after a million years together. I worry that I'm imprinting upon you. I worry that I'm stealing you from your destiny to meet someone else.

Did I fail you? Was I supposed to work harder, to make you happier? Was I supposed to let you slip away from my complex history and my own burdens? Maybe if I did, someone else might have brought you happiness I couldn't. Maybe if I did, you wouldn't be dying, tumbling away from me as we speak.

'You don't have to bring me flowers,' you say at dinner. 'To the grave, I mean.' The dim light of the late sunset is still evading the shadows of our house, slipping inside through the cracks of the windows. On the radio, an old jazz song is playing. I add some Arabian spices to yesterday's Chinese leftovers and reheat them.

'Are we back to that topic?' I say, tired, sleepy, trying to eat my food in peace, not in the mood for another debate. Death abandons the table, answering phone calls from his agents around the world. 'How many times do we need to have this conversation?' I say once again. You silently watch as my emotions get tangled on my face. I hold my tongue for a second, but a final statement escapes: 'It's pointless to talk to you sometimes.'

At night, you show your true colours. You take off your smile like a wet raincoat. Your morning cheerfulness is a beautiful nothing, like a counterfeit coin. You get trapped inside the darkness of your fate, lying helplessly in bed, waiting for a sleep that will never come. You start dreading that moment just before sundown, as the reality rushes faster to you that this will be another sleepless night. This will be another night when the pills and potions will be useless. I see you, like a vampire, metamorphosing into a dark creature greedy for attention and conflict. Your mood slips into the blackness of the night, just like the sun on the final lines of the horizon, changing colour from warm fuzzy orange to dark, gloomy blue.

Depending on the night, this is either the time of day when you and I get together and commiserate, or when I tell you a story that will silence the beast within you and allow us a steady stream of motion to a warm friendly bed, where another story sends you to a blissful sleep. These glorious nights, however, are numbered.

After an appropriate amount of sulkiness on my side, matched by an equivalent amount of bitterness on yours, I decide to test the waters and see which way this evening will go. 'When we're at odds,' I whisper from the other side of the table, 'I feel like my life is a slightly tilted painting on a white wall. I can ignore the painting for a short while. But at one point I have to give in, reach out of my comfortable chair and adjust it.' In my hand rests a glass of whisky that I filled in a theatrical way moments ago. Is that a crack of a smile I see on your lips? Will it be a night of peaceful dreamless sleep? I push further. 'You're my most valuable painting, my rebel against angles and lines. I can't leave us in a moment of unbalanced anger.'

I don't tell you, but although our fight started with your constant reminders of death during every meal, which are getting obnoxious, another reason why I never leave things tangled between the two of us is that I am too capable of seeing how Death occupies our future as he does chores around our house. What if I carried on a fight and woke up tomorrow without you? Since every moment between us could be our last, each moment has to be a grand finale.

'Have I ever told you about the morning I got lost when I was a child?' you say from across the table. I smile: yes, you have. 'No, you haven't. What happened?'

'I know what reminded me of it,' you smile. Your eyes brighten as you recall the distant memory. 'It was all the talk about graves.'

You say that as if you're not the one who brings all that talk to our dinner table.

You were eleven, maybe thirteen, when you woke up one day in a state of trance; you felt the need to explore the limits of the unknown world around you. It was a morning when your mind allowed you to wander as far as you could within the protected zone, the bubble your family surrounded you with. You had travelled within it far enough to reach its inner walls. Everything outside looked colourful and easily reached, and you wanted to pop the bubble and explore what lay beyond it.

You didn't want to escape, like I did. You felt comfort in your kingdom, and you wanted to expand. Your family gave you the world. Your mother, who spent her nights giggling in her sleep, dreaming of ways to treat you better, always made your favourite meals on Mondays and Thursdays, foul b'zayt and mlokhieha. Your older brothers were there to teach you how to hunt for mice and how to care for cats, and where to buy the best meat for your mother's kebbeh nayeh. Your aunt, married to a distant cousin, would come back from the deserts of Saudi Arabia carrying gifts for you: Nike shoes and toys that required batteries to work. She singled you out among all the youngsters of the family with that magnificent blue horse figure: it galloped upon a touch of a button, then neighed and snorted at the end of its race. The world around you was a safe haven. Damascus opened her arms to you, and you rushed to her embrace.

At the time, Syria was enjoying a change of course. The country was blooming economically after President Hafez al-Assad ended years of tense relations with the West and accepted an invitation to a peace conference with Israel. In the eighties, the lines at the government-subsidized markets had been long and tiring as the country ached under US-led sanctions, but now people stopped buying cheap rice and sugar that never sweetened their tea from the government, and started to buy imported goods. Your father's factory, producing paper to print books on and to box gifts within, was profitable again. He returned from his long day at the office carrying apples, oranges and kenafieh from the Nabil Nafiseh sweetshop at the corner of Malki and Arnous streets. He even bought a car for your older brother, a 1961 Mercedes that roared across the street and scared the girls in hijabs as they left the Islamic school in Bab Sharki.

Damascus felt clean, soapy and filled with possibilities. The people shed their seven-year-old jackets with rotten elbows covered in fabric patches and managed to afford some new clothes. The shops in Hamidiyeh were filled again with children's toys and decorated backgammon sets.

The furthest that you had explored was when your mother took you to Zanket el-Setat market. Women bought fabrics there to make their own dresses. The market was narrow and filled with tables outside the shops, making it even more crowded. Women pulled the hands of their children and powered through the crowds looking for their prized fabrics and the latest styles in hijabs and niqabs.

Your mother bumped into an older woman who she knew well. The old woman was carrying a lot of bags; she had blue eyes and a sweet smile. 'This is Samira the tailor,' your mother explained. 'She is the best in her business. She makes dresses for the rich wives of police officers and government officials.' You looked at the old woman as she walked away, and forgot her name instantly.

Your mother pulled your hand into a corner in that tight street, avoiding the eyes of the men bargaining and advertising, and slipped with you into a shop with a low door that she needed to lower her head to enter. Inside, on the walls and under a glass table, you saw women's lingerie organized neatly according to size and colour. Your mother pointed to one of them; it flickered with gold and fake diamonds, and she asked for its price while your face turned red.

'Tomorrow, your woman will also buy herself stuff like this,' your mother whispered wickedly in your ear, a smile on her face. 'Don't be shy, son. This will be your marital right. Your woman will be the queen of all brides. She will wear all the gold in the world for you.'

You walked out of that shop knowing that you were a righteous king on the throne of your future. Damascus became your kingdom, and you wanted to explore it further.

That fateful morning the rain, generous back in those days before the drought, covered the old streets with a layer of sparkling water puddles and you wanted to jump in each one of them. The smell of jasmine around your old Damascene home was tickling your senses with sweet promises. The fountain in nearby Abaseen Square was still pouring water, and the yellow taxi cars – their paint cracking under the spring sun and giving layers of metal skin to the wind – roamed around it. The smell of the apple blossoms coming from Ghouta rode on the breeze and filled the hills of Damascus with an inviting fresh aroma. The giant Umayyad Sword statue in the middle of the city shone with the colours of the rainbow under the warm late-spring sun.

That morning, when your sense of escapade peaked, and you wanted to accomplish more on your own, you convinced your sister. 'We need to go visit our grandfather's grave,' you told her.

What made this enter your mind? You're not sure. You were too young to give reasons for things you wanted to do. I would say that you wanted to relive the experience of the Ramadan feast. During the last Ramadan, your father took you in the early morning to the graveyard near your house, to visit your grandfather. The tradition of visiting the dead, wishing them a happy feast, is the gloomy opening to a long day of treats and cash gifts, followed by eating too many sweets and singing racist songs on a swing.

'Ali will never die, for his daughters are black and ugly like monkeys.' We sang those songs for the Ramadan feast, way before feasts forgot to visit Syria, unaware of how inappropriate they were.

You and your younger sister walked hand-in-hand in what you assumed was the right direction. When I heard the story for the first time, I knew you would get lost; you have a horrible sense of direction. You walked down the covered street of Medhat Basha, your nose stuffed with the smells of exotic spices from all the shops on both sides. Then you took a left toward Qanawat Street. Back then, the old men used to sit around and drink black tea while playing tawlieh; they swore at each other over a wrong turn of the dice, and each pulled puffs from his beloved arjileh. Each one of them brought his own, proud of the beautiful design of the arjileh he had bought. You and your sister walked by them, unaware that those old men would soon be replaced by thrift shops opening on the corner of every street. The thrift shop owners would spend their days shouting back and forth with old women buying cheap clothes for their sons and daughters, bickering over five Syrian pounds' difference between the price she wants to pay and the money he wants to make. Those thrift shop owners were similarly unaware that soon they would be replaced by people protesting against the Syrian regime, carrying green flags and screaming their lungs out for freedom. The protesters were equally unaware that they would be replaced by soldiers carrying guns and swords, shooting people on sight.

Deep in the old streets of Damascus you walked; the streets were painted with the sweet light of early morning sun. Your sister shivered a little, but you have always been resilient to cold. The cold weather waved within your soul as you walked down that road. It brought fresh bursts of energy within you. You felt alive and all-knowing, like a god on his throne. Your smile broke into a grin when you saw the entrance to the old graveyard. It was the doorway into the forbidden, the far-away and the special. As you took your first step into the graveyard, you wondered for a second if someone would ask you and your sister if you should be there. Someone would tell you, 'But it's not the Ramadan feast yet, son,' and send you back to your parents.

No one stopped you as you entered the graveyard.

In the morning, these places lose their scare factor; they become quiet calm places, where the distant noise of cars passing feels muted. You walked on the right side of the graves, saying the Islamic salute to each one of them, like your father taught you. The tombstones were embedded with Quranic phrases and names of the bodies resting underneath. The tombstones in Damascus are always formal: they write your first and last names, the name of your father and the date of your death, followed by religious prayers. It feels impersonal and lonely.

But then comes Eid and people pour into the graveyards. They carry flowers and myrtles, and they gather around their loved ones' tombstones. They tell the dead stories, follow up on the news of their loved ones, pray for them and read passages from the Quran. Fathers tell their sons stories about their dead grandfathers and exaggerate the details to fill the imaginations of the children with a glorious past.

'My grandfather had four wives,' your father told you upon your first visit to the graveyard, as you stood there listening intently. 'He used to own a little piece of land on the outskirts of Ghouta, near Mashrou Dummar. He built a house over there, surrounded by gardens. He planted two trees of each fruit he loved so they could mate and reproduce.

'He called it Noah's Garden,' your father said, amused; in the background you heard the distant prayer of a crying woman.

Your great-grandfather's wives used to gather in that garden, where their husband had built a pool. They loved each other, your father attested, and were close to each other like sisters. 'They used to swim in the pool, all four of them surrounding my grandfather, bringing cherries, apples and figs for him to eat while he rested in the cool water, escaping the heat of August.' Your father explained that even while swimming in the water, his grandfather never took his white hat off. Your father assumed that he kept it to hide his receding hairline.

You realized, a bit too late, that you were drifting within your memories of your father's stories and had lost your way in the graveyard as you walked aimlessly with your sister. Fear slipped into your eyes and your hand tightened upon your sister's. Suddenly you freaked out. You realized that you had taken too big a bite from the world; you were suffocating with it.

Your sister saw your tears and automatically she produced some of her own. You started running around, trying to find an exit. Instead of comforting her, you scanned your surroundings, looking for someone else to deal with her. You knew nothing of how to care for her, and instantly thought of your mother, who was always there to carry your sister on her lap and bounce her until she calmed down. By then your sister was crying loudly. Her weeping was heard across the graveyard. The tombstones were towering over you both. You saw them as towers denying your view of others who might come to your rescue while she imagined them as monsters that would devour her. The thought drove her to a hysterical cry.

Suddenly an old man appeared behind one of the tombstones; he was wearing a white shirt and a little white hat. You approached him, and something familiar about his long face, big white moustache and black-framed reading glasses made you feel comfortable and safe around him.

'Uncle, please tell me, where is al-Bezorieh?' you asked him, and he smiled.

'It's far. It's far away.'

Your little hearts dropped to the ground, but while your sister started to cry out loud, you remained calm, if only on the outside. 'We want to go to school, Uncle, take us to school, please.'

The man walked and gestured for you to follow him; among the graves he peacefully floated, touching each one, saying As-Salaam Alaikum to all of them. He spoke to them as if they were old friends, long missed. You both followed him, trusting his knowledge. In seconds, you found yourselves at the doors of the graveyard. 'You go down this road,' he pointed with his finger, shaky and bony, 'and you will find yourselves in familiar places.'

Late to school, you started to run, but you gave a final look behind your back and the old man was nowhere to be found.

'I miss Damascus,' you tell me and I detect your change of mood; I'm losing you to the darkness once more. Death has decided to join us again, as we roam the house in a rhythmic act of final moments. He helps us turn off the lights and make sure the fire of the stove is not left aflame. You and I continue our conversations as we dance that early evening dance. I pass by the yellow carpet, and you turn off the lanterns in the seating area. I pass by the kitchen, while you take your medicines in the bathroom. The dogs, old like us, attempt to follow us at first, then sit down in a corner, pile up and sleep.

'You miss *your* Damascus; I have been telling you that it's gone for years now.' I remember having this same conversation three weeks ago. 'The Damascus you know, where grandfathers come back from the afterlife, the one where jasmine grows on beautiful red-haired women's balconies, and where we met, has been devoured by the war.'

I exit the room and I find you standing, depressed, in the hallway. I realize that I pushed you further down the rabbit hole of memories. 'You will keep it alive,' I say as I come to your rescue and hold you closer. 'We will keep it alive together.'

Death, from a corner, smirks before examining the ears of the sleeping dogs. It's not their time just yet.

As you enter the bed, and before you turn off the light, you welcome the cold sheets on your body and then turn to me. 'Will you bring flowers,' you say, 'to my grave?'

'No. I will bring my stories,' I say, and you adjust your head on my shoulder. Before you ask, I begin telling you a story. Like the sultan, you know your wishes for entertainment are my command. 'Once upon a time there was a man who went far away from his beloved land, and when he returned, everything was changed.'

In the name of Allah, the merciful! One! Two! Three! Four! Five! He was still half-asleep when they broke down his door and entered his room. He didn't move from his bed as they searched his apartment; he honestly believed that he was dreaming. They ignored him as he sat on his bed, scratching his head with his fingernails, trying to understand what was going on around him. He did not try to resist them until they grabbed him and started to pull him through the door. He saw them climbing the stairs to the roof of his little house. He used to carry canvases up to his rooftop, where he had turned a small, abandoned room into a studio.

He used to close the black curtains and work in his small studio until the early hours. He realized that this was not a dream when the reality sat upon him that one of them was carrying a bluish painting under his armpit, and the sweaty armpit was mixing the colours, adding an artistic touch to an unfinished work.

As he was pushed inside the trunk of a car, witnessed by women in scarves wallowing on balconies, the morning sun was still at ease, but its rays promised a long, hot day.

Six! Seven! Eight! Nine!

When he arrived at the police station, he couldn't tell what they were arresting him for. He never showed his paintings to anyone, so he knew they must have come to his house for a different reason. He tried to understand their problem, and what led them to this anger. He tried to grasp his mistake; he knew that he must have made some sort of a mistake. He was afraid and he started to recall the events of the previous week, only to find it uneventful. He might have offended a member of the royal family unintentionally; maybe he cut one of them off while he was driving his car. He squeezed his thoughts and tried to remember, but his efforts were in vain. *I knew this car would lead me to a catastrophe one day*, he thought. He knew his ability to drive was laughable, but sometimes he would just jump in his car and drive as fast as he could. It allowed him the sense of escape that he always longed for, allowed him to feel that he was in total control of his life, and maybe also his death.

When the investigator entered the room carrying one of his paintings, he knew that whatever the original reason they came for his arrest, that was no longer the problem.

Ten! Eleven! Twelve!

He didn't know that after they delivered him to prison, they spent some time talking about his paintings, about the naked women drawn in the strangest positions, while calling for Allah's mercy because they glimpsed these paintings while they were arresting him.

He knew better than to draw the women's faces; he wanted to protect the identities of his muses. The men could see that he had mangled the faces of all the women in the paintings. The eyes were the hardest part;

they were full of hopes and dreams. They had demands and aspirations. While painting those women from memory, he painted their faces in full and then used a small brush to mute the eyes, the noses and the significant facial features.

A week or two later, the police storage officer was doing inventory in his facility when he realized that all of the paintings were missing but one. He stood there, puzzled by the disappearance of the paintings, and took another look at his papers. There were supposed to be seventeen paintings in here!

The officer took a step away, preparing in his head the list of paperwork he had to fill out, but then flipped the painting around to take a look at it.

The painting portrayed a young naked girl from the back, standing inside a house, gazing from the cracks in of a closed wooden window to the world outside. The officer gazed as well; his eyes were eating the well-drawn corners of her full buttocks and her naked back, drawn like the stretch of a violin.

As he headed back to his little office, the officer had the painting hiding under his shirt. When he was in the safety of his office, he pulled it out, opened the lower drawer and encased it inside, before locking it with a key. He had his key inside his pocket as he headed toward the makeshift kitchen in the storage area to make some tea.

Thirteen! Fourteen! Fifteen! Sixteen! Seventeen!

The artist's lawyer slipped him the ointment underneath the table, so the police guard wouldn't see it. He told the artist that he would be deported the next day. The artist didn't understand why and asked the lawyer if he could keep his job. 'You got fired,' the lawyer explained. 'Your boss fired you when he heard about the paintings.' The lawyer said that someone had reported him for reckless driving, but when the police found the paintings they decided to jail him for indecency. Without his job, he didn't have grounds for a working visa any more, and he would be deported.

He gazed for a second at the ointment in his hand before he slipped it into his underwear. He thanked the lawyer before he headed back to his prison cell.

On his way back, as the door to the prison cell opened for mere seconds, the eyes of the other prisoners gazed at the small circles of light that entered the darkened room. The door closed, leaving them without a hope of light, and he searched with closed eyes for an empty spot on the floor until he found one.

He slipped his tired body on the floor; the cold, moist stone floor felt nice on his back, easing the burning he felt there. The smell of shit and vomit filled his nose for a second, oozing from the bucket in the corner of the cell, but he ignored it. The smell gradually became familiar, before it disappeared into the back of his mind.

He felt the heavy breathing of the many prisoners on his forehead. A week ago, when he came to this place for the first time, he had feared the other prisoners. Rapists, thieves and murderers were gathered in one room, and he was a weakened man. He tried to hold his urge to piss for so long, shying away from their gazes, knowing that the only release he had would go into that bucket. Then the call of nature overwhelmed him and he had to walk slowly to the bucket, avoiding eye contact with anyone, and relieve himself. The smell that exploded on his face made him dizzy and he almost fell to his knees.

Eyes wide open, he turned around looking at the other prisoners, waiting for a rapist to grab him or a gang to kill him. Instead, he saw them avoiding his eye contact, looking in different directions. He suddenly realized that they feel equally naked, and that he was safer in here than outside, in the hands of the guards.

He was on his back, and he could feel the pain there. It felt like a V-shaped burn rotting away on his back. He imagined it as a bird, carrying him away from this place, taking him back to his homeland. Out of nowhere, a hand reached for his chest, causing him to jump back in agony, but his eyes, now capable of seeing in the dark, managed to see a young boy, fifteen or sixteen. The face of the boy was covered in dry blood, and it seemed that his nose had been long broken. The artist smiled a weak smile and got closer to the boy, allowing him to touch his chest once more; the boy rested his head there, wet drops of tears raining endlessly.

Eighteen! Nineteen! Twenty! Twenty-one! Twenty-two!

He was hoping that Amal would be waiting for him in the airport, but she wasn't. Only Abdul-Salam, his high school friend, and Bassem, his brother, were there. He looked them in the eyes, and didn't ask, and they didn't try to explain.

He returned with them to his old house, where his mother welcomed him with kisses. Her eyes were teary and her heart was skipping a beat as she pulled him closer and gave him a hug. She smiled at him and stepped back to allow him to reach his father's wheelchair. He approached his father without speaking a word, and kissed his father's fingers in a respectful gesture. The father, however, looked away before demanding Bassem come and take him to his bedroom, closing the door behind them with a slam that sounded like a bullet.

Twenty-three! Twenty-four! Twenty-five!

The artist woke up frightened in his old room and looked around to make sure he was in his family's home. He jumped off his bed, but that made him dizzy. He opened the curtains, allowing his homeland's warm, calm sun to enter the room, and he felt it like warm water spilled over his body. He smiled and scratched his chest with his fingers. He took a step back and looked at his reflection in the mirror before he started to take off his brother's pajamas and put on the same outfit he was wearing yesterday.

His mother entered the room, unannounced, while he was still in his underwear, and she gasped in surprise, commanding him to stop what he was doing this very minute. She left the room and came back with a set of clean, shiny clothes. She started to help him put them on, just like when he was a child still learning how to button his shirt.

He felt serenity that he hadn't felt in ages, and he tilted his mother's head to his chest and printed a kiss on her forehead before going outside with her.

As he entered the living room, he saw all of his family members sitting there: his father, brother and his widowed sister's daughters. He felt their eyes examining him, so he avoided their gazes and reached for the landline, calling the embassy to ask for his stuff, which they had promised to send to him. When the phone went on ringing without an answer, he remembered that today was one of the glorious national holidays, celebrating a revolution of the past.

Twenty-six! Twenty-seven! Twenty-eight! Twenty-nine! Thirty! He tried to reach Amal on the cell phone that he had sent her on her last birthday, but he couldn't reach her. He remembered asking her to put a ringtone especially for him on her new mobile: 'Kiss', by Prince. He didn't know its lyrics exactly, but he had seen it once on a TV show, and the TV presenter translated the lyrics, providing him with a vivid lyrical memory of the whole song. He could imagine her shiny new phone, asking for a simple kiss from the love of his life, over and over.

When she didn't pick up, he knew he had to call her mother.

The old lady picked up the phone, but she wasn't the carrier of good news. Amal had left the house and escaped with a lover days ago. The old mother was in shock when it happened, slapping her face repeatedly and crying the name of her daughter time and time again; but now, she had come to accept the news, after speaking about it seven thousand times to seven thousand different female neighbours. She told him that Amal had taken all the money he sent her for their wedding and escaped with Saad, who was barely twenty-one years of age.

He wished the mother well and hung up the phone before he started laughing hard.

Thirty-one! Thirty-two! Thirty-three! Thirty-four!

He opened his old painting case, pulled some white paper from the drawer and started to unleash the colours from their little prisons. He tried to speak to the colours the way he used to, and he tried to imagine each one of them stretching out perfectly over the white paper, drawing a new naked body aching for freedom.

After an hour, he lost hope; he had just splashed his colours on the painting, creating a faceless figure of colours.

His back was acting up again, so he went to his parents' room, knocked softly on the door and opened it. From the small crack he managed to see his sleeping father and his mother sitting on a chair, giving him her back, gazing out of a wooden window with her hands touching softly in her lap. He murmured her name and she woke up, as if coming out of a coma, and followed him to his room, where he took off his shirt and she grabbed the ointment.

Thirty-five! Thirty-six! Thirty-seven! Thirty-eight! Thirty-nine!

While his mother was placing the ointment softly on the burning wounds on his back, his mind wandered, against his will, to the moment when they took off his shirt in the middle of the desert. There were two men witnessing him sitting on his knees and begging for mercy, while a judge was standing apart. 'For your crimes against the decency of society, you're sentenced to forty lashes,' the judge said. 'May Allah have mercy on you.'

A man wearing a black mask held the whip high, praised Allah the merciful, and started counting.

Forty!

'You slept?' I say, whispering.

. . .

'Are you awake?' in the quietest range of voice I can possibly produce.

. . .

'I love you,' I say, not expecting an answer.

'I love you too.' Your voice comes from a land within a dream.

3

THE TALE OF THE MAN WHO
NEVER SLEPT FOR THE REST OF
HIS DAYS

'Where did you leave the doughnuts?' I hear you screaming from the kitchen.

'I haven't the foggiest!' I respond, sitting by my desk, rolling a joint.

'The show must go on,' Death says, in his deep voice. From the Greek tales he comes, and decides to join me for a puff. I finish rolling the joint with experienced movements, licking the paper and smoothly attaching it to form the perfectly shaped tunnel of happiness, held together with a paper roach.

'If I don't entertain him,' I ask, 'who will?'

I worked my magic on the smoke detector in my office years ago. When friends come over the scent of marijuana, mixed with the smell of old furniture and whisky, is the first thing they notice. Some of them never ask, others ask directly. 'Do you smoke up?' they say, with wide anticipating eyes and a wicked look on their faces. I smile, and I usually answer by opening my small stash and rolling a new joint.

I used to have a dealer here in Vancouver; it was the first contact I asked for when we immigrated here. He was this tall white man with a sweet smile who always came by on his bike and delivered the weed to our house. He carried a big bag on his back and when he opened it, the smell of weed would fill out my whole house. He spoke beautifully about the different strains he brought, expertly explaining the effects of each, suggesting a certain sativa for the early morning hours, a specific indica for an intimate late-night gathering. 'Love Potion,' he murmured admiringly, pulling out a jar filled to the brim with well-sealed bags of eighths, 'this little bitch has got me into so much trouble.' We used to laugh, and I used to buy whatever he suggested.

I buy my weed from big pharmacies now; I walk there, and I carry my little prescription permit card. A young girl with a tattoo on the side of her face asks me to tap my credit card on her machine, and never cares about what I bought; she never tells me stories of sexual encounters fuelled with the grey smoke of marijuana.

Death, anxiously waiting for his puff, provides me with the lighter. 'Light that bitch up!' he says. I pull the first smooth line of smoke, reaching deep within my lungs, rushing with my blood, hitting the inside walls of my skull. I cough and Death, eager to please, tells me, 'Salamtak – bless you!' I take another pull. It fires my eyes. My phone rings, some silly message from an advertisement service; I disregard it. I pass the joint to Death, who holds it in his fingers. 'Watch those cold fingers,' I smirk. 'The joint might set you ablaze.'

'I've done that before,' Death says, as he places the joint between his teeth and pulls a puff. I see the smoke escaping into his bony mouth, then I see it filling his ribcage, hovering there for a second or two, before Death exhales it all out. 'Not to myself, of course,' he says. His deep voice cracks. 'If you die stoned, your soul tastes like blueberries.'

'I remember we used to have code names for our weed back in Damascus,' I reminisce. We used to call hash 'Sawsan' – like the name of an innocent sister or a young child. 'Bring Sawsan and come over,' I would say to a friend over the phone, worried that the government monitored my number. 'Sawsan is tired today; maybe she will come tomorrow,' the friend might say, sending a disappointing wave over me and the visitors to my home in Damascus. 'Marijuana was never available,' I point out to Death as I take another puff. Rumour has it that Hezbollah, the extremist group in neighbouring Lebanon, ruled the drug market in Syria and financed some of its work through its hash sale. 'They left the good stuff for export,' I joke. Death laughs.

Like an old song I've heard a billion times before, the smoke fills my head with old memories of times past. I can never let go of things that I've done. The moments that linger are always the shameful ones. A constant memory of mine is the moment I was discovered reading files in the manager's office of a tourism centre I worked for as a boy. I was fourteen.

During summers in Syria, when children are not in school, many parents find their children temporary jobs. After I escaped my mother's home, my father spent two nights looking for me in the cold streets of Damascus until he found me sleeping on a long chair in al-Sibki Garden, hungry, surrounded by stray cats and sad gazes. He carried me to my grandmother's home. He left me there and rarely came to visit, except when I became old enough for a summer job.

He asked me to wear my best shirt and pants, and took me on a twenty-minute ride to Arnous Street. I thought he was taking me to Damer, the delicious ice cream shop there. I thought he wanted to buy me something sweet to eat, or have a conversation about my return to my mother's home. We ended up in an office, meeting a friend of his. My services as a busboy were offered. They were accepted. I cleaned dishes and made coffee and tea for guests in the tourism centre. One day, while cleaning the manager's office, I saw files written in English.

I was learning the basics of the language at the time; I was still reading Russian literature and Greek mythology translated into Arabic. I couldn't make sense of the sentences I was reading in those files. I didn't understand many of the words, but I was curious. I wanted to know that language.

Alaa, a man the size of an elephant and with a similar sense of humour, walked in. He screamed at me, called me names and pushed me around. I was seriously sorry; I really did not mean to read the secrets of the company. I didn't want to make coffee either, but that's beside the point.

I was fired that day. The moment when I was told I was fired for the very first time in my life stayed with me. That silly, small memory of a momentary shame that should have been forgotten the next day still reaches into my mind every now and then. It reminds me of my very first failure. Every time I want to start anew, that memory swims to the surface of my consciousness, explaining how I will be publicly shamed in front of eight giants, women with tall legs and fancy handbags and men with well-groomed moustaches.

Death, listening to my thoughts, leans toward me and smiles while smoke pours out of his eye sockets, and hands me the joint. I tap on his cold fingers as I take it. If the souls of the stoned taste like blueberries, a joint smoked with Death himself should taste like heaven.

'You know,' he says, 'you don't change. I've skinned pieces of your soul from your body once or twice before. Yet, deep within, you're still a child hoping for acceptance and curious for more. Throughout your life, you've fought against your own destiny over and over again; you want to be the stronger one, the harsher. You want to take control and never let go. You see yourself as incomplete, and you see all around you as perfect. The only way for you to feel complete is to be the strongest.' Death stops for a second, catching a breath; I pull a puff from my joint. 'What you never seem to understand when you look at yourself: you always see only your own failings.'

Death speaks to me through the clouds of green smoke. 'You're a reversed version of Dorian Gray: hidden within you, there is a picture of yourself coloured with your fears and insecurities, and it prevents you from seeing the real you.' He takes the joint from me. 'Deep at night, when you're lonely and scared, while he is sleeping after a story, where do you hide from your fears?'

'I hide behind the smoke,' I say. Seconds later, we are both giggling.

I should tell Death the truth. At the end of the day, he knows it already. Since that day I ran from my mother's house, I have never stopped running. They tell you that when faced with a dangerous situation, mankind has the tendency to fight or flight. I guess I started my flight into a safer place, but never found a moment of peace to actually acknowledge that I have reached it.

'You overcomplicate things,' Death says. 'The truth is simple; you have built a kingdom of peace within your own imagination.' He explains that in reality, there is a third option to that fight-or-flight dilemma. 'You can freeze,' he says. 'You can pause the world around you like you pause movies on your old VCR, and just slip into your own safe kingdom.' The weed has played its games with my mind. I see myself as a child carrying a wooden Damascene sword in the face of a bee; but my shadow is that of an Arabian knight carrying the sword stolen from Ali Baba's cave, anticipating the fierce attack of the giant roc.

'Whenever the world dims my lights,' I murmur, 'I escape to my land of shadows.'

Silence fills the office. Death and I hear your footsteps as you walk around the house, intentionally avoiding my office. You know I'm smoking my second joint of the day and the smell bothers you. It makes you wrinkle your nose and mumble words of disapproval before you disappear back into your own thoughts.

'Tell me a story,' says Death, lazing back into the rocking chair he favours in my office. 'You tell all the good ones to him. Tell me my own story.' I smile.

'Once upon a time,' I say, 'I was stoned in the streets of Beirut. It was dark, but I managed.'

Death, while listening, continues to swing in that rocking chair.

S toned as fuck, you walk down the street you know well. The lights of the street lamps, and those of the cars, mesmerize you, shining up in the sky like little suns. *You know how it goes; relax, let your body lead you in the right direction, slowly now.*

There are three homeless women on the sidewalk of the road where you live. When you moved here eighteen months ago, there was only the one, that one sitting on the left-hand side of the road, begging passersby for a dollar, while attempting to control her two-year-old child, who was running around in the busy street. Syrians too! You can tell from their accent when they ask you for change. They gradually raise their voices as you come closer, in a broken-record manner, repeating prayers wishing that your mother may live forever and that your work will be fruitful and blessed. As you walk further, their voices fade away.

Your hand is putting slight pressure on an envelope you're carrying, leaving sweaty blackish fingerprints on both sides. Inside, there are two concert tickets. The music from the shop next door is too loud; its Arabian tune is played on the oud, stereotypically heard in the restaurants of Beirut. You need a Red Bull, relax, ask for one, pay money, hold the blue-and-silver can with your other hand – *This is complicated!* Take a sip. It tastes stale, yet fizzy.

You hail a taxi, negotiate the price; you jump in, pulling a cigarette out of your pack.

The taxi driver is chatty; he is from Syria too, and you feel suffocated by his accent, reminding you of back home. You wonder for a second if your assumption that he is Syrian is accurate, or if it is simply one of your own illusions. What if he is speaking Lebanese and you're the one hearing voices while glimpsing lingerie ads, well-lit on the side of the road? *What is the colour of the Queen of England's underwear?* The driver won't shut up. You need to buzz into your own thoughts.

'Brave son of a bitch,' the driver says, while you try in vain to block him out. 'It must be the good manners his mother raised him with, that motherfucker pilot who just shelled a school in Aleppo.'

'Kess ekhto shu sharmout,' you answer, cursing, surprised that you managed to wire your mind to your tongue to pronounce the sentence.

You remember the morning: it's clearly appearing in the background of your head, and you can see yourself waking up. Next to you your lover lies, his eyes sparkling with love and emotion, and he asks you, 'OJ?' You smile and you tell him, 'OJ! But roll the jay!' From the little drawer he pulls a ready joint. You grab it from his fingers and fetch your lighter. One of you says that it's a wake and bake, but you cannot remember who said that.

'The school was planning a small exhibit of children's drawings,' the driver continues, unhinged by your minimal responses. 'Instead of hanging paintings on the walls, the little children's body parts were everywhere. Some of them might have carried their paintings with them to Allah up high and asked for a final judgment.'

You allow your body to rest in a more horizontal position on the bed as your lover relaxes his body next to yours. Each of you is wondering if you should make the first move. You hesitate – are you ready to re-establish that connection?

Is this the answer? You turn around and allow your fingers to slip inside his T-shirt, slowly playing an imaginary piano on his back. He is the key to your music, the instrument of your creativity. When you make love, you feel that you belong.

'The pilot will get a trophy for his bravery, killing innocent children, hitting the right target,' the driver says. Tears are gathering in your eyes; you are not sure why. The lights around the car are fading away. 'The Syrian propaganda will come out to announce, proudly, that the Syrian regime won a war that wasn't a war, and faced the universal conspiracy that is targeting the integrity of the Syrians as a whole.' You want to tell the taxi driver to shut the fuck up.

You restlessly grab his head, pulling his lips toward yours, and you drown in the abyss of his kisses. Lonely and lost, you feel the need to dig deeper into your life with him. The endless wait for answers to questions you don't dare to ask, the feeling that you want to hold him near while listening to songs you know the lyrics of; you wonder if he will still love you tomorrow. You adjust your body closer to his. 'You won't be needing that,' you say, while helping him take off his T-shirt.

'This will only lead to more killing, you know.' The driver continues his monologue, driving you insane. 'Someone from the other side will strap a bomb to his chest and will perform a similarly heroic act against the people supporting the regime,' he says, waving his cigarette in your face, so you blow yours in his. 'And more people will die for nothing.'

He reminds you of a land that never was yours. 'I still love you,' he says.

'I never questioned that,' you respond. The tangling movement stops, he looks in your eyes, and he asks you, 'What is wrong?'

You're in pain, you are growing old and tired of the constant struggle to keep moving forward, and the positive energy that normally fills you up has been absent for weeks. 'Just pass the joint,' you tell him.

'The martyrs will go to Allah and ask him for justice,' the driver says, as he stops by the concert hall. 'Allah will then damn everyone: the government, the people and the world.'

You push your hand over the side of the bed and the glass of water that you left on the nightstand the previous night tips over the edge, shattering to a million pieces on the floor. You and your lover jump to the mess and you pick up one of the pieces. The blood from your finger streams on the glass, shining. 'Are you scarred?' he asks you, jokingly.

'Probably more than I know,' you respond.

You leave the car, walk toward the makeshift walls surrounding the entrance to the concert hall. Inside, you can hear the sounds of people cheering and you can see the light system working. You're late to the party. The music is playing. You realize, a bit too late, that you forgot the tickets in the cab.

Death isn't pleased with the story, I gather. His robes are shivering, his bones producing clicking noises that give me goosebumps. 'Why would you tell me that story?' he protests. 'It's a profession. It's the job that I do. I'm not to blame.'

I relax back in my office chair. 'You need a therapist, my friend,' I say.

Death's body is shrinking; he looks like a small dark child, reading files he wasn't supposed to. 'I was hired by lunatics,' he explains. 'They wanted the job done; I don't have control over it. They threw their bombs. I collected the souls. The hundreds of thousands of them. I worked hard. They were random with their missiles and bullets, but I was organized. I had everything under control.'

At first, it was the Syrian regime: the ruling family wanted to stay in power. 'They killed many. They dropped explosive barrels from the skies upon sleeping families.' Death's deep voice is cracking deeper; there is a stutter in what he says. Chemical weapons and poison gases were used. Death had a lot of work on his hands.

Then the Sunni extremist Islamists came, who found new ways to explain terror. Headless bodies were crucified in public squares. Children sang songs about cutting heads off the Alawites, the Muslim sect that was ruling Syria. Those same children, weeks later, were carrying the promised heads. 'It was a slaughter, they went insane,' Death explains, 'and I went insane with them.'

The story never ends. It goes on forever, and it gets complicated and tangled. This is a story I can't tell.

'Hakawati,' you call me from downstairs.

'I'm coming!' I shout. My eyes are red.

Death is now a kid, maybe fourteen; around him stand a million giant Syrian souls: tall, dark haired women, men with well-groomed beards, and children. Death never forgot the children.

4

THE TALE OF THE
ENSORCELLED PRINCE

I wonder if all of this is a curse placed on me by my evil stepmother for not attending my father's funeral. If I, like her, will have to sit alone in the darkest corner of my house, ruminating on what possible future I could have after my partner passes away into the depth of death. If I, like her, will sit on a small chair by the door as strangers carry your beautiful body down the stairs in a closed coffin. If I will be lost for words at your funeral, the way she was at my father's funeral so many years ago.

My stepmother gave me a frantic phone call that night, thirty-something years ago. You remember, don't you? We were in bed, naked, your body curved within mine, and our white dog, old and grumpy, was using my leg as a pillow. It was a peaceful, uneventful night. I didn't feel a pain in my heart and my ear did not ring; the emotional connection that they speak of, tying fathers and sons across time and space, was already severed between my father and me. You and I had just slipped into bed, unaware of what lights were left on, or if we had turned off the TV in the living room. We exchanged sleepy kisses, and you brushed your forehead on my shoulder. You mumbled some unintelligible words, and I shushed you back to your land of dreams. It was another long winter night in Vancouver and we weren't accustomed to the rain yet.

We were living in that apartment building on West Georgia, hearing the zooming sounds of cars as they rushed under the rain throughout the night. Our apartment was small back then, a tiny little space that hardly gathered us, and I hated its windows that barely cracked open. You disliked the kitchen and found it utterly weird that the kitchen was not divided away from the living room. 'How can I cook in peace here, while people are watching my every move?' you would say, standing topless in the kitchen, taking another chance at replicating your mother's Syrian recipes. 'I can't make a mess here.'

My mobile phone rang and her voice came from the other side. I was half asleep, and I hadn't spoken to her in eight years, but I recognized her the minute she said her first hello.

On the TV in the living room, a song was playing. *Anywhere, I would have followed you.* I must have left Spotify on my Evening Chill playlist. I could hear it through the cracks in the wooden wall behind our bed. *I'm feeling so small. It was over my head, I know nothing at all.* Her voice came from the other side of the phone line, traversing deserts and oceans. She sent the words across and they flew like Anzû, the ancient Sumerian bird with the body of an eagle and the head of a lion. *I will stumble and fall. I'm still learning to love, just starting to crawl.* For a bigger effect, she was exaggerating every detail about the last moments of my father's life, claiming that he dramatically called my name in agony. Her words were monstrous and massive, just like that mythological bird. The only tree big enough to hold her vicious nest of words was the tree that straddled the seven heads of the river of the sun.

I came to learn, years later, that my father passed away peacefully. He went to sleep one night and never woke up.

On that night, Death visited our apartment for the first time. He politely knocked on our front door and asked for our permission to walk in. He has never left since. He travelled with us on our vacations, slipped through our bags when we moved, until he found his favourite rocking chair in my office in this home of ours.

I made Death coffee and I asked you to leave us alone. Death and I sat around our kitchen table and gloomily drank black coffee. I didn't cry. He asked me if I needed anything and I gave him a dirty look. Within his dark robes, flashes of memories came racing out: they were moments of deep regret, but at their edges, I could see the sweet memories of a time long past.

'Say something. I'm giving up on you.'

It was June in 2000; heat had finally arrived in Damascus, prompting people to wear short sleeves, but never shorts. Syrians rarely like shorts; shorts reveal the knees of men, reducing their manhood and cupping their private parts. Damascene weather was unusually high in temperature and I craved a popsicle. My father and I decided to walk the empty streets of Damascus, looking for an open shop. It was the third day after Hafez al-Assad, the former Syrian president, passed away peacefully. They say he was on the phone with the Lebanese president, or was it the Egyptian? I can't honestly remember. His last words, supposedly, were those of peace and dignity, fighting the good fight against Israel, the bogeyman the Arab government used to herd its people. They say that he died a hero, as he lived.

At the time, I was taught not to think much about politics or question the motives of our great shiny leader.

The empty streets reflected the sun upon our faces. My father's face was becoming red. I was sure that he was cursing the moment he came up with the idea of going out. 'Who goes out days after *he* died?' he whispered, mostly to himself. 'We won't find any open shops anyway.' My mind was somewhere else.

Samer, the seventeen-year-old boy who stood up for me when I was bullied back in school the year before, had come over to our house the previous week. It was a silly thing, really. I was listening to the latest Backstreet Boys song on a small Walkman when the boys at school noticed me. They grabbed my little Walkman, which I had paid for myself with my summer job, and started to throw it to one another. One of them pushed me and I dropped to the ground. A teacher was smoking a cigarette on the other side of the road. She mumbled something and walked away.

Syria was a world where everything ended eventually. My love for dogs was killed when my mother threw away the little puppy I brought home from the streets. So I wasn't surprised to be witnessing the devastating end to the Walkman I cherished. I could have shouted and screamed and tried to defy those greater forces, represented by the three bullies. I explained my cowardliness to myself: *At the end of the day, the true measure of our lives is in the relationships we form, however they may end. I shall remember my Walkman with love songs sung by a group of handsome young men.*

Yet hope came with the arrival of a seventeen-year-old man armed with a bad-boy attitude. I remember that he used to pull up the sleeves of the school's military-style uniform to show his biceps. They were roundly filling his sleeves and covered with soft, youthful black hair. He didn't have to scare the boys away. He just asked, 'What's going on here?' and the boys gave it to the winds, but not before surrendering the Walkman to him. He extended his hand toward me, and I was lifted off the ground. He smiled, and he said that his name was Samer.

I knew his name. I had asked about him before from afar, and a friend with a brother in Samer's class managed to get me his name. He was two years older than me and he was always there in the schoolyard around the time we had our midday break. Both of us wore the military uniforms forced upon us by the school system. On him, it looked magnificent; he wore it with a rebellious touch, the shirt always open to reveal the black Metallica T-shirts he wore underneath; he pulled the sleeves up and tightened his belt around his waist. His uniform was well-fitted and formed the shape of each and every one of his muscles.

My uniform, on the other hand, was baggy and always a size or two bigger than me. 'We will buy you one that is a bit bigger than you,' my father had said while we were standing in the school uniform shop in Hariqa Street. He didn't wait for my approval. 'That way, you can wear it for two years.' My father looked my thin body up and down with a disappointed gaze before adding that he was sure I would grow larger to fit into it. I looked miserable in that uniform, like a sad clown who had lost his way to the circus, and by the time I grew an extra inch or two, it had become dirty, ugly and unusable.

My father and I finally reached the shop owned by Uncle Abu Saleh. He was an old man with a bald head and a grey beard. Before I entered the shop, I grabbed the promised popsicle from the freezer – strategically placed outside the shop for children to see – and followed my father inside. Uncle Abu Saleh wasn't really my uncle. He was my grandmother's favourite cousin. I'd heard murmurs in our family that back in their day, my grandmother and Uncle Abu Saleh were supposed to get married, but he was called to the army and later thought dead. My grandmother, young and helpless, sat by the radio, her only friend back in the early forties, and waited to hear his name among the lists of the dead.

Six months later, she was married to another according to her father's wishes, and Abu Saleh came back from the army just in time to attend her wedding.

'Let *him* go to hell,' Uncle Abu Saleh said to my father in a loud voice.

My father's heart dropped to the ground. 'Let's not talk about that.'

'You were young, you don't remember,' Abu Saleh insisted. 'It was dark days when he took over.' Abu Saleh spat in a tissue, and threw it into the trash. My father gestured to him to calm his voice but Abu Saleh wouldn't listen. 'He killed so many people in Hama back in the eighties,' he added, his tone getting louder. 'He only kept the historical sites, and destroyed everything else.' My father's face was turning yellow. 'He brought his own people to repopulate the city.'

I was sixteen; I did not know what Uncle Abu Saleh was talking about. I had been a mere thought in my father's mind when the Syrian regime ended an uprising led by the Muslim Brotherhood movement in the early eighties. The Sunni Muslim movement, representing the majority of the people, was standing against the Alawite-led government, which took over power in a coup back in the seventies.

Abu Saleh accepted his fate as the man who came too late, and retreated to the background of my grandmother's life. He married a respectable woman picked by his mother, just weeks after my grandmother's wedding. He had never met her before the wedding night, I'm told. He only saw a picture of her presented to his mother by a matchmaker. He treated her well, and she performed her duties as his wife for dozens of years. She respectfully prepared his dinner every day, ironed his clothes and washed his white gallabieh with laurel-scented soap. She carried his son, Saleh, for the full term of nine months, and raised their only child with endless love. She barely left her home, and never visited our family. Abu Saleh never took a step in my grandmother's home except for the funeral of my grandfather. He showed up at the door, firmly held the hands of my uncles and father, read a couple of verses from the Rahman Quran sura loudly, drank the dark, bitter coffee quickly and left within twenty minutes.

B y this time in their conversation, my father started to take multiple steps back, increasing in frequency and speed. 'We shouldn't talk about *him*. You never know who is listening,' my father said, his voice shaky. He placed his hand on my shoulder, as if to protect me.

Abu Saleh died eleven years later; his house was raided by a group of armed militia who killed him and his wife. Those who killed him were rumoured to be part of the 2011 uprising against the Syrian regime, which now had Assad Jr. as its leader. His son, Saleh, was drafted into the Syrian Arab Army in 2012, where he was assigned to fight the terrorists in Aleppo. He eagerly joined the army, wearing the dark green uniform and carrying a gun on his belt and an AK-17 on his shoulder, posing for a final photo that his friends took of him. He went to the war and no one has heard of him since.

'You will see,' Abu Saleh said, as we escaped his shop. 'One day this regime will fall and all this evil will be over.'

W e walked, Samer and I, every day for hours. We used to skip school and go to a nearby garden and just talk about everything: I told him about my collection of comic books and he told me about his love of kittens. I played with the kittens he managed to catch. I helped him with his English lessons and he helped me understand some math. Besides his firm shoulders and his soft hair, I enjoyed the fact that he really laughed at all my jokes.

He told me about his dreams of leaving. He wanted to get on a plane and travel away, and I wanted to be on that same flight with him. We didn't know exactly where we would go – the geography we were taught at school seemed to ignore the existence of the rest of the world – but we wanted to go away nonetheless.

Like a Damascene mosaic piece, built one stone at a time, there was a feeling growing within me. There was an unmatched joy that came from seeing him walking toward me in the early morning winter sun. He brought warmth to my chest. He filled me with a lover's anxiety that would reach out to my throat and break my newly found man's voice while I talked to him. Before Samer, that feeling only came when I was listening to my old Backstreet Boys cassette. I felt an uplifting, yet sinful, sense of joy as I heard their youthful voices singing silly songs about unrequited love and broken hearts. With Samer, that feeling started to take shape. The feeling smoothed and blended within me, like the stones on the surface of the mosaic.

One day, while we were lying on the grass in Jahiz Garden outside our school, I told him about my mother. I showed him scars, both visible on my skin and hidden within my heart. He listened as I told him about the knife she carried, and gasped when I told him about the burned photos. In the corner of his eye, I saw a tiny tear slipping on the side of his face, until it dripped to the shiny grass. Without a word, he grabbed my hand and squeezed it. The simple act sent shivers up and down my spine and for a second, it tensed all of my body. Then, as I relaxed again, with the sun breaking through the clouds and covering my face with a blanket of warmth and happiness, I knew that I was in love with him.

M inutes before we reached home, I looked at my father. I stopped walking and just gazed at him. It took him a while to realize I was left behind. He always comes to that conclusion a second too late: when he left me with my mentally ill mother for three years, when he demanded perfection one very single visit he made to my grandmother's house, when he came back to visit my mother's bedroom once in a while, producing more children to suffer with his eldest. He was always a second too late to come around and realize his faults.

'Daddy,' I said, 'I'm gay.'

I was the first one to kiss. Samer and I were sitting in his room watching *The Mummy*. He was laughing at Brendan Fraser's jokes; I was scared of the skeletal mummy. I got closer to him and he placed his arm on my shoulder. I looked up at him and I went for the kiss.

And he kissed me back.

'I attended Samer's wedding six months later,' I tell Death, sipping the last sip of the coffee. The sunrise is shyly giving colour to Mount Seymour outside our window.

'I attended his funeral six years after that,' he replies.

M y father didn't react. The empty, sunny street echoed my admission, yet he couldn't hear it. He walked back toward me in slow steps and then stopped walking midway toward me. We exchanged looks of disbelief and confusion. I regretted what I said that very second. 'What did you just say?' he whispered from afar, but I could hear him. I didn't reply. 'What did you fucking say? Tell me, you son of sharmouta,' he insisted. I silently looked at him with tears gathering in my eyes. I didn't move a muscle; I didn't say a word. He looked equally confused. He looked around the empty street, as if looking for an answer to his questions. His face was turning red. His eyes were sparkling like a lighter that had run out of gas. He turned around, took a deep breath and started walking away. I remained motionless for a second or two, waiting for his reaction. Suddenly he stopped walking; he turned around and rushed toward me. He grabbed me by the hair and pulled me behind him. I walked backwards, tears gathering in my eyes; my skin was tightening and the pain of his grip on my hair was swaying inside my head like a pendulum. He didn't speak and I didn't scream, not until we reached my grandmother's building and he started to pull me up the stairs. I lost my balance and fell, but he continued to pull me by the hair as my body hit the stairs one after another.

He opened the door and rushed inside. When my grandmother saw us, she gasped. She floundered and demanded my father let go of my hair at once. 'What's happening?' she screamed, and my uncles started to gather in the hallway. My father didn't say a word; he pushed her away and she fell on a nearby chair. I screamed, fearing for my delicate grandmother, and then couldn't stop screaming. It felt as if my throat was a dam and it broke, and the flood of screaming wouldn't stop. My father pushed me into the first bedroom he saw, my grandmother's room, and locked the door behind us.

My father pulled out his belt and repeatedly whipped me on my side. He slammed me on the ground and called me a louti, a faggot. 'I raised a man,' he said. 'You're not my son. You're not a man.' My father punched me in the face, dislodging one of my teeth. My grandmother was knocking on the door hysterically, demanding he open the door. My uncles were debating whether they should break in or 'leave the father to raise his son as he pleases.' My father demanded to know who the other boy was. Two hours and a broken nose later, he found out. He left the bedroom to find my grandmother sitting on the floor by the door, crying her eyes out. He walked over her and reached for the phone. With his fingers covered with my blood, he dialled the phone. He called Samer's father and they talked. Six months later, my father was invited to Samer's wedding.

I unbuttoned Samer's shirt while his hand was scratching the skin on my back. I took off my T-shirt and he kissed my chest. I slipped my fingers under his belt and pulled it. He kissed me deeper. His hand grabbed my hair and pulled me back; he looked me in the eye for a second. Was he second-guessing? Was he wondering if it was wrong? But the second was over and his lips were locked upon mine. I pushed him back and kissed every hair on his chest; between my teeth, I softly bit his nipples. He gasped.

Brendan Fraser was screaming something obnoxious in the background.

I pulled down his pants and he pulled down mine; we were both naked at once. Then we honestly did not know what to do next. What happens now? How do we react? What is the next move? We were stuck, deep within a kiss, touching each other. For the next hour, we hugged, kissed, bit and touched each other all over until we suddenly relaxed back, breathlessly touching each other with soft, rhythmic strokes.

He pulled me toward his chest, and I rested on his arms. He smiled and caressed my naked body with his hand. 'I will call you my prince,' he whispered. 'You'll always be my prince.'

My father locks my grandmother's bedroom door on me for three nights. My grandmother sneaks in at night to help me get to the bathroom, and then returns me to the bedroom in the hopes that my father won't find out. She brings ice cubes wrapped in a towel; she places it on my broken nose without a word. She strokes my hair while tears slip down her face.

On the fourth night, my storm starts. I'm leaving. My grandmother knows. She comes to me that night carrying my clean clothes in a pile, and leaves them by the side of the bed. She leaves the door unlocked.

My books are disposable. I only keep my favourite. My clothes are not many; I only pick the ones without a stain of blood or a stain of memory. The bag, which used to be my school bag, is filling up fast with my stuff. In my pocket, there is money. My shoes are waiting for me by the door.

I take a final look at my grandmother's room with its queen bed, the rose mattress, her wooden windows, her shelves of books – some broken, some intact. The small praying mat and the fireplace, my grandfather's black-and-white photo. I say my goodbyes, and I never see them again. 'Do you want to tell him a story?' Death asks me. He puts down his coffee cup and I realize that we're not in the past any more. Death is pointing to you as you descend the stairs. We are old now; the conversation between Death and me at the kitchen table, sipping coffee and sharing memories, extended through time and now we're back in our home, and you're old, grumpy and sick. 'I might have to,' I answer. My voice cracks – I'm tired.

I see Death's shadow; it grows taller. It gets darker. It stretches on the wall, and reaches the ceiling. 'What are you doing?' I ask Death, but find no answer. I squeeze my eyes and I look at the shadow. It's now a shadow of a man hanging from a noose. The body sways left and right in the same rhythm as the sound of your steps as you walk down the stairs. He returns to life, lifts his arms to grab the noose around his neck, unties it, and slips to the floor. The shadow walks towards me. I welcome it into this world. It is dark, heavy and full of sorrow. It sits in my lap; it infuses within me. My hands are its hands; my tongue is its tongue. It wants to tell its story.

The shadow of Samer, eager to please, starts telling his story.

When my time came, they carried my body down to the cold, wet earth. I was wrapped in linen cloth; it was white and harsh on my dead skin. The four men placed my body with my head turned in the direction of Kaaba, hoping that my soul would find its way to the righteous direction. They stood around my body down in my grave, and they said a final prayer before climbing back up. My father stood there with red eyes, breathing deep sighs into his lungs. My uncle was smoking a cigarette, puffing its smoke in the air in a repetitive movement. My wife, who found my dead body hanging from the ceiling, refused to come to my funeral.

The late evening rain started to drip upon the small gathering of men around my grave. It was accompanied by a strong wind, carrying the smell of death from freshly dug graves around us. The four men stood aside, waiting for my family to say their final goodbyes. My father took a final gaze at my dead body before waving his hand for them to finish their work. They lifted their shovels, filled them with wet soil and started to pour earth down on me.

'A shameful funeral,' my father whispered as he started to walk away.

'An unmarked grave,' my uncle responded, following his steps.

No one carried my dead body to one of Damascus's mosques. No one prays a death prayer for a man who killed himself. No one gathered in my family's house. No one read the Quran's suras, or talked about my life. No one cried for me, not even my wife. She carried our young son and returned to her mother's home on my death day. My body was carried in the dead of night to a nearby hospital and then deposited in a grave before midnight.

Within a month, all who knew me forgot about me. My stories were never to be told; my name was never to be uttered. My body rotted in my grave and worms found their way to my insides, eating away at my rounded arms covered in black hair, pulling on my tongue and yanking away my brown eyes.

That night, she returned early from her family's home. She was supposed to spend the night there, but her father and mother had another fight, and she couldn't bear the screaming matches and the ear-piercing cries of her young child. She silently slipped away through the door, hailed a yellow cab and told the driver to take her back home. She turned the key slowly, fearing to produce a sound that would wake me up. She feared me; I knew it. I left the mark of my palm on her face once or twice before. She hated me, but she accepted her fate. 'A man has to teach his woman how to treat him,' her mother told her when she complained about my fists and my heavy hand. 'The beatings from your husband should taste like raisins in your mouth.'

She took off her modest heels, pulled her hijab off her hair and walked on her toes to her child's bedroom. She placed the sleeping boy in his crib and looked at him in the darkness. She cleaned his nose with a tissue before smiling. He stopped snoring and went back to his peaceful sleep. Finally she walked slowly to our bedroom. She opened the door and walked in without turning on any lights. She didn't want to wake me up.

When her eyes adjusted to the darkness, she could see the shadow of my body lying in bed. She could see my head resting on my pillow, and she could see my naked leg uncovered on the corner of the bed. Then she saw the other body in bed with me. She gasped, rushed across the room and turned the lights on.

I squeezed my eyes. Annoyed, I woke up, unaware of what was going on around me. I pushed the head resting on my shoulder away and tried to open my eyes in the blaring light. Then I heard the scream.

'There is a naked man with you in bed,' she screamed. 'A naked man in our bed!' The man, whom I had picked up from Shallan Park a couple of hours before, jumped from bed. 'You're married,' he shouted. 'You didn't tell me you were married!' He stood there, naked in my bedroom screaming at me, while my wife stood by the door.

She pointed her finger at me, and then at him. She didn't blink. I could see the realization filling up her mind. Her features were changing; her surprise was morphing into anger and betrayal. She rushed out of the bedroom and I could hear her crying out loud. Our son woke up, heard the noise and started to cry as well. 'I'm going to call your father,' I heard her scream from the other room. 'I'm going to tell them that they gave me a defective man.' I jumped out of bed and started getting dressed. I called her name once, twice, but she didn't reply. I looked at the naked man and whispered to him that he should leave.

The naked man stood there for another second, then gathered his clothes silently. He slipped out without a word. I heard the front door open, and close.

'Open this door,' I screamed at her as she locked herself inside our son's bedroom. 'I swear to God, I will bring this house down on your head if you don't open this door.' She didn't reply. Instead, I heard her dialling a number on her phone, and heard her start a heated, tear-filled conversation. I kicked the door with my foot, but stopped when I heard the howls of my son crying.

I roamed the house like a caged animal. I returned to our bedroom. My brain was rushing; I remembered the nights I had spent getting beaten up by my father, I remembered the pain I endured and the promises I made never to be sinful again. I remembered crying in the mosque, in a late-night prayer, asking Allah to take away this trial from my mind and body, to release me from the pain of my sinful attraction. 'Never again,' I whispered. 'Never again will I go through this.'

I pulled out my belt and tied it up to the fan in our bedroom. While I heard the escaped words from my wife's conversation in the other room, I tightened the belt around my neck. I stood on the side of the bed and pushed myself down. I felt the weight of my body on my neck. The fan ached under my weight. I struggled to breathe as I felt the noose tightening. The leather of the belt was slicing into my flesh. My tongue popped out of my mouth as my lungs tried to pull in air. My legs spasmed, trying to reach the side of the bed. I stayed alive for six more minutes. I could feel my heart rate rushing, then slowing. I could feel my toes arching, then relaxing. I could feel my piss covering the front of my pants, hot and burning, dripping down my leg, down to my feet. Then, I didn't care to feel.

I was smoking a cigarette with three other friends on the corner of Shallan Street, near al-Madfa Park, when he approached me. His reading glasses, dark attitude and wicked smile brought back a distant memory of a lover long gone. He asked me for a cigarette and I gave him one. He knew one of my friends. They had slept together last month. He had asked my friend about me and figured out my name.

We walked down Shallan Street and ordered french-fry sandwiches from Baguette Sandwich at the corner of the park. He told me his name, but I forgot it. He slipped his finger along my biceps, admiring their youthful hair. He asked me if I'm a top or a bottom. His face lit up when I said that I'm a top. 'A manly guy like you should surely be a top,' he said, placing his hand on my thigh.

We didn't have conversations about kittens or comic books; we didn't exchange war stories about insane parents. He didn't know who Brendan Fraser was. I took him home, knowing that my wife would be sleeping at her parents' house that night. While we were driving there, he unzipped my pants and slipped his hands inside, pulling my penis out. He squeezed it a couple of times between his fingers. 'I've always wanted to do this,' he whispered while he directed his mouth toward my penis. I didn't feel good about it: the act felt vulgar and uninvited. I wished he would talk to me – ask questions about my past or shyly express his love. But I knew the night wouldn't have that connection. I knew that the past couldn't be replicated, no matter how much I might try.

I opened the door for him and he walked inside. I pushed him against a wall and reached for his lips. I couldn't keep up the make-out session for too long; I could smell his bad breath and it filled my head. I pushed him to the bedroom, unbuttoned his shirt and pulled down his pants. I pushed myself inside him and he moaned. There was no skin-scratching and no finger-slipping. There were no deep kisses or hair-grabbing. No long gazes in each other's eyes and no lip-locking. He didn't kiss every hair on my chest.

By the time I came on his back, I was tired, disgusted and filled with ghosts of the past. I flipped around and fell asleep.

My father and the sheikh were sitting in the guest room in our home. I was sitting in the corner. My jaw was aching and my side was covered in bruises, but neither man looked at me. They whispered to each other intently. The sheikh's face was gloomy and dark; his white beard was trembling as he *tsked* repeatedly with his tongue. After a moment of silence, the sheikh called me to come closer. 'You know what Allah did to the people of Lut?' he asked, and never expected an answer. 'He reached with his mighty hand and grabbed their village. He lifted it to the highest of the seven skies, then turned it upside down and smashed it on the ground.

'That's how the Dead Sea was created,' he added, shaking his head. He explained that my acts were sinful, and that my punishment should be severe. 'We are instructed to take you to the tallest building in town and throw you off the edge to a crowd of spectators,' he said. 'Then we should drop rocks upon your dead body until you're covered in your makeshift grave.' I've always feared heights.

Redemption is possible, though, the sheikh pointed out. 'This is a test placed upon you by Allah in his skies; he wants to see if you can come out of this life pure of body and soul,' he added.

'You'll marry your cousin. I already spoke to her father,' my father said in a decisive tone.

'You shall pray,' the sheikh said. 'You shall ask for forgiveness every day of your life until the day you meet the angel of death. You should hope that by returning to the righteous path, you will find mercy from Allah.' I dropped my head down in agreement, and a tear slipped from my eyes that I quickly swiped away.

Before I was told that I would marry a woman, before I came on his back, before I woke up to the lights and screams, before I placed the belt upon the fan, before they placed my body in a grave, before my brain rotted under the wet earth, my last dream was a memory of a man I kissed once. 'I will call you my prince,' I whispered to him once again. 'You'll always be my prince.'

'You love him,' you whisper. The night is almost over, and the rooster is about to announce the morning light.

'I pity him, I guess.'

'You can write the beginnings, but you can never know the endings,' you tell me as you slip down the bed, preparing to fall asleep.

'Maybe,' I reply, 'but his ending could have been prevented.'

I toss and turn, trying to find the right position to fall asleep. I finally find a comfortable corner of the bed and I rest my head on my pillow. In my mind, I remember the jokes he laughed at, the kittens he caught and that very first kiss. I smile. I imagine him riding a flying horse toward a country whose name we couldn't pronounce. I imagine him escaping the world that hated him and finding another home. I imagine him living forever. I immortalize him in my stories. He will always be my prince.

5

THE HAKAWATI'S VOYAGES IN THE LAND OF WOMEN

You know I'm hurting, haunted by a ghost of a boy I once knew. You decide to leave me alone for the rest of the night. You turn around, reach for the light switch and turn off the last glimpses of the room around us, now occupied with my dark thoughts.

I always second-guess my own path in life. Maybe if I had stayed in my mother's home, accepting my fate as her forever caretaker and punching bag, Samer wouldn't have died. Maybe if I had let her slide that knife into my throat, leaving me bleeding among my comic books on my blue mattress, he would have been saved.

How could I have known that escaping my mother would have all of those repercussions on my life and the lives of other people around me? People always ask me to tell her story, and I rarely do. They assume that such a topic would be easy. That I can account for my history with her the same way I can recall which medicine I should give you when. I heard that she passed away years ago. She was alone in her old Damascene house when clashes took place in the streets. It was during the final years of the civil war and she was forgotten in a corner, alone in her family's old house, filled with memories and regrets. There in the capital of the civil war that became a catalyst for so many wars after, she sat as a blind

witness to the end of a life she understood so little of and the birth of a
life she didn't understand at all.

In the flashes of memories I have of her, I recall her sometimes
being sane for days, but those days smelled of her medicine and the
dust gathering in the air, filling my lungs. I also remember her being
the insane woman she was. She was outside hanging her blue jacket on
the clothesline on her balcony to dry when a stray bullet found its way to
her. I was told that no one noticed her disappearance for days. She had
slipped to the outskirts of social life years before that, and hardly anyone
remembered knowing her.

But enough about *her*.

My grandmother was the woman who practically raised me. Samira,
as she called herself, was a short, blonde-haired old woman with blue
eyes. She was a loving, strict woman capable of anything, including
making the best riz b'haleeb in the land of Syria and the whole Middle
East, and forcing me to sleep at eight-thirty every night, so I wouldn't
hear the news on the only Arabic TV channel the country had at the
time: Syrian Arab Television.

When my grandfather died in the late-eighties, leaving her alone with
six teenage sons and a daughter, she pulled out her sewing machine
and decided to do something about it. She paid a taxi driver to sneak
her some fashion magazines from Lebanon, and she started imitating
the latest fashion trends in Paris and selling the dresses to old ladies.
The women especially came around during springtime, when weddings
are traditionally more common and many women are in need of a
good dress.

In the early morning I would abandon our dark house where my
mother roamed like a caged animal and go to the sunny small house of
my grandmother. I used to knock, and she would open with her white
prayer cover on her head. 'Your blessing?' I used to say, extending my
hand. She would gracefully place hers in mine and I would print a wet
kiss on it and lift it up to my forehead, showing my respect.

My grandmother loved her plants. She had dozens upon dozens
of them. She and I would spend the morning watering all the plants
around the house. I used to climb a little ladder for her and water the

small ones she hung from the ceiling. 'Plants give fresh, cold air during summer days,' she would say, water dripping from between her fingers. She used to drop the water on her hand, shaping her fingers like small tunnels, targeting the right root. 'They are also creatures of feeling. They are created by Allah with one emotion to feel: love for those who water them, second only to their love of Allah himself.'

My grandmother, an old, traditional Muslim woman, found her way to understand life. 'Everything has a purpose,' she told me as she poured olive oil over the mint-covered labneh. 'Every single thing was created for a purpose, in the grand structure of fates.' Every bird in the sky and every animal that steps on the ground have a common connection in my grandmother's head; they all have a rhythm with life that they understand. They hear it like the beating heart of earth itself. Allah blessed each creature with a set of emotions, allowing them to judge right from wrong and give thanks when due. 'Except for humans,' my grandmother would say. 'They forgot how to listen.'

When Samira was fifteen, she was forced to marry someone other than the man she loved. She had been in love with her cousin Abu Saleh since they were little children. When she was seven, her mother told her that she would marry him one day, and that became a fact of life. She would watch him passing outside their windows; she stood inside her house, gazing through the cracks of a closed wooden window to the world outside, and saw him leaving his home. He was tall and she enjoyed seeing him wearing the fez that his father bought him when he turned eighteen. She thought he was handsome, and that he would bring her all the desserts in the world if she asked.

On one late summery day, she heard his door open. She rushed to her window, avoiding her mother's questioning eyes, and looked out for him. She saw him standing outside his family's home with his father. The father mumbled, and Abu Saleh nodded his head in agreement. He was wearing a grey military uniform and carrying his old hunting rifle. The father then pulled Abu Saleh in and hugged him dearly, before he sent him walking down the street, avoiding bike riders and tripping under the heavy bag he was carrying.

She was told that he went to the war against the British invaders. Her father told her that the British called it Operation Exporter. The war was over in a couple of months, and life returned to normal, but Abu Saleh never returned. She waited by her window for hours every day in vain. She hoped to see him coming back, knocking on his old door, yet he never did. 'You're turning sixteen soon,' her mother pointed out. 'We need to get you married.'

It was a strange day for her. A matchmaker, a khattabieh, knocked on their door and Samira's mother welcomed her with a cup of coffee.

It was 1941; she knew that from the radio. She had heard it once in her father's room and startled to hear a stranger's voice coming out of it. The radio was never allowed to be touched by anyone but her mother, who would take some feathers to readjust the dust on it when her father was not in the house. However, when her cousin Abu Saleh was missing in the war, Samira was allowed, for a short period of time, to listen to the radio announcements. She wouldn't want to know much about the radio otherwise; she was raised believing that curiosity is not a good trait for a girl, and she didn't care to break that rule.

The khattabieh sat with Samira's mother. She was a stranger from a different neighbourhood in Damascus. Back then, it wasn't customary for a woman in old Damascus to enter a new neighbourhood unaccompanied by a man of her family; however, for that day, only women were gathered and there was no place for men.

Samira's mother and the strange woman were sitting in ard dyar, the little garden surrounded by the rooms of the house from every corner, shielding it from the eyes of strangers on the street. The two women were exchanging compliments and trivial chat. Samira walked in wearing her best dress, as instructed by her mother. She smiled as she presented the coffee to the stranger lady. 'Min eed ma n'dama,' said the lady with a smile. Samira could never understand why 'from a hand that shall never be cut off' was considered an endearing compliment. However, she smiled politely and replied with a soft 'thank you.'

Samira sat silently between the two ladies, then suddenly felt a cutting pain: the khattabieh was pulling her hair. 'Ma shaa Allah! It's so beautiful,' the woman said, and Samira's mother understood the gesture. 'It's all natural as well, ya khanoom!'

The lady put Samira through all kinds of weird tests. She brought her a nut and asked her to crack it open with her teeth to make sure the teeth were real. She pulled out a little piece of paper with tiny words on it and asked Samira to read it to see if her sight was perfect. She accidentally poured water on Samira's dress and spent an extra minute or two feeling Samira's thighs while helping her dry the water. Samira was uncomfortable, but the look in her mother's eyes made her go through it all willingly. At last it was time for the final test. 'I want a madas,' the strange lady said, and Samira's mother decided to put an end to it. 'Her breasts are real and you don't need to touch them to know that, khanoom,' Samira's mother said, while Samira's face turned red.

The strange lady examined Samira's body with her eyes for a moment, then decided to back off.

Two weeks later Samira was in a white dress getting married to Ahmed, the son of the woman who had sent the strange lady. She had never met Ahmed before the wedding night. The invitation card, which my grandmother showed me once, was a piece of yellowed paper that used to be glamorous, and instructed the people attending that no children or maids were allowed to come.

After two older sons, Samira gave birth to my father. Twenty years later, I called her tetta as my first word ever. Ahmed passed away thirty-five years after the wedding and my tetta continued to mourn him until her death.

I miss the conversations my grandmother used to have with her customers. The women would come late in the morning and they would sit around the balcony, sipping coffee and exchanging gossip. 'He was a cheap one,' my grandmother said one time, talking about my dead grandfather. 'He would measure the size of the orange cake I made him to make sure no one else ate it.' My grandmother would look up constantly and whisper 'Forgive me, husband' before continuing her gossip session with her customers.

You would hear him walking to the kitchen carrying his ruler to see if someone had eaten an extra piece of the orange cake. Minutes later, you'd hear his voice coming from the deep end of the house. 'Who ate my bloody cake?' he would ask, and no one would answer.

The next morning, my grandmother would cut me another piece of the cake.

After the gossip was done, my grandmother used to take her customers to a small hidden room where they would all take their clothes off, down to their colourful undies, and try on the new, unfinished dresses. Sometimes they laughed, sometimes they seriously discussed the form and shape of each dress using adult words I had never heard before.

'It shows too much of my boobs,' one woman would say.

'Oh, show a little boob, honey. The last time that breast of yours saw the light was the day your husband took off your bra for the first time.' My tetta was always ready with a response.

By the time I was old enough to understand, I knew that tetta had become a big deal. Her customers told their neighbours about her beautiful dresses and her jasmine trees, and the neighbours told their sisters, who told their friends, and suddenly everyone in Damascus knew Samira, the tailor with the magical touch. Middle-class women would come in the early morning, knocking on her door and presenting her with cooked meals and plants. Fast cars carrying heavy, wealthy women would stop by my grandmother's building, and the driver would open the door for the women and help them leave the car. They would watch over them as they walked up the stairs.

My grandmother used to grow jasmine in that room where she held her meetings with her customers, until the day my uncle felt that he was too old for his mother to provide him with money. He took away the sewing machine and the smuggled magazines. He threw the pins, the zippers and the buttons in the garbage. He only kept the jasmine. My grandmother protested, but he rejected her pleas. 'I'm the man of the house now,' he explained. 'I can't walk in the street with my dignity if people know my mother is the tailor who spends money on me.'

My grandmother refused to water those jasmines. They passed away slowly and painfully.

I leave the bed, trying not to wake you up. This is one of the very rare nights when I stay up after you sleep. Slowly I escape the bedroom, aiming for my office.

There I see Death sitting behind the desk. He looks at me. 'Tough night, huh?' I walk toward my bookshelves and I pull out my stash. I open it and the smell of marijuana fills the room. Death's eyes sparkle with a greedy, needy look.

'I don't feel like sleeping,' I say, pushing him off my chair. 'I wish someone would tell me a bedtime story.'

'Let's play a game, then,' Death says. He waves his hands and around us, the stage of the famous fifties TV show *To Tell the Truth* appears. A cartoon figure with a raised hand is drawn on the curtain behind him. He looks at it and winks. The curtain lifts. Behind it, I see the figures of three women hiding in the shadows. Death starts explaining the show. 'What is your name, please?' he asks, and the light hits the face of the first woman. It's my grandmother.

'I'm the woman in this man's life,' she says, pointing at me. Death smirks and then asks the second woman the same question: she's my sister. She says, 'I'm the woman in this man's life.' Finally the light hits the last woman behind the curtains.

'This is not what I signed up for,' I whisper to Death, and he smiles.

'You need to see her for who she really is.'

I refuse to look at the third woman. She is my mother. 'What's your name, please?' Death asks.

'I'm the woman in this man's life,' she replies.

'These women will tell you memories of yours that they witnessed,' Death explains, stretching his Es and Os, imitating a game show announcer. 'One of the three memories is false, while the other two are true.' I don't want to play. I want to escape my office, but its colours around me have turned to black-and-white. I stand up, dropping my stash on the floor, and I look for the door but can't find it.

'Ah, ah, ah,' Death says, 'no escaping from my game. I'm doing this for you. You need to face your demons. You will relive your memories with these women.'

He turns to the three women and whispers, 'Do you solemnly swear to tell the truth, the whole truth, and nothing but the truth?'

'I do.'

'I do.'

'I do.'

MEMORY 1

I'm seven years old. My grandfather is sitting with his friends in the saamlik, the men-only section of our old Damascene home, and my grandmother is peeking in from the hallway door every now and then. The room is spacious, decorated with old mosaic pieces on all of the walls. The wooden chairs are carved to form flowers, branches and mandalas. The ceiling is high, and a chandelier that used to carry candles and oil lamps hangs from the middle of it. I can see the electric wires that climb the walls like vines and reach the chandelier, filling it with electric light and stealing away some of its beauty. One side of the room has no wall; it opens directly to ard dyar, with a couple of steps leading down to the indoor garden.

I'm sitting next to my grandfather, listening to the conversation while playing with a wooden horse and a small knight toy. My grandfather repeatedly coughs and his brother, who is an even older man with a small cane that he uses to walk around, passes him a cup of water. The cane has a head that looks like a monkey's face. I've always loved that cane. Two other old men are there; they look blurry, as they play no role in this memory other than listening intently and smoking tobacco from old pipes. My grandmother brings coffee for everyone. They eat cookies with their fake teeth and talk.

'Oh, I remember, I remember perfectly,' my grandfather says, as he puts another cookie in his mouth. His white moustache is stained with little crumbs of cookies and the black coffee. 'It used to be so original and new. I took my wife to the cinema; I can't even remember the title of the movie.' My grandfather describes a scene that he did not enjoy in a movie he doesn't remember. 'Here she was,' he says, 'a woman holding a gun at a man and screaming her lungs out.

She looked so scared and unaware of the powerful feeling of the gun.'

His brother is coughing hard. I look up to him, staring at his monkey cane, and I hear him saying, 'Those were the days; that blondie was the first woman to ever hold a gun in the movies.'

My grandmother walks in, holding a tray with lots of fruit. My eyes automatically lock on the blueberry juice she is bringing for everyone. She is moving swiftly, trying to reduce the time she spends in the company of men. She covers her head with her white scarf and wears her praying dress in modesty.

I calculate the number of glasses versus the number of people. I feel delighted to discover that I'm counted in to get my share of blueberry juice.

'Women should not hold guns, not in the movies nor in real life,' one of the men says. 'They are not going to be able to control it, and you never know. They might even use it against their husbands.'

'Es-Allah, what a memory!' my grandfather says, while he picks up the blueberry juice, which I'm looking at with widened eyes. 'Those days are never coming back. We live in a bad time in history: women are holding guns and going to work and supporting families.' He continues his rant. He explains how he forced his wife – my grandmother, who is still in the room – to cover her eyes when that actress picked the gun up and pointed it toward the man. She looks at him from the side of her eyes, but she knows better than to add a comment.

Agreement comes from around the room, while my grandmother finally hands me my precious glass of blueberry juice.

MEMORY 2

I'm nine years old. My mother is walking down Hamra Street in Damascus, holding my hand. It's the late eighties, and the shops are regaining some of their old glow. The clothes shops are adding more mannequins to their storefronts. They place colourful children's clothes on the smaller mannequins, imitating children playing or dancing. A couple of shops even dare to place provocative, skin-showing nightgowns on their female mannequins. My mother looks at each of them, then explains to me how much she adores the colour of one of the dresses, or enjoys the cute cut to a skirt. I am enjoying an ice cream – vanilla ice cream covered with chocolate and dipped in sweet honey, a taste so complete I don't think I've ever really enjoyed it since I got older. Somehow, when you get older, you forget how to taste the small things and to enjoy them the way you used to when you were a child.

My mother's hair is dark brown, just like mine. It has no cover. It's wavy like a sea, beautiful and long. I've always thought that my mother has dreamy hair worthy of a princess or a jazz singer. I'm enjoying my vanilla ice cream and walking beside her, while she window-shops.

An old man (at least old in my eyes; he might not be older than thirty-five) is walking beside us. He pushes me as he passes by. I'm falling to the ground and my vanilla ice cream is falling too. I end up face-down on the ground with the ice cream all over my T-shirt. The man continues on his way without even looking back.

'Hey! Watch where you're going!' my mother shouts at him, as she picks me up and helps me to stand. My eyes are teary. Painful pulses are coming from my knee and my elbow, but they cannot compare to the painful feeling of losing the vanilla ice cream that I loved so very much, and getting it splashed all over my shirt.

'Are you talking to me, ya mara? Huh?' the guy says, turning around; he looks angry and unpleasant. I want to ask my mother to step away. She holds her breath for a second, and calculates in her head the possible outcomes of this interaction. 'You pushed my child!' she says. 'Watch where you're going! He might have gotten hurt.'

The man looks furious. He has short hair on the crown of his head and longer hair on the back of his neck. He speaks with an accent that implies he is from one of the coastal cities of Syria. He terrifies me, and since that day, that haircut and that accent still send shivers through my spine.

'Know your place, woman! You can't talk to me like this!' he says.

'Well,' my mother responds, 'you should know your place. You could have hurt my child!'

The guy, now with an amused smile, is coming closer. People from the shops are watching the exchange without doing much. It hasn't yet developed to the point where another man has to defend the helpless woman that's my mother. For now, they just sit and watch.

The guy smirks. Then suddenly, he slaps my mother on the face. I hear the sound of the slap seconds before I actually see his hand moving toward her. She is shocked.

My mother looks at him, her face red. I look at her; she is squeezing my fingers between hers. A second later, my mother gets closer to the guy, who is still standing close by, smiling, and punches him in the nose.

My mother holds my hand and starts walking, while she hears the noise from behind her. She never looks back at the guy as he stands up, trying to follow us, while the men from the shops hold him down. She smiles at me and tells me that we are going to buy some more vanilla ice cream.

MEMORY 3

I'm twenty-seven years old. A man is sitting across from me who does not belong to our family. He looks nervous. We're gathering in my grandmother's home. It's one of the few times I've returned to visit, always followed by the disbelieving and disapproving eyes of uncles who know that I'm too old now to be handled. My father has given up on fixing me and just ignores my presence. I try to avoid his accusing eyes, and I wrinkle my nose, hearing the cracking of the smashed bone he left me with.

The stranger sits there, sweaty, confused. Around him, my five uncles, my aunt's husband, my father and I are sitting. The man's father, uncle and brother are here as well. We are gathered for a reason today: this man is about to ask for my sister's hand in marriage.

The man does not know my sister; he first saw her in my father's house when he visited a couple of weeks ago, accompanied by his mother and grandmother. His female relatives had already seen the bride-to-be a week earlier. The meeting is going well, according to my father's standards, but I'm personally displeased.

The stranger and I got to talk earlier in the day. We stood on the balcony of my grandmother's home on the top of the hill in Mezzeh, overlooking the big Huda Mosque. We watched the cars zooming to the highway that stretches all the way to Beirut. I asked him a simple question: 'How would you deal with a disagreement with your future wife?' He replied that there was already a disagreement between them. 'You see,' he said, 'she doesn't want to wear a mantouh.'

I held in my laughter at his trivial example. He was talking about the long jacket that covers a woman's body from her neck down to her feet. Together with a headscarf, a woman would be completely covered in the traditional Syrian Islamic outfit. 'I told her that we can talk about it later or when we are married,' he told me, and then took a moment of silence. The cars passing beneath us filled the air with their noise and reflected their lights on the windows and glass door of the balcony. He finally added, 'She has to wear it anyway, because it's the most important base of the marriage.' To sound smart, he finished his argument by saying, 'We'll surely talk about it, but we will decide that she will wear it.' I stared at him, wondering how serious he was. I remained silent, and he swam in the awkwardness of my gaze. He was tongue-tied. I pulled open the balcony's door and invited him to walk back to the family gathering.

My eldest uncle, who is married and rumoured to have up to two mistresses, starts the traditional, well-planned parade. 'We are giving her to you, but only if Allah is giving her to you.' The verb *give* sounds heavy in my ears. 'We are giving you a woman from a good family of men, not a woman with no father or brother.' He finally adds, 'She has never been kissed by anyone but her own mother,' to discreetly explain that she is still a virgin.

My sister was at the time sitting with my stepmother, my grandmother and my other sister in the kitchen, preparing blueberry juice for the men deciding her fate.

'I don't want to play with you any more.' I stand up, escaping tears and heartache. 'You're an asshole.' I finally find the door, hiding behind a black-and-white curtain. I break out of the room as the set of the dreadful *To Tell the Truth* breaks apart. The three ghosts of women slowly fade away.

At first, Death seems unaware of how much damage he has caused. He looks dazzled and confused. He slips down in his chair, erasing the scene. 'I'm sorry,' he whispers. 'I didn't realize it might bother you this much.' I turn off the lights and I walk away angrily; he follows.

'You knew it would hurt,' I say, tears gathering in my eyes. I remember the moment my mother was slapped on the face in the middle of Hamra Street. She slipped to her knees and started weeping in the street. The man looked upon her victoriously and walked away. Other men from nearby shops came to her rescue, but she pushed them away. She started accusing them of touching her, and gathered half of the street upon us. That night, my father came to the police station to pick us up from the cell we were locked inside. He drove us home while she wept silently in the back seat. He dropped us off at her house and left. I slept wearing my ice-cream-covered T-shirt.

'I just think you should face your past and try to see the beauty in it,' Death explains, grabbing my arm. I feel the chill of his touch on my skin.

'I think you should leave me alone,' I whisper, looking away. I slip into our bedroom and lock the door from inside.

6

THE CONCUBINE AND HER
GLASS ROSE

In my dreams, I have just enough time to say my goodbyes to you. In my dreams, we put on our best and we go for a dance on the green grass in our front yard. We lie down on a bed of roses and I spend my days sending you away with songs instead of stories; you slip into your own private dream land and you're gone, like a beautiful flower that dies as the sun gets too hot. Yet this time it's not a sad moment, it's a moment of rebirth: you're going to rise from the ashes soon. In my dreams, you're forever.

These are never the dreams that I remember when I wake up. I only remember the ugly and the strange. Today, I dream of my own death. As I toss and turn in bed, waking you up in the wee hours of the night, I dream of the end of my life. I feel the pain of my soul leaving my body, I release those final deep breaths and I find myself in my grave.

'Baby,' you call me from the land of the living. I struggle to leave the bed of my tomb; it closes in on me. Skeleton hands grab my clothes and tie me to the wet, muddy land of my nightmare, where the raindrops are little balls of screaming mouths with rotten teeth. 'Honey! Wake up.' I hear your voice: it's in the thunder, in the screams of every raindrop, in the sharp fingertips of the skeletons.

Wake up! Wake up! Wake up! Wake up! Wake up!

The nightmare is reversed: the raindrops are forming on the surface of the ground, slowing turning into balls of scream, lifting themselves to the skies. The skeleton hands are slipping back into the mud. The nightmare is rewound backwards through time: I'm jumping out of the tomb and back to the green fields and the beds of roses. Back to you.

I open my eyes. 'You were having a nightmare.' No kidding. You hand me a glass of water. I greedily drink it.

Physical death has become the norm for me; I have experienced it so many times before. Emotional death was a once-in-a-lifetime experience that I never want to come back to. I don't like to remind you of the time you caused me to remain dead for three years. I don't like to remember it myself. We were still young; we had just arrived in Vancouver after our two years of refuge in Lebanon. Upon our arrival, we had a honeymoon phase of love for the city. We walked with a spring in our feet, as we championed the rain and the muddy corners of the city we had just been introduced to days ago. Like a new lover, we embraced Vancouver; we didn't think of our futures or hopes, we just lived the moment.

We would catch the SkyTrain from our first apartment in Richmond, where airplanes passed by our building and people rarely listened to loud music. We took the train all the way down to Yaletown Station and walked up the staircase until we came upon Davie Street. We walked up the hill and refused to jaywalk the streets, even when there were no cars. We wanted to be model citizens and we feared that breaking any law might cause them to take away our new city from us. We walked until we reached the rainbow crosswalk, met people we had never met before and became instant friends with them. We ate poutine and pretended to like it, even when the greasy sauce turned our stomachs upside down.

Months after our arrival, we started to sense it. There was a feeling we had never felt before growing within our bodies. We started to have more fights, pushing each other away while pulling each other closer. It was a twisted tango that we danced. I wanted you near me, and you couldn't stand being away from me, but we couldn't be in the same room for too long before our screaming matches covered the forgotten music of our joined heartbeats.

At night, my nightmares used to wake me up, and I felt disoriented and out of place. I felt unbalanced, as if the world around me was colliding and I couldn't breathe any more. Neither of us could admit it, but I missed our home in Beirut, while you missed your family home back in Damascus. We felt a longing for places we knew well, and the new, beautiful city we had just fallen in love with felt like a big concrete prison that we wanted to escape. I became easily startled. We were becoming more and more disconnected from each other and from the world around us. We didn't realize this until years later, but deep down we felt rejected by the society around us. Whenever we met someone new, all they wanted to talk about was the weather and the traffic; it was part of this new strange culture we found ourselves in. Back in Syria, when you want to push someone away, to reject them and keep them at bay, you talk to them about the weather and the traffic. You reduce them to mundane conversations until they take the hint and leave you be. Our attempts to build friendships were lost in translation.

You became reluctant to leave the house and refused to meet new people. You retreated into our bedroom and closed the door behind you. You gazed at me in disbelief as I locked our bedroom door upon myself when I returned from the small newspaper I worked for as an editor. We had promised each other years before that we would never sleep in separate beds, but for weeks, I couldn't sleep next to you, I didn't feel safe. And you resented me for sleeping on the couch.

The worst part was: neither of us knew what was wrong. The counsellor, suggested to me by my office management after I burst into tears in the middle of a Monday morning meeting for no apparent reason, told me that it was culture shock, coupled with post-traumatic stress disorder. 'You have been through a lot, your body is used to a level of stress that you have built within you your whole life,' she told me. She was a First Nations woman with a smile on her face and deep eyes that looked into my soul. 'Your stress remains with you, protecting you from the new and the unknown. Everything around you now is new and unknown.'

'I dreamed of my own death,' I tell you, breathless still after the nightmare. 'I think it's Death's way of apologizing for what happened yesterday.' I think he allowed me a sneak peek at the end of my own road in life. You see, Death has a wicked sense of humour. 'I dreamed that I died lonely; it will be a cold death, on a metal hospital bed. My back will be exposed to the icy surface of the bed frame, but my body won't be able to produce those shivers I get when I'm cold.' My soul will ascend over the surgeons' tables and escape their tools, leaving the body to fall apart, like a doll. I feel that from now on, I'm only living life through glances of my end. My death is now foretold and set in stone. It's a gift from Death, to show me his good intentions. I appreciate that. He knows my sulky mood well.

You are alert; the stories of death are the most interesting for you nowadays. 'Kish bara w b'eed,' you say – 'may it remain outside and away, what a horrible dream.' I smile. You tilt my body around, letting me rest in your embrace. 'Tell me more.'

After eight months of endless fights, you came to my office one day and waited for me on the corner outside. You asked if I would like to go for a walk. I walked behind you, trying to ignore my urge to run in the opposite direction. I felt that our souls had been tangled for too long, then suddenly stretched apart until they broke. I didn't know which pieces of my soul were left within you, and I felt strange pieces of your soul residing within my own.

We reached Sunset Beach, and you told me that you wanted to break up with me.

I expected that line. I knew that ending would come. I felt a sense of momentary relief. 'There is nothing wrong between us,' you whispered, 'but at the same time, I feel that everything is wrong.' We walked, hand-in-hand, on the seawall. The rain started dripping on us as the sun sat down early, the clouds covering the skies and the tips of the buildings around us. We didn't talk for an hour, but when we reached our home, we knew that it was over.

For the following three years, we each navigated the city alone. We would meet at big events and common friends' gatherings. At first we tried to be friends, but then we couldn't stand talking to each other. Honestly, I couldn't look you in the eyes without falling in love with you once more. I couldn't stand being so close to you, without calling you mine.

There were moments when I felt betrayed by you. 'We deserved to be together,' I would mumble to myself, as I looked out of the window of my small studio apartment on Cardero Street. 'He broke up with me because he couldn't handle my pain, while I was there for his.' I hated you. All the photos of us I saw on my Facebook were blaming me for trusting you. All the poems I wrote for you felt like unattached words, divorcing each other and walking in different directions. 'I feel cheated,' I told a one-night stand, lying naked in my bed, bored as he listened to me narrating our story to him. 'I spent years drinking his cheap white wine, pouring it into my body.' I felt as if we had built castles upon clouds; and when you left, the clouds gave in and our castles smashed to the ground. After you, I twist and turn in pain and agony among the ruins of our castles, unable to walk away.

'I didn't break any rules,' Death tells me. He is sitting on the bedroom sofa that I only sit on when I'm tying my shoes. 'I'm not telling you when you will die, I'm just showing you how.' I've always thought that the Islamic concept of the relationship between the body and the soul is rather cartoonish. 'The soul is the glue that holds the body together,' Tamer, a young Egyptian member of the Muslim Brotherhood, told me once. Of course, later that day, Tamer and I had sex in my apartment's bathroom, but that's a story for another time.

I spare you some of the earlier details of my nightmare: it all started with your own death. My dream started with you and me in golden fields: I fall asleep next to you in a dream land, but the moment I open my eyes again, I realize that you're gone. A moment of panic takes over me. I am torn between the urge to pull you up by the shirt and demand your immediate return to this life and the need to curl up in the bed of roses with your corpse. I want to snuggle up next to your cold body and rest my head calmly on your shoulder and wait for my old friend Death to bring his horsemen for a visit.

'He died of a broken heart.' That's what the medic will say about me as he walks into my dream to pick up my body, wasted away within your rotten flesh. The green fields of our dream around us are drying up, turning to brown. The imaginary medic will think to himself that it was a smart remark, not realizing how clichéd he sounds.

No! I refuse the direction this dream is taking; I refuse to believe that my end is engraved within your body. Like a child, I believe that I can change the way this dream is unfolding: I grab my own face, my eyes weeping silver tears of sorrow over your dead body, and I carry myself inside our home. Calmly, I pick up the phone and type random numbers, calling people I don't know who should know about your passing. Some of them act surprised that you're gone; others assure me that it's all for the best. You went through so many lovers in those three years. I heard stories of you hanging out with the cool kids in town. A friend of mine told me that you went down on a guy in the shower in his building's gym. He told me that the guy you slept with was a model, and I felt replaced. I felt like an old shield that had been carried by a courageous warrior, protecting him from arrows and swords, then dropped in a corner, forgotten, replaced by a beautiful new shield that didn't carry the scars that I did.

Men enjoyed your exotic looks and your wheat-coloured skin. They fancied you an Arabian knight who would make their sexual fantasies come true. You enjoyed the attention, loved their hands reaching under your shirt in XY and Junction. You went to after-parties and engaged in their drug habits. I hear that you were the star of an orgy or two.

I barely went out. I hid my head between papers and poems and books, and refused to look up. All I could think of was how much I missed you.

My counsellor told me that I wasn't missing you. 'You're missing the feeling of connection you had with him, the feeling of belonging to someone from your own culture, who speaks your own language, who knows you best.' She connected the loss I felt to my PTSD, explaining that it all went back to my childhood. 'You loved him because he loved you like your mother never did, he accepted you like your father never did,' she pointed out. 'You loved him because you were addicted to finding his love for you between the layers of his silence. Sometimes, you could see that true love. Sometimes, it was just your own imagination.'

Then, after two years struggling with issues that I didn't even realize I was going through, there was a moment of clarity. On a day in early May, while sitting on the sands at Third Beach, I looked to the sunset and I whispered to myself that it was beautiful. I must have done that a billion times before, looked at the sky as with its burning colours, and told myself that I found it beautiful. But that day, that sweet beautiful day while I was alone on the beach, feeling a breeze gliding through my jacket, on the soil of a land I wasn't born on, I didn't just say the words, I felt them. It felt as if my soul were a phoenix, finally ready to enter a new cycle of life, after all of its flesh and feathers burned to ashes; the sunset had agitated its fires once more, and it was reforming and reshaping. I felt reborn, and it made me laugh out loud.

That same day, you missed me. The feeling surprised you; you hadn't thought of me for over six months. You were on a camping trip on Vancouver Island, and suddenly, all you could think of was me. As if the return of my soul to my body, after three years of walking dead, had suddenly reconnected my soul to yours across space and time. As if our souls had found their own way to re-establish our connection.

You told stories about us to a blond boy you had met on that camping trip. You told him how sad you were that we weren't talking. The boy, hiding with you between the tall grasses of the Pacific Rim Park, was more interested in touching your body and slipping his hand under your belt. But you spent the hours of the early evening telling him stories about you and me, stories you hadn't thought of in years.

'I dreamed that I was alone. You left me alone for some reason,' I tell you in the living room. It's early morning; there is no point in returning to sleep anyway. 'I dreamed that I lost interest in life, I dreamed that I dried up like a fish out of water. The dogs dried up too – they either disappeared or died. Your life was bringing life to our lives. When you are gone, everything else is gone.'

'Don't talk like that,' you tell me. I feel ashamed – I know I'm nagging.

'I know. I shouldn't. But that's what I dreamed about.'

I find it ironic that the possibility of outliving you never crossed my mind. It was somehow comforting knowing that, with my history of addiction and my multiple vices, I would be the first to go. I wouldn't mourn you. I wouldn't be the one sitting alone in a corner missing you. I selfishly always wanted to be the one who dies first. I have lost so much in my life before you, and I have lost you once or twice before; I'm not ready to lose you again. I'm not ready to be the one standing while you slip away. I cannot handle your departure one more time.

In my dream, we die on the same day. You die in our bed in the morning, and I die in the hospital before nightfall.

In my dream, I meet a doctor who wants to save my life on the same day you die. She is a young doctor, and she tells me to stay if I can give more love to the world. She whispers the words in my ear as I slip in and out of my dream coma. That pretentious bitch and her pretentious quotes that she must have murmured a million times to a million different patients. I'm sure she watches too much *Grey's Anatomy*.

I give up. I die. It isn't tragic, it isn't cinematic; none of the doctors cry, not even the pretentious bitch. One second I'm alive, and by the next I'm gone. The dream decided to linger in that moment of silence, my dead old body abandoned in the centre of faint lights, my eyes open, my shirt torn. Your body is one floor below it, dignified, in your comfortable sleeping clothes, almost smiling.

After three long years, while I was having dinner on my own, eating leftover food from two nights before, I heard a knock on my door. It was a rainy Vancouver evening and I was alone. The rain was pouring on my window, and the ocean I could see between the buildings was waving angrily. I opened the door to find you outside, drenched by the rain. Your hair mingled on your forehead. 'I miss you,' you said. 'I miss talking to you in Arabic. I miss nagging at you to open the windows while you smoke. I miss arguing with you and making love to you.'

It took you three years to gather all of your words in three sentences and to bring them to me. It took you three years to face your own emotions and to connect with me again. 'Get in, you'll get a cold.' I opened the door wider and you came in. That night, you slept in my bed, and I spent the night awake, looking at you. By the time morning came, the sun was out and I woke up to find myself curling up on your chest.

'You can't tell me you're not the least bit curious about my dream from yesterday,' I say, while we're tucked in bed. The dogs are piled up by our bedroom door, Death is resting on the shoe-tying sofa in a corner, the fireplace is roaring with warmth.

'How about you just tell me a new story, Hakawati.'

That dream is a bore anyways; I must have dreamed it ten times or more. I smile, and I tell you, 'Once upon a time a woman fell in love with her wedding dress.'

What made her happiest on that day was the colour of her wedding dress. The white of the fabric glowed like a snowflake forgotten by December on the windowpane in her childhood room, like the summery cloud that passed over once while she and her mother were watering the jasmine in the little Damascene garden outside.

The dress was white, the same way clouds remained white throughout her journey through life. The first time she noticed the clouds was when she was four; she was on the rooftop, playing with the snow that had gathered there after a stormy night. She slipped and ended up on her back, covered in soft snowflakes. Suddenly she noticed the skies for the first time. They were light blue, with breaks of white snow-carrying clouds. The white of those clouds was the same white as her wedding dress.

The dress was also soft, just like her brother's cheeks after his first shave. She kissed him softly on the forehead after he returned home with Father from the barbershop. He pushed her playfully, for he was a man now, and could not be touched by her ever again.

She was afraid to touch her wedding dress. She was allowed to spend a couple of hours with Waleed, but not without the company of three of her maiden aunts and her now-too-old-to-be-kissed-on-the-forehead brother. She feared to touch her wedding dress the same way her heart almost stopped with each sneaky little touch between her fingers and his.

Once when she was handing Waleed his coffee, he touched her fingers. It surprised her, but she wished she could squeeze his fingers within hers. She was too shy to do so.

On the shoulder of the dress rested a lovely rose made of glass; the flower seemed to contain the happiness of the dress. She wanted to kiss the little glass rose and hold it close to her heart. Her sister opened the door and slipped in; they laughed, but never too loud – they feared their father's punishment.

They both lay on the bed, eyes to the ceiling, and her sister asked, 'You're getting married today?'

'I'm getting married today,' she responded.

Waleed insisted on carrying her up the stairs until they reached the door of their new home. When he carried her, slipping his hand softly around the wedding dress, allowing her to rest completely between his arms, she heard his heartbeats. His strong, loving heart was beating loudly into her ear, which was resting on his firm chest. She could feel the love pouring out of his heart into her mind.

Bum . . . bum . . . bum . . .

He struggled trying to open the door with his key while still carrying her. He finally gave up and carefully lowered her to her feet. 'Enter with your right foot,' he told her, 'for good luck.' She held her dress up, like a princess walking through wet grass, and started running around the house, entering one room after the other. She was a magical fairy jumping flowers; her laughter brought beauty to the house, turning it, spell-like, into a home. He stood there, smiling, watching her tour her new house. She came back to him, untying her hair, which slipped onto her shoulders like a nightly waterfall. He reached with his finger and lifted some of the hair hiding her teary eyes. Suddenly he picked her up once more; she laughed.

They entered the bedroom. He sat her down on the bed, and sat next to her. Her face was now shy and red, like a flower exposed too early to the sun; her eyelashes slid down over her eyes. He shared her shyness. His forehead touched hers. His hand was slowly drawing imaginary lines along the glass rose on the shoulder of the dress. 'I love you,' he said. 'Do you love me?'

'I love you,' she said. Both their hearts beat, forever rhythmic. *Bum . . . bum . . . bum . . .*

Another rainy day! Fairuz, the Lebanese singer she loved to listen to in the morning, was explaining that she has complete trust in their love, and that's enough.

The girls had gone to school earlier in the morning. They jumped for several minutes on the bed, waking her and Waleed up. They laughed, and she laughed with them. Waleed held one and printed a million kisses on her nose and forehead. The other jumped onto her mother's shoulders and demanded to be carried to the kitchen.

She added a couple drops of olive oil to the little sandwiches for her daughters as she heard them giggling in the bathroom, throwing water and bubbles on one another. She didn't want to add too much olive oil. The girls could get their fingers covered in the sweet green oil.

Waleed put on a suit and prepared to drop off the girls at school. She gave them three kisses: two on her daughters' foreheads and one on her husband's lips.

They left, and the chaotic hurricane of their existence calmed down. A silence filled the house; she could feel its weight on her shoulders. Fairuz was telling her, once more, that love is all she needs. She called her mother, she cleaned her kitchen and she finished her chores. She watched a silly Egyptian TV series. Now what?

The blue closet was due for a cleaning. She opened its doors and the dust filled up her nose. She coughed. The closet was filled with old-fashioned dresses, forgotten books and candles. Within it, the white wedding dress stood out. She took it out of the closet carefully and smiled to it like an old friend. She touched it, searching for the glass rose. It was still there, magnificent, vibrant. Some of the glass crystals had abandoned it, leaving white threads behind them.

She was worried she might destroy the dress, but she couldn't resist the temptation. She slipped her legs into the dress, one after the other, and pulled it up slowly. She felt heavier but the dress still locked on her body like an old, warm glove. She looked in the mirror and untied her hair. It was still a nightly waterfall, but it wasn't what it used to be: it was decorated with grey meteors, slipping through her hair over the years without permission.

She looked at herself in the mirror; her face reflected her old dreams. She wondered for a second if she still looked as beautiful as she used to. 'All the love stories end with you,' Fairuz told her.

She started hoarding her memories like an insane person. Her face told stories of stories untold. Her daughters were married now. Waleed was dead. The phone would ring any minute, and her elder daughter would be on the other side; she would tell her that she couldn't come to visit. 'My son is sick,' she might say. 'I'm very tired,' she might add.

She slowly lifted her reading glasses from her face. She stumbled and almost fell as she walked away. She looked for her glasses, then realized they were hanging around her neck. This was not the first time she had lost them and found them there.

She left her little chair and stumbled toward her bedroom, using the furniture to help balance her tired steps. With every touch, she remembered something old. This was where her daughters used to study; this was where Waleed used to sit.

She entered her bedroom, now lonely and dark. She felt the air pressuring her lungs to pull harder. She tried to reach her bed, but her hand instead slipped to the doorknob of the blue closet.

Inside, only her wedding dress remained, the only evidence that she ever did anything in her life. She felt wasted. She pulled it out of the closet, hugged it for a second. On its shoulder there was a dry glass rose that used to be shiny. Her fingers twitched for a second, then she managed to pull the shoulder, destroying the rose. She cried, she grabbed the dress viciously, she screamed.

That night she went to sleep with her face snuggled into the dress. She never woke up. She wasn't found for days.

In the dark, I finish my story. Your hand has stiffened up on my shoulder. Your fingers are cold. Your pulse is weak. I look over my shoulder; my eyes adjusted to the darkness a while ago. Death is standing there, in the corner, looking guilty. 'Are you going to take him now?' I ask Death. He doesn't respond.

I slowly turn from your body. I feel frozen deep inside my own thoughts. Now what? Is this my moment to let you go? Should I end my stories and stop pulling you toward life? Am I being selfish forcing you to stay with me? I should nod my head in agreement, and let Death pull you away from my arms. I should let you go, and accept your fate. I should break my attachment to you and face the world without you.

But the castles we rebuilt are holding on. They float on our clouds of medicines and fantasies. I can't smash to the ground once more; I can't lose my way to our bed once more. 'What happened in the story?' you ask in a weak, sleepy voice. Death cracks a smile; I forgive him all of his mischief. 'Nothing. She lived happily ever after with her husband and her children,' I tell you. You smile. 'That's nice.'

I turn back to you. My head feels heavy. I just want to sleep, but the touch of your chest drives me into old memories of passion and love. I slide deeper in your embrace. My ear is now on your chest. I hear your heartbeat.

Bum . . . bum . . . bum . . .

7

THE TALE OF THE QUEEN'S ZOO

Waiting for death is a job for the lonely. You, as a human being, are unfinished still, but your time on the planet seems to be finished. You feel as if you're anticipating sadness with sadness, sitting there, awaiting an end, reacting with sorrow even before it happens.

I sometimes allow myself to wander away into an old paradise of memory. Sweet stories, young and old, gathered together in a stream of happiness. It started, I guess, with the imagined memory of my first teardrop as I cried for the first time – a new soul taking in air, fresh and cold. That teardrop must have felt like a waterfall, since it was the first of its kind to ever slip on my face. It's the thrill I felt as I climbed the stairs on my own for the first time, inspired by other two-year-olds around me, up that little plastic garden slide. As I allowed gravity to take over and pull me toward the ground in a speed new to me, I felt a joy that I had never felt before. My kingdom wavers between the realm of imagination and the world of reality: in corners, there are doors that lead between them. Knocking on one door is usually enough during the escapes I take down memory lane, while you're taking a long shower or while I'm watering the garden. Some of these doors lead to memories from my life, others lead to alternate realities or olden times.

I'm sitting in my chair, coughing constantly, while listening to you tell old stories from across the coffee table. I slip in and out of my kingdom. I hear pieces of sentences from you, some names and some adjectives. By now, I know your stories too well: a slip of the tongue is enough for me to know which story you're telling.

A moment of silence takes place between us; it allows me a short dip into a recent memory, the sweet mango margarita I had last night. In my kingdom, I see myself holding that cup, icy with the cold drink, and I feel the sweet syrup arrive in my mouth. I hear your voice from the background and it fishes me out of the pool of my memories.

'Do you remember Maryam?' you ask me.

'Maryam? Damascus's Maryam?' I ask. In my head, a picture of the short-haired lesbian with the big smile appears. We would go out after work to the old bars of downtown Damascus. In my head, her face is in the corner of the photo, while an old, magnificent house takes up most of the image. In her hand, a beer always rests, and the skies behind her are stormy with the colours of the sunset.

We call her 'Damascus's Maryam' to differentiate her from Aleppo's Maryam, who was a nasty woman with a childish sense of humour and a voice so thin it felt like nails scratching on a blackboard in the centre of my nervous system. The two women dated for a while. It wasn't my place to point out to Damascus's Maryam how unfortunate this relationship felt to me, so I kept my mouth shut and faked my smile.

Their relationship lasted for a year, maybe eighteen months? I can't remember. Damascus's Maryam travelled constantly to Aleppo and I joined her on those four-hour rides every once in a while. We used to bring a bottle of vodka on the bus, pick the last two seats and drink blindly. We opened the windows and smoked on the bus ride while exchanging dirty looks with other passengers. We would reach Aleppo in the early morning hours, and we would find Aleppo's Maryam waiting for us, alongside two other lesbian friends we knew well. The two of us drunkenly laughed and hugged everyone twice. I remember kissing a woman I'd never met on the lips as I mistook my way to her cheeks. 'Don't worry about it,' I told her, my words slurring, 'I'm gay.' She shushed me down, laughing, and whispered in my ear that she was a lesbian. We laughed it off, and we became instant friends.

On one of those trips, Damascus's Maryam ended up in her girlfriend's bedroom. They were supposed to go up to grab sunglasses, as we were planning a walk to Aleppo's Citadel. They ended up making out on the bed, while two other women and I were waiting downstairs. Aleppo's Maryam grabbed my Maryam and pulled her to bed, and the two women started licking each other's lips and exchanging words of adoration. Aleppo's Maryam's mother walked in on the two women, who managed to separate just in time for the elderly Christian woman not to see them embracing, but to notice the flustered looks on their faces.

A week later, the mother demanded that it was time for Aleppo's Maryam to find a husband for herself. Her daughter instantly made up a lie. 'I didn't want to tell you this, Mother,' she said, calculating every word, 'but I'm already seeing someone.'

Aleppo's Maryam made up this whole story about a man called Anas who lived in the United States, studying economics and hoping to come back to his city of birth to marry a devoted Christian woman. 'He is so religious, and goes to church every Sunday,' Maryam explained to her mother, whose eyes were getting wide as she heard the delicious news of the upcoming husband. Wedding bells were already ringing in her head.

When the mother demanded to see a picture of that promised man, Aleppo's Maryam went to my Facebook and showed her one of my pictures. 'Oh, he is a looker,' the mother whispered to her daughter, already imagining the well-raised, well-educated children who would have an American passport and live a happy, comfortable life.

I didn't know about any of this until a month later, when the mother finally asked to speak to the man on Skype. I got a frantic phone call from Damascus's Maryam, who came clean with the whole story, and then asked me if I was willing to be Anas for that Skype call.

'Are you serious?' I said, sitting up in my bed in my little house on the outskirts of Damascus. 'I'm not lying for your stupid girlfriend.'

Two days later, I was on a Skype call with an elderly woman in Aleppo asking me about my life in New York City. 'New York City is beautiful,

Aunt,' I said, while standing in my bedroom, Damascus's Maryam monitoring the conversation closely. 'By Allah, it's the most beautiful city in the world.'

Maryam looked at me with frustrated eyes. She grabbed a notebook and wrote: *Anas is Christian, stupid.* I looked at her and gestured how uncomfortable I was.

When they finally broke up, I took Maryam out for beer. We walked around Bab Sharki, gazing at the old houses, staring at the fluorescent red lights on every corner and discussing the doors around us. 'Why do they sink deeper in the ground?' she asked. We looked at a door that was no more than a metre high.

'They remain the same, my friend; the world put layers upon layers of concrete and asphalt on the roads leading to them, strangling them and denying them the ability to be wide open as they used to be.'

Maryam met me in a dark year of my life. I had just returned to Syria after a long, lost battle in Egypt. Defeated, in pain, I took her hand and she got me to feel happiness again. She was all I had then. I walked the streets of Damascus, cold with water drops from late-afternoon rain, hand-in-hand with Maryam. We talked about everything. She looked like a petite boy, so getting her into my small bachelor apartment, where women were forbidden from entering, was very easy.

She introduced me to the underworld of Damascus: the magical drunken trips we took together were countless. Damascus opened its arms, and we embraced the city. We both adored its corners and its alleyways. We loved to go to the old Damascus souks and fill ourselves with kenafieh and ice cream from Bikdash, a shop in the heart of the Hamidiyeh Souk.

'Any idea where is she nowadays?' you ask me from across the coffee table. I take a second. 'I need to check,' I say. I knew Maryam was a lesbian the day I saw her for the first time. I had just started a new job with a small newspaper. Our offices were across from one another, and we bonded over the fact that we both spoke English fluently and were the only smokers in the office. When I saw her for the first time, I thought that she was a boyish-looking man, and referred to her as a man as I said my first hellos. 'I'm a girl, damn it,' she laughed, 'but thank you. I like it when people mistake me for a boy.' Supposedly private, the newspaper had a policy of reprinting every single political and social article published on the government's Syrian Arab News Agency. We sat together exchanging knowing looks as we copied the articles from official government sources. We knew we were spreading government propaganda and we never tried to justify it to one another. On the balcony of our office, we exchanged cigarettes, drank hot Turkish coffee and talked.

It took me a week to tell her that I was gay and that I knew she was a lesbian. A conversation-starter of 'Hey, I'm a homo. You're a homo?' would've been too awkward, so we both fished for clues in each other's small hints. All week long, we'd slipped our positive opinions about homosexuality into the middle of unrelated conversations.

'I love the coffee here,' I'd say.

'Yes. I love it too,' she would say enthusiastically. 'You know what else I love?! Gays! I love gays.'

Her sense of subtlety was questionable, but everyone let it slide; her wide smile and happy persona made them forgive her bluntness. We finally came out to each other one afternoon on the balcony. We both laughed at the silly games we had played over the week. Then we decided to go for a long-awaited beer.

One afternoon in late September, we were both fired. As the war started to take shape in the early days of 2011, the newspapers lost their budgets as media companies channelled their funds into historical TV series glorifying the Syrian identity, filled with plots in which those who stray away from the orders of their leaders die horribly. We stood there as our editor-in-chief explained the cuts and wished us happy hunting for a job in a country where no one was hiring. We left the office feeling defeated.

The city reflected our feelings; the streets of late fall in Damascus are cold and harsh. The grey colours of the buildings encage your soul sometimes. We felt suffocated. We escaped the metal and iron city to the old city of Damascus, with its white houses and narrow roads and its green lights: green street lanterns, green minarets, decorated red and green doors. The old city, like us, was a prisoner of the new one. An ancient wall surrounds the old city of Damascus. Sadly, a new city has developed around the ancient one, with dirty bridges and unfriendly buildings. The new city pushes in deeper, trying to squeeze the life out of the old one. An ancient wall protects the beautiful city, adorned with seven green doors, where army upon army has stopped, and couldn't enter. Each door has a story to tell; each door leads to a souk and each souk has its own personal smell. Some doors stood tall in the face of conquerors, while Christian armies broke others during the Crusades. In the centre of all that chaos and war stands an old mosque. The Umayyad Mosque used to be a church, which used to be a synagogue, which was built upon the holy site of an old religion, lost and forgotten.

Maryam and I were children of Old Damascus. She grew up near the door of Bab Toma, while I was born close to the door near Saroja, on the opposite side of Old Damascus. Like the city, walls of war surrounded us. We were doors that used to open wide, and now the asphalt of the roads around us had started to strangle us.

The door near Maryam's birthplace, Bab Touma, takes you to the Christian neighbourhood in the city. Laws in Syria deny any Muslim from opening a bar; only Christians are allowed to open bars or sell alcohol. This turned the Christian neighbourhoods in Syria into avenues of hip bars, built upon the sites of the old bars of the 1960s.

I used to imagine myself in one of the Damascene bars in the 1960s, wearing a suit and a tie. Back then, the colours of Damascus were livelier: Damascus smelled of jasmine and was surrounded by the colour of wine. The deep red painted the beautiful faces of the women and the fezzes of the men. I walk into a dark alley covered with the shadowy lights of candles. There, in the deep, there is a door. Inside, I hear the old-fashioned music of the oud and darbuka. Women are wearing wigs and diamonds, drinking and dancing with men wearing fezzes and smoking cigars.

In a corner, I see him. Háfez al-Assad himself; he must be in his early twenties. He is spying, with wide-open eyes, on a group of middle-aged men talking politics and hitting the table with their fists. I can see it in his eyes: he is planning a long series of coups to take these men, one after another, until his time comes and he gets his chance at holding the chair of presidency.

He has hungry eyes, like those of a wolf. He comes from a religious minority in Syria that barely has any power, and has been looked down upon for centuries past. He carries with him years of sectarianism and classism. He joins them. He smiles to them in a friendly, well-studied manner. This is the moment everything starts to go down the drain. This man will grow to become the military leader of a country that will believe a big, fat lie for forty years.

'Did she ever go to South Africa, in the end?' I hear you asking.

I abandon the old bars with their dancing ladies and smoke-filled air, and I return to our reality. 'I don't think she ever did. But who knows?'

The war in Damascus limited our travels, and we started to spend more time in my house. We used to smoke Marlboros, then they became hard to find, and even when we found them, they were too expensive for two unemployed people. We switched to Lucky Strikes, then to Winstons. Finally, despite its disgusting smell, we switched to al-Hamra Tobacco, locally made cigarettes that reminded me of the smell of asphalt; their only benefit was the fact that they were cheap. I found a nail in one of those cigarettes once. Maryam laughed so loud I thought the neighbours might knock on my door as she pulled the nail out of the tip of my cigarette.

'Let's hope the factory doesn't fall apart,' she said.

I was never a smoker when I was young. I learned the habit later in life. When Maryam asked how I started smoking, I told her, 'My uncle used to sneak in Marlboro cigarettes from Lebanon in the late eighties. I hated the smell of smoke back then, and couldn't stand him smoking.' On a visit to my grandmother's home, I went to his bedroom while he was out. I remember finding a whole carton with twelve packs of smokes, and I started to open them one after the other, pulling cigarettes out and breaking them in half. 'My uncle came later that night to find a pile of tobacco on the floor, and he knew instantly it was me,' I said, amused. I remember hiding in the bathroom while my grandmother stood outside the door, begging my uncle not to hit me.

Years later, I explained to Maryam, I took my first steps around the hallways of the Egyptian hospital. My lungs still hurt, my shoulder felt foreign to me. I walked the hallways alone, knowing that no one would come to visit me. I craved human connection, and wandered until I found myself at the back door of the hospital. In the corner of the parking garage stood a tall man smoking. I walked toward him, stumbling around, losing my balance. 'Hello,' he said, and it was the first word I had heard from another human who was not a doctor or a nurse in weeks. 'Do you need help?'

I looked at him, and I couldn't gather words. Strangers felt dangerous, promising painful kicks and sharp stabs in the lungs. He smiled, and shook one of his cigarettes out and offered it to me.

'I remember taking the cigarette from him,' I told Maryam. 'I remember the fire of his lighter burning the tip.' That shared experience made me comfortable. 'I coughed for what felt like an eternity,' I joked, pulling another cigarette and offering her one from my pack. 'He tapped on my back with his palm, and it was the first human touch I had felt since that night.'

Once, between the jokes we endlessly exchanged, Maryam told me that she would one day build a zoo in South Africa. She said she would bring elephants and bears. 'But we will not build cages,' she told me. Her smile was wicked and sad. 'No one wants to be in a cage.'

Somewhere along the way, Maryam lost her smile. Her face carried the stories she didn't want to speak of. The regime forces arrested her seventeen-year-old brother. No one knows why; he went to school one day and he just never came back. Ten days later, they finally found out that he was in prison. Her mother slapped her own face in misery and her father held back tears. 'He is seventeen,' her mother kept repeating, 'what does a seventeen-year-old have to do with anything going on in this godforsaken country?'

He was released after two months. He was all right, although he had lost a lot of weight. At first they celebrated his return, but as days went by they noticed something strange. 'He doesn't sleep,' Maryam whispered to me while rolling a hash-filled joint. 'He never sleeps! I walk into his room at all hours of the night and find him awake, eyes wide open.' She tried to talk to him in those moments, but he never responded.

After two weeks, he finally managed to sleep. Maryam told me that she went to his room in the middle of the night and couldn't find him. She didn't want to freak her parents out, since she knew he hadn't left the house. 'He would have passed by me in the living room if he left,' she said. A thought crossed her mind for a second, and she looked out of his window down to the ground seven floors beneath them. She sighed in relief when she didn't see his crumpled body on the ground.

She finally found him. He had placed pillows inside his closet, cornered himself in an uncomfortable position, closed the doors upon himself and fell asleep. When she opened the closet, he shrieked and demanded she close the door at once. She closed the door, slipped to the floor and cried silently. One evening, she took me to the room a gay friend of hers rented in an old Damascene home in Saroujah; the room had a wooden ceiling with a column in the middle to carry the weight of the years the ceiling had to endure. We smoked hash and cigarettes there, then she left me alone with her friend when she realized that we had spent the night flirting. She waited in her car, smoking a cigarette and reading Paulo Coelho's *The Alchemist*, while I drowned my face in the tattoo covering her friend's back. She texted me, telling me to take my time, explaining that she enjoyed spending hours in her car, parked on Thawra Street, watching the city changing colours like a bride on her wedding day, from the white, sunny afternoons to the red evening lights.

The next day she parked her car under her favourite tree at the entrance to her university and returned to find that the car next to it had exploded. The explosion killed six people, destroyed her car and set her favourite tree aflame.

She once stayed on the phone with me as I sat alone in my house while a battle between the regime forces and the rebel forces took place outside my house. She heard me whisper what I thought would be my final words. I was crying, she was crying. I had bought myself a bottle of whisky that I was planning to drink with her the day after, and I ended up drinking the whole thing on my own. Power had been out for two days by then, so the ice in the freezer had melted ages ago. I didn't care.

By three a.m., I was completely wasted. 'I will go out and ask them to stop fighting,' I told her on the phone, and she asked me if I'd gone insane. 'No. I just think that if I went outside and politely asked them to stop fighting, they might consider it,' I explained. 'I want to sleep, Maryam, I cannot sleep while they are killing each other outside. I just need to sleep.'

When I met her for coffee the next morning, I made her promise never to repeat that conversation.

'Remember the first time you met Maryam?' I say.

You smile. 'It was when we went to that party in Damascus.' It was your first time at a bar ever. We had started dating weeks before, and I wanted to introduce you to my friends. You smiled politely when you met Maryam for the first time, and asked if it was okay to shake her hand. She looked at you in disbelief and grabbed you for a tight hug. We got in a yellow taxi and demanded that the taxi driver turn on the fare meter; since most of the traffic police had been given guns and sent to fight terrorists, taxi drivers had begun ignoring meters and demanding as much cash as they pleased.

You were nervous; you had grown up in a family that rejected alcohol as sinful. Your only ideas about drunk people came from the movies; you had an idea of men and women gathering in an orgy-like setting, burping loudly and speaking with slurred words. When we reached the bar, cornered in behind the Barada swimming club and the Rukn al-Din Highway, you grabbed my hand and asked me if I would be drinking. 'Hell, I will be pouring drinks into myself,' I said, and Maryam laughed.

You refused to drink and sat in a corner watching over me while I danced with Maryam. The bar was filled with young men and women in their finest outfits, and the music was loud enough to cover the sounds of war echoing from the nearby Muhajireen neighbourhood. The lights were dimmed and black curtains were placed on all the windows so the last lights of the sun wouldn't sneak in. Remember? I told you that I loved you for the first time the morning after that party.

The party started at five p.m. and finished at ten-thirty. A curfew that the government didn't enforce, but people realized they had to obey. Everyone would rather be home before eleven. That was when the possibility of death started to grow higher. At these parties, everyone got insanely drunk while it was still seven p.m. It's one way to forget that you were within a conflict zone. The club lights and the shaded windows kept us up with the beat – drinking, smoking and dancing.

You stood in a corner and looked on all of this with dazed, confused eyes. It was your first time, and it was overwhelming. You kept trying to ignore the loud music, playing songs you enjoyed, but you couldn't hold your feet from tapping to the beat of music.

'Remember that deaf crew?' I ask you. I came over to you and pointed them out, screaming my lungs out so you could hear me over the loud music. 'Look at them!' They danced to the beat of the bass in Rihanna's songs. They couldn't hear the song itself, but they felt the beats coming from the ground, or when they sat on the large speakers. It reached within their skulls. They heard the music, some maybe for the very first time. They danced, for they could not express what music is with words. They jumped so high going through the joyful motions of dance, but couldn't wait to hit the ground so they could hear the music again.

'They are enjoying the music tonight. They are leaving the world behind them,' I told you then. 'Damascus is gone. The world is small and pointless. They are here. They dance. Look at them.' Happiness spread on their faces. Maryam was saying hello to one of them. They shook hands with one another and then laughed.

'Come, dance with me.' I reached out my hand. I pulled you away from your seat, and we moved to the centre of the dance floor. I showed you some of my dance moves, while you laughed awkwardly at me. I hugged you, and I wanted to kiss you right there; it might have been another one of our stolen kisses. But then I decided against it, fearing the eyes of people around us. By ten-thirty, anxiety was clear on the faces of everyone at the club. Quick goodbyes were exchanged, and last kisses were printed on faces. 'Keep your eyes on yourself,' we said to one another, hoping that the road back home wouldn't be troublesome. We knew, in the back of our heads, that every time we said goodbye to a friend, it might be the last time. Slowly, we absorbed that knowledge and normalized it; we accepted that the heartache would come, so there was no point in anticipating it.

Maryam asked if we could share a cab downtown, and we agreed. You jumped into the front seat, while Maryam and I sat in the back, giggling at drunken jokes, lost in the city around us. You smiled a broken smile as you looked upon us through the car mirror. 'Where is your address?' you asked, and Maryam stumbled upon it; she laughed, she gagged and almost threw up. The cab driver wasn't impressed.

We finally made it to her building and I helped her out of the cab. The both of us hugged under her building, and I was helping her open the door while she was waving goodbye to you. Then, like a giant bird that had given up on flying, a body smashed into the ground right next to us. Her hand froze mid-wave, your eyes widened, and the taxi driver cursed as the blood hit the side of his car and his face. I looked in horror upon the body of Maryam's brother, his head twisted in an impossible turn, his knee exploded and the bones of his lower left leg penetrating his thigh. His feet were arched, and his fingers were twitching. In his arms, he held a white pillow.

Maryam screamed, and her scream echoed in my ears and woke my senses up. I turned to her and pushed her inside her building. She fought me, hitting me on the chest repeatedly. 'Let me go,' she screamed, 'Fuck you! Let me go out! I want to see him.' Her face melted, the light of her eyes shattered. She suddenly stopped crying, froze in her stance, and her eyes stopped blinking.

We both sit silently for a moment. 'Do you know where Maryam is nowadays?' you repeat. I pick up my tablet. A couple of clicks away, I say, 'She is in South Africa.' The image in front of me is of her grey face and white hair. She is standing by a safari car carrying the logo of a natural habitat zoo. 'She owns a zoo called White Pillow,' I say. I look at the photo again. She has her smile back.

8

THE KING AND HIS THRONE

The clouds of Vancouver gather closer to the ground. Even when I leave the windows wide open, they rarely let light in any more. The grey skies, adding a gloomy filter to the colours of everything around us, feel too close for comfort. I feel claustrophobic. Even so many years after we moved here, I still can't come to terms with the way the days get shorter and darker in winter here. The streets of the West End, filled with topless tourists and gay men in short-shorts back in the summer days, are now empty and covered in a sheet of rainwater. They look like mirrors, reflecting the lights of the street lanterns. The constant growling of the rain as it hits the ground becomes the background noise to our lives.

You retreat to our bedroom earlier every day, and I have too little daytime to prepare a story for the night. Death and I are still not on speaking terms. He sulks in a corner, looking at me with the side of his skull. Does he want to apologize? Is he waiting for the right moment? Despite the wet world around me, I feel dry. I spend too long in the shower, welcoming the hot water and the steam on my body, shivering at the thought of leaving the hot bath. I miss the sun, and I find myself going through seasonal depression. 'Years you spent here, and you still go through that?' you ask me. I'm a fragile soul. I'm easily touched by sadness and sorrow. My eyes reflect the grey world around me, filling me with an endless need for warmth, for sitting in the sun. I welcome its cleansing rays, filling my heart with a temporary peace.

O n rainy nights like this, Death likes to play games with the souls of the dead. He brings one or two around for chitchat. I see his gesture as meaningless, but decide to engage in the game. 'If you're going to play no matter what I say, I might as well enjoy it,' I say. I escape you as you drown yourself in Skype conversations with people you barely remember, and I go to the living room. I carry a cup of hot chocolate, preparing to enjoy the show Death is putting together. I sit down on my favourite chair, across from our roaring fireplace. Death dramatically enters the room, waving his cloak. He silently pulls the soul from the darkness of his cape, like a magician pulling rabbits from a hat.

'They called him "the beast",' the dark soul says, after it escapes Death's grip. It stands there, glowing green shadows in the corner. 'That's what they called my grandfather. It made me feel proud.' He is faced with blank stares from both Death and me.

'What do you call yourself?' I demand an answer from the damned soul.

'My name is Hafez al-Assad,' it says.

His father, Ali Sulayman, had eleven children. Hafez was the fourth from his second marriage. By the time he was born, his father had already managed to gain the respect of the little Alawite city they lived in. They called his father al-Wahish, the beast. 'My father was among those who signed a petition with the French, calling for a detachment of the Alawite majority areas from Syria,' Assad explains. 'We wanted a land for our own. We had the right to our own glory, our own flag.' It wasn't in the cards for the Alawites to detach themselves from the land that had been occupied for so many centuries before them that borders and lines were mingled and lost. The only line that remained was the unity based on religious faction, and like humans do, they gathered around a shared identity and rejected everyone who didn't identify with it. The Sykes–Picot agreement had already divided the lands of the Levant between the British and the French. 'Our call for our own land was a fight against imperialism,' Assad adds from the corner. 'It was a glorious act of rebellion that was ahead of its time.'

'Yeah. Sure,' I whisper.

By the time Hafez was his father's age, he knew better. 'Why should we detach Alawite regions away from Syria when we can turn the whole country into an Alawite-controlled land?'

Before he joined the Syrian Arab Air Force in 1950, Assad joined the Ba'ath political party. 'Everyone was joining a political party then, it was the right thing to do,' he explains. Syria was shaky at the time; the young country had been born only months before. It had been under occupation from outside forces with different agendas for the past twelve hundred years. 'Our country has been under Islamic, Ottoman and French occupation before,' he says. 'It was my role to bring it back to its real glory, to create the Syrian identity and make it a national one.'

Death seems bothered by his continuous commentary.

From the dead of night, the soul of Khaled comes to join our chat. He slips through the open doors of our old home and sits on a comfortable red sofa in a corner. He makes no sound. He politely crosses his legs. He smiles at me with his white smile and takes off his shoes. When he died, Khaled was twenty-nine, but he has that dirty student hippie attitude. He smiles like he's seventeen.

Assad doesn't mind the audience.

'I wanted to be a doctor,' he says, 'but my father couldn't afford to send me to study in Beirut.' Hafez asked his father what he should do instead. 'You should join the military,' his father said in his heavy accent, made worse by his large moustache. 'The military academy offers free food, a bed and a salary.'

'Sure. Being a doctor would have been amazing,' Assad says, mesmerized by the fire in the fireplace, its flames reflecting upon his eyes in his dark corner. We can only see the light in his eyes. 'But being a military man meant power, status, access.

'Which I used for the good of the people, of course,' he adds.

Assad wanted to fly; he was commissioned as a lieutenant in the

Syrian Arab Air Force in 1955. 'I won a trophy then,' he recalls. 'The best aviator trophy.' He pauses. 'I deserved it.'

I met Khaled in a bar at two a.m. on a cold night in the late winter months of 2011. I had arrived in Damascus days before. In my closet, I didn't have many winter clothes. I had just arrived back in Syria unprepared, forgetting how cold its winters are compared to the soft winters of Cairo. The cold of Damascus was breaking my bones. I was a creature of the night, mending my broken heart with a pathetic search for love, and a series of empty bottles and one-night stands. It was a time when I'd meet anyone and would think to myself: *Yes. I can make this work. Let us try.* I was desperate and lonely, and I met Khaled. He was sitting across the bar with three other people; I knew his friends. They were common friends with Maryam and me. I walked over. I said hello.

I didn't know that you, my dear one, were passing outside the same bar on your bike at the same time, coming out after your late-night workout and heading back home through the rainy Damascus streets, championing the cold and the storm.

'I on the other hand, am not a fan of conquering storms,' Assad says. 'This is my wisdom and my strength. I know when to take cover and wait for the right moment to take action. It's the trait of a leader, really.' He muses. He continues the story of his military career. 'I saw it as my first step toward a political career,' he says from the corner. 'I grew stronger and I grew bigger. Abdel Nasser found me.'

Gamal Abdel Nasser realized that the young Syrian man was a force to be reckoned with. At the time, Nasser was holding down a shaky union between Syria and Egypt. The union, which lasted for three short years, favoured the Egyptians. Many Syrians were not happy. The president thought that the only way to handle such a powerful, young military figure as Assad was to send him to Egypt. 'He could tell I was the right man for the job,' Assad says. 'He saw me for what I am, and feared me. He knew I was capable of making Syria a great country, and pushing away the Egyptian influence.'

'I met Hosni Mubarak then,' Assad adds. Death sighs. The future president of Egypt and the future president of Syria enjoyed a night out on the Nile and had a talk.

In my corner, I am fighting the shadows of my own short story with Khaled. At the time when we met I carried my soul gently, as if I were carrying a wounded animal. Everyone could see it. Khaled could see it. I hid it underneath bundles of pointless jokes and philosophical questions. Khaled asked me that night if I wanted to go home with him, and I said yes.

Khaled told me his mother had left the country months ago, when the revolution started. He lived alone in their home, after he refused to join her in her journey out of Syria. He abandoned most of the old French-era house, with its wooden windows and high ceilings, and decided to stay in his childhood bedroom. It was a tiny room with a small door and two small single beds. He used to share it with his older brother, now a fellow in an American hospital. In the room, little comic book action figures were spread across shelves and corners. I smiled and grabbed one of them. 'When my father found my stash of comics,' I told Khaled, trying to hide my envy, 'he reacted as if he had found a stash of porn magazines.'

'Why would you keep all of these under the bed?' my father had asked, puzzled by the paperback collection of the adventures of Batman, and the weirdly designed outfit – too tight for my father's taste – of the Flash. The layers of superhero books, which I spent most of my allowance on, were piled under my bed, hidden away from the sneaky eyes of my sisters, whose sole purpose in life was to destroy my favourite books and draw purple cats on the insides of their covers.

My father couldn't understand them. How could he? He was raised in a Syria that was locked in, where other cultures were rejected and a wall was built around the country, refusing to allow in any people, books, movies or documents that might enlighten people. He grew up in a Syria that was struggling financially, and he spent his allowance on candles to light in his room when the power got cut off. He grew up when entertainment was watching the silly adventures of Ghawar al-Toushieh on TV in black-and-white. The superheroes must have looked demonic to him, and the fact that I spent my money on someone else's drawings must have been mind-boggling for him.

'No one could foresee the future then,' Assad says, interrupting my thoughts, 'but both Mubarak and I knew that the union would not last and that a total change of the system would take place in both of our countries.' They both knew that a new wave was coming. They had each other to rely on, and others: friends and family members, those who would stand with them when they took over countries.

Syria entered an age of coups; people weren't sure if they would wake up tomorrow to the same president they elected this morning. Lu'ay al-Atassi was president for four months; Ahmad al-Khatib was president for another four months. Governments came and went, but Assad continued to fall through the cracks and find ways up the ladder. 'I continued to reach up until I got to my goal.' His ghostly face smiles – he ages rapidly as the story continues. 'One day, after one last coup, I finally rested in that office; I had finally found the power that would allow me to make Syria the greatest country in the world.'

Assad survived multiple assassination attempts, some announced by the government, others hidden to avoid worrying the people. He enjoyed listening to Fairuz while drinking coffee each morning, and so the Syrian stations would only play Fairuz music in the morning. In 1982, two years before I was born, he ordered the killing of thousands of residents of the city of Hama to end an uprising against him. 'The whole city had to go,' he tells us. 'They were standing against our righteous work to make Syria a great country. They wanted to end my epic journey to turn this country into a land like no other.

'I only wanted the best for my Syria,' he explains.

'My mother had a sister, her sister had a daughter, her daughter had a husband, her husband had a brother,' the ghost of Khaled whispers from across the room. 'That brother was working in Hama. He was a young doctor who was sent there by the regime. He never came back.'

Assad ignores Khaled. 'I was suspicious of everything,' he adds. 'Evil forces wanted to destroy the country I worked hard to build. I had to protect the glory of Syria, I had to make sure it stayed the Syria I had made.' He decided to moderate and monitor the use of fax and internet. 'They could use them against Syria.'

'I think you feared for your precious chair,' I say, cutting his bullshit.

'I adored my office, I adored Fairuz and I adored Syria,' he insists angrily. 'I'm the father of this country. I gave it its name, I made its flag and I turned it into the most beautiful country in the world! No one will take that away from me.'

'The secrets that people keep are all the same,' Khaled adds from his corner. 'We hide from one another what we all are suffering from.' I remember telling him that same sentence, years ago.

He saw me gazing at that little Superman. 'Superman has always been my least favourite,' I told him. An alien comes from across the universe and takes control of the world without election, bringing all kinds of monsters who truly only want him, while the people dying around him are collateral damage.

'Your eyes are carrying words,' said Khaled. I smiled. I survived on that tortured-soul attitude for years in my twenties. It helped me get laid at times; it also helped me get things off my chest.

In his little clean room, surrounded by old dusty rooms, Khaled and I kissed. I grabbed his arm, pulled him toward me and pushed him against his wall of childish posters. I kissed him and he kissed me back, hungry for my lips. In my arms he slowly relaxed, allowing his body to curve within mine. For some reason, Khaled trusted me. We slowly slipped into his bed; his sheets were printed with images of Thor and Loki. The Asgardian brothers were fighting viciously.

My father was holding one of the books, the latest edition of the adventures of Thor. On the cover, the handsome blond character was drawn in colour, designed to look angry about the actions of his brother Loki. His name was written in Arabic letters. My father waved the book in my face. 'These books will distract you from your studies,' he said, shaking the book violently. A loose sheet escaped the comic book. On it, a conversation between Thor and his father Odin was taking place.

'Dad, I like my books,' I tell my father in a shaky voice, fearing for his heavy hand on my face. 'I really enjoy reading them, Dad. They're harmless.'

'I made you, I'm your father,' he insisted. He kicked the pile of books and they flew all over the room. 'I gave you your name, and made you the man you are supposed to be. When I tell you that these books are not good for you, you listen!'

'I understand your father's point of view,' Assad says, from across the room. I look him in the eye, deny him access to my inner demons. 'He worries that his son will not amount to much. I realized once, ages ago, that my citizens needed management. They need government permission for everything, and to get it, they go in circles upon circles of endless lines and pointless employees. Everyone feels like they need to accomplish something for themselves today or else the world will end for them: everyone is on the edge of life. When you're hanging on the balance of your life, you never look up to see who is pulling the strings. You're too busy surviving the falls.'

'Let me remind you of your own children,' I say. Assad lost his first daughter, Bushra, when she was an infant, and went home and tried again. His second offspring was also named Bushra; she got married to Assef Shawkat, the deputy chief of staff of the Syrian armed forces and the former head of military intelligence. Bushra lost her husband in a bombing in Damascus during the second year of the Syrian civil war. She fled with her children to the United Arab Emirates. 'Please don't,' Assad says. I continue: his eldest son and his favourite, Bassel al-Assad, originally appeared to be the frontrunner for presidential succession in the Assad kingdom. When he died in a car accident in 1994, my grandmother cried. I heard her whisper that night, while I pretended to be half-asleep, 'Yes, I know. I know. He would have been an insane president. But he is a human being.' I heard her sigh. 'I'm sad for his death.'

Assad quivers. The ghost of his lost child appears in the corner for a second. He is wearing his signature sunglasses; his full beard covers his face. 'I missed him, I cried for him, I blamed myself for his death.'

THE KING AND HIS THRONE • 125

Assad almost weeps, but he holds his breath. He looks at me with tired eyes.

'Bashar, my second son, never wanted to be part of this,' he says, changing the topic. I don't believe him. 'Before Bassel's death he was an ophthalmologist. He had a British girlfriend and just wanted to be left alone.' Bashar al-Assad became the president of Syria upon his father's death in 2000. When Hafez met my old friend here, people thought that the end of the world was upon them. Then the parliament changed the law, allowing the new president to be elected by an unopposed ballot despite being only thirty-four.

'Can I offer anyone a drink?' Death proclaims. 'We need to calm this conversation down, or else we could startle you-know-who. This is a precious time we have together.'

Khaled cracks a laugh from his red sofa and slowly stands up. His beard is artfully designed to look forgotten and unshaved; his smile is clear as day. I remember flashes of his body; he was shy and self-conscious. He wanted to turn off the lights. I smiled and told him then that people share the same secrets and suffer the same demons, each one alone. I helped him take off his shirt; I remember his smooth chest muscles. I slipped my hands down his back; I remember the small, tender curve at the end of his spine. I grabbed his hair; it was soft and smooth. Slowly we slipped into hours of intimate bliss. We were happy.

Then the morning came.

In the morning, both of us were done. We had had our share of our addiction; we had played the game. We had reached the heights and we tasted blood. With our backs to one another, we dressed silently. He didn't attempt a conversation. Neither did I. That morning we had a cup of coffee, we joked a little, then I opened the door and I left.

'Syrians at the time were lost souls, my friend,' Khaled tells me. His face escapes the shadows. 'We were all too afraid to let our guard down. We were scared of one another, suspicious of what pain a new person might bring to our lives.' Khaled and I were there for one another that night. We both needed a temporary love affair that came and went with the night. We had a sip of love, security, depth, and then we were ready to abandon all in favour of keeping to the familiar and escaping pain.

My father played the game too. That comic conflict was the moment my father realized, maybe for the very first time, that his thirteen-year-old son was not the traditional Syrian son he had hoped to have. The piles of books, still pouring from under the bed for him to kick around on the floor, were clear evidence that his son was not interested in football, cars or women's boobs. As he flipped through the pages, looking displeased with the designs of the warlocks and villains, he started explaining to me in detail how these books, which he had never actually read before, were ruining my personality, my educational future and most importantly, my ability to reproduce.

'Listen to your father,' Assad says, mocking. 'He knows best.' Assad, who was also called 'father' in Syrian slogans and under his many photos covering buildings in downtown Damascus, was busy all the time as he aged. He rarely travelled, even within Syria. 'I was worried that if I left my comfort zone, I might lose the power to keep this country strong,' he explains. He would spend eighteen hours a day in his office in a small villa facing his Presidential Palace. Assad opened his office doors and a stream of diplomats from across the world came seeking to stop a war between Syria and Israel. Did Assad really want to fight Israel? No one knows. But he sure got a lot of favours and a lot of international support for being the gentleman with great wits and greater political stamina. 'I negotiated with them like a professional poker player,' he says, 'and I won every time. I kept Syria strong, I kept it relevant.'

'Syria remained relevant,' Khaled smirks. 'It became the focus of every presidential debate in the US for years to come.'

I was alone in my small, smelly house in Damascus when a friend called me. 'You shouldn't call Khaled,' he said. 'He is visiting his aunt.' The code was familiar and terrifying. It meant that the Military Intelligence Directorate had arrested him.

The day he was arrested, Khaled went for a walk outside wearing a white T-shirt. Did he know that there was a call on social media for people who wanted democracy and freedom in Syria to wear white and walk outside proudly? No one knows. He felt a harsh grip on his shoulder; he was pulled toward a parked van.

Weeks later, a video of that day's arrests spread across social media;

when I saw it, I recognized Khaled among the people arrested. There was a deep cut on the side of his face, his eye looked dark and blue and he had plastic cuffs around his wrists. 'You want freedom?' the plain-clothes soldier screamed at him, kicking him in the chest. 'This is freedom. Here is some freedom for you.'

His mother came back to Damascus. She opened her door and found me. I introduced myself. 'I'm Khaled's friend from college,' I said, thinking that telling her the true version of events would destroy the poor woman. She wasn't crying. She seemed weirdly calm. She opened the door and allowed me in. Inside were eight gay men, some of them friends of mine, all sitting there, all pretending way too hard to sound straight, all there to help the mother during the crisis. Some had brought flowers.

I remember my father. I slipped deeper within my covers as he continued his temper tantrum. Under the pillow, hidden between the covers, I had my favourite thing in the whole world: the only copy I could find of Captain Marvel, the wonderful young boy wizard who, by speaking the word 'Shazam,' could transform himself into a grown man with superpowers given to him by the Greek Gods. I was lost for words, I didn't know what to tell my father any more. I wished for a second that I could transform into a superhero and jump out of the window, escaping the guilt that I didn't understand. Why was it a problem that I had all of these comic books? Why should my father be so taken aback by them? Slowly he realized that his verbal attacks and questions were not going to be answered.

Then I remember Khaled's mother: she was seated behind her laptop wearing her reading glasses and her phone wouldn't stop ringing. She kept a brave face for a while, welcoming us into her house and presenting us with sweets while calling her son a batal. A hero.

I think I was a bit jealous to see the love pouring from the mother's face. She accepted her son's assumed decision to join a peaceful protest. She celebrated her son's differences.

Saturday morning came and Khaled was still missing. Khaled's mother was roaming her house silently, tired from hearing rumours.

Everyone was spreading rumours: some said Khaled was being treated well, others spoke of blindfolded eyes and roughing people up.

'He is not getting out today,' someone said, and I agreed. 'And tomorrow is a national holiday; he might get out by Wednesday.' Khaled's mother told me that she might be able to send clothes and food to her son through a contact. We waited for the contact to call and the hours lingered.

The phone rang; it was only a relative. As Khaled's mother spoke, I saw the tears sliding down her face. She continued to speak in a normal, steady voice, but her tears were pouring. The teardrops were so big they slipped off her face and landed in her lap.

By Wednesday, Khaled's mother was marching around her house, chanting anti-regime slogans and curses. She didn't care if anyone heard her any more. It took three adult men to hold her down and stop her from screaming anti-regime chants out of the window. 'Let me go,' she screamed as we tried to calm her down. 'I want to be arrested. Let them arrest me – that way they will take me to my son.' After that morning, Khaled's mother refused to allow us to visit her. I attempted to go a couple of times but she never opened the door. 'She told me you came,' the ghost of Khaled says. 'She left you the Superman figure on the doorstep.'

I never got that Superman figure from Khaled's mother. Someone might have stolen it while it waited for me on the doorstep. Khaled never returned home. His mother waited for him there, making both of them breakfast every day until the day she died and joined him in the afterlife.

Sunrise is approaching; I see it lighting the corners of my curtained windows. 'This night is almost over,' Death whispers. Slowly the ghosts of the past return swiftly into his dark robe. I see a glimpse of a final smile from Khaled.

9

THE HOUSE WITH THE
BELVEDERE

Our house is a work of wonder. I understand it now as if this house and I were old friends who had spent years attempting mischief together. I hear it complaining about you sometimes; I hear it complain about me. When we bought it back when we were younger, the house was young too: a clean, dry, beautiful dark-red house with elegant touches, mixed with a funky feel from the furniture and the drawings on the walls. The house remains clean, minus the dog hair. It remains beautiful. It shows the reality of our souls that our faces don't show any more; it tells a story about you and me. Houses have stories to tell but sadly, not many of them speak loudly.

I lived in so many houses before I found the one that I finally called home. I lived a nomadic life. I travelled. I stayed around when I felt welcome and ran away when I felt threatened. My life revolved around escapes and I was an artist of escapology. Back then, when I moved into a new place, I felt like an invader of a space that wasn't mine. I walked shyly across the halls of those rented, shared apartments; I kept my stuff in one corner.

I was born in my grandfather's house in Damascus. My father was nineteen and my mother was seventeen. He heard my mother's scream, he heard a short, snappy cry and saw the midwife leave the room holding a blanket covering a red being that made vague gestures with its hands. 'Pray in his ear,' the midwife whispered. 'Kabber in his ear.' My father – young, silly, unaware of what awaited him – held my body and whispered in my ear, 'Allahuakbar, Allah is great.'

In the mid-eighties, you would only hear those Allahuakbars spoken outside of mosques when a baby was born or when they were screamed out loud as a sign of total astonishment. For example, when my uncles watched a football match on the old, staticky TV, they would throw things in the air and scream 'Allahuakbar!' when their favourite team scored. The next morning, one of them would be sitting with friends who had seen the same match, smoking arjileh under the white neon lights of a café in old Damascus. They would be drinking tea and my uncle would be telling his friends about the goal they had all seen the night before. 'We weren't sure that we would make it, ya zalameh,' he would say. 'Suddenly, Allahuakbar! We won!'

The meaning of words changes with time: thirty years later, Allahuakbar scares the world and injects fear into the hearts of millions. Dark-featured fighters carrying long swords were beheading people while screaming Allahuakbar with the same amusement my uncles felt for their football matches.

'I remember a Ramadan night I spent in my grandfather's house,' I tell you. The four-, maybe five-year-old me was trying to be helpful by setting the plates on the table. My grandfather, who happened to distrust TV iftar announcements, was listening for the deeper voice of the Umayyad Mosque's muezzin on the official Damascus radio station. He always called the sunset prayer two minutes too late.

I remember the laughter of Ramadan as we gathered around the iftar table. We always prayed together first. 'O my Allah, for thee I fast, and with the food thou givest me I break the fast, and I rely on thee,' my grandfather said, and we all replied with a loud, deep *amen*. 'In the name of Allah, the beneficent, the merciful, O he whose indulgence is boundless, forgive me,' he added, and we repeated it behind him. Once I tried to speak it too fast. I was hungry and ready to devour the feast in front of me. I reached out for a piece of bread, and I was faced by an angry look from my grandfather, so I took my sinful hand back.

My mother, a happy-go-lucky twenty-something-year-old back then, was more supportive than my grandfather about fasting. 'You're too young to fast throughout the day,' she told me. 'You can take the minaret stairs toward fasting.' It was an easy system for children to get used to fasting. I fasted until the noon prayer for a couple of days, and then challenged myself to fast until the afternoon prayer. By the last week of Ramadan I was fasting like the grown-ups, until the sunset prayer was called. I felt proud of myself. During my shorter days of fasting, my mother relied on me to be the decision-maker on the taste of the food. She called my name and I came running to the kitchen, where she and two or three other women were gathered.

'Taste this,' she said, stuffing a spoon full of hot soup into my mouth. 'Does it need more salt?' I personally hated salt; she loved it.

'No. It's perfect,' I said, enjoying the hot taste burning the tip of my tongue.

'Great,' she said, adding more salt to the soup.

After the dua was done, my grandfather allowed everyone to eat, and we started to munch on the yummy food the women had spent all day cooking. We started with the heavy lentil soup, which always tasted better with a squeeze of lemon in it. The women alternated between fattoush and tabbouleh salads throughout the month, but they got creative as they came up with main dishes: mlokhieha was my favourite, and waraq enab came as a close second. Maqloubieh was my mother's favourite, but I didn't enjoy eggplants as much as she did.

My uncle was known as the joker of the family. He brought a plastic cockroach once and slipped it into my mother's salad. 'There is a cockroach in my salad,' she said calmly when she unveiled it with her spoon. She grabbed it out of her dish and looked at my uncle. 'You don't fool me easily, Brother.' She returned to eating, while the iftar table shook with roaring laughter.

After iftar, the men of the house left for the mosque for taraweeh prayers. I was dragged with them, but I wanted to spend the evening with the women drinking hot tea and watching TV. My only solace was the fact that the men would buy sweets on their way back to the house, and I got to decide which dessert to pick. 'Nabilseeh, I want nabilseeh,' I said, pointing to the cheese-based dessert, covered in milky cream.

It seemed to me that I stayed up very late that night. I must have slipped into dreamland long before midnight. At three a.m., a loud knocking from the street awakened us. 'Al-mesaheer,' my tetta Samira said, opening the door to our small room. 'Who wants to see al-mesaheer?'

The cold pinched my little face when I opened the window that looked over the narrow street outside. An old man appeared from afar. He was wearing traditional Syrian sherwal pants, a black jacket and a red fez; he held a little drum near his chest, knocking on it five times in front of each house.

'Wake up for your suhour, let the month of Ramadan visit your homes,' he sang loudly under each door, calling people to eat the pre-fasting meal. 'Abu Mohammed, wake up for your suhour.' The minute the mesaheer's silhouette was close enough to see the details, I saw his son walking sleepily behind him holding a small lamp.

I stood inside the warm, wooden house of my grandfather, where I was born, as were my father and his father before him. I looked up as the man walked by, ignoring me, calling out for more people to wake up before the light of his son's lamp dimmed. The smell of fried eggs, mixed with a spoon of flour, and the sounds of life behind me took me back inside.

My grandfather's house isn't there any more. The old Damascene house with its own fountain of silver-shining water and its forever smell of jasmine was destroyed by the government in 1989 to expand al-Thawra Street. My grandfather took his wife, Samira, his six sons, his only daughter, his daughter-in-law and me and moved us to a small countryside house on the last hill that the government hadn't seized from him. My grandfather lived for two years in the hill home; he was never happy with the new house, complaining that it was too cold, or too hot or too smelly. I think that he just missed the place he had called home for all of his life. He remained unhappy until he died.

I loved that hill house. As a family, we had a large studio that my father built on top of my grandparents' home. I loved the balconies overlooking Damascus, the summer breeze on the rooftop, the cold drips of water from the cracked ceiling in the winter, the blue wallpaper. I took my baby cradle into a corner, covered it with an old rug and called it my room, where I pretended to fall asleep after bedtime and I learned the Arabic alphabet.

I was five or six, and my mother had barely crossed her mid-twenties. I was her toy, and she was too young to be a mother yet. She must have thought of me as a speaking, moving, wonderful doll. She brushed my hair six different ways per day, and picked a mini-tuxedo with a red bow-tie for me to wear during Eid. She would heat milk for me, and make herself tea, and we would sit and have tea parties that she dressed up for. She went toy shopping with me on a weekly basis, and spent more time than I did trying to decide between the different choices, in the end always picking games played by two.

One afternoon, my mother sat me down. She pulled her wedding dress from her blue closet, and she showed it to me. On its shoulder, a glass rose rested, and she feared to touch it. She worried that the glowing, glimmering pieces might fall off the dress.

In the darkness of the night, I used to hear my parents whispering loving words. They used to tell each other stories. My mother used to write down Fairuz songs in a large blue notebook. On the balcony, my father built her a swing using old clotheslines and an abandoned pillow. Every morning, my mother sat on the pillow, listening to Fairuz, drinking her coffee, slowly swinging back and forth, enjoying the warmth of the sun as it filled Damascus with life. She used to pick me up in her arms in the early afternoon hours, sit me on the clothesline swing and push me higher. My feet never touched the ground; I imagined myself a grey dove spreading my wings across the hills around sleepy, calm, sunny Damascus. In my child's mind, the world was limited to what I could see of Damascus from that swing, rising higher than the walls of our balcony. I could see the latest blooming jasmine flowers in our roof garden. I could see the Barada River dividing Damascus in two. I believed that I could see the edge of the world, while I was sitting on the edge of that makeshift swing.

My mother had the brilliant idea of planting seeds in the pillow of the clothesline swing, and they grew stronger with the winter rain. She sat behind her window, sipping on her Turkish coffee, listening to Fairuz and watching the jasmine tree growing from the cotton pillow, climbing the clotheslines, until it created a fairy tale swing, beautifully braided between the jasmine flowers and the clotheslines.

Spring came, and she returned to using her swing in the early morning hours. As she pushed the swing higher, she felt like she could fly; she was a princess with long, smooth hair, a beautiful dame with love for the sun. The swing took her high, and she felt capable of anything. She heard the sound of cars beneath her as she playfully looked down the three-floor building. She used to fear falling from the balcony, but she didn't care any more. I enjoyed watching her from inside the studio. I heard her laughing and telling stories to herself. I heard her having conversations with herself in languages I didn't understand, following up on chitchats she had with imagined people. When I was a child, her laughter and her conversations felt like a game, as if she were playing with an imaginary friend. Her imagination took her to places I had never seen; I could glimpse them in her absent-minded eyes as she swung from the clothesline swing, and I wanted to know those places too.

My father, on a quest of expansion, decided to buy another home and move us into it. We abandoned the small, sunny suite with its clothesline swing for a spacious, dark house that took stairs upon stairs to climb to. It was the last house I shared with my parents. In that dark house, I never heard my parents whisper love songs. I never saw them happy. My mother sat in that house for days and did not move.

My father rarely came to visit, excusing his abandonment with work commitments. Her imaginary friends must have turned to demons; her funny chitchats that used to end with laughter back on her clothesline swing turned to arguments with unseen ghouls, ending with hysterical episodes of crying. The house filled with the dust of our lives, and the kitchen was never used to cook iftar meals during Ramadan. My father's visits became shorter. Her conversations with her demons intensified. She sometimes picked up the telephone, which was a luxury we didn't have in our old home, and had intense conversations with people on the other side. I picked up the other phone from the kitchen one night, trying to see who she was talking to. I heard her whispering that she would escape. 'I will fill a bag full of my clothes and come to meet you. I will wait for you. Don't be late. No. No. I don't want to be here any more. I don't want to be with him any more.' From the other side, I only heard the ready chirp of the phone line waiting for someone to dial a number. 'I'm scared, I'm lonely and scared,' she added.

I returned to my grandmother's home a couple of years later, and I slept on a sofa in the living room. I had a little closet where my covers and sheets were to be gathered every morning. My grandmother made me a sandwich of oil and za'atar to take with me to school every morning. She woke up at dawn to pray the morning prayers, and she woke me up with her. We sat together after the prayer, and she made us a cup of coffee to drink. We read the Quran together, and watched the sun coming up from behind the mountains of Damascus. The clothesline swing was long gone. An uncle of mine, who turned the studio into his own bachelor pad, found no use for it and cut it down.

After I escaped my grandmother's house, with a broken nose and a bruised side, I slept in gardens, parks and on the corners of streets. Men and women with children would drop coins in my hat, and I would gather them. I silently looked at them with grateful eyes, and they never asked questions. I used the money to buy myself food, and tried to save most of it. Once, the man running a small sandwich shop where I bought myself my sole meal of the day asked me to tell him my story, but I didn't reply. I gave him a dirty look and walked away. Two weeks later, he offered me a job. 'You can clean the shop, and you can sleep in it at night,' he said, but he didn't trust me enough yet. 'I will lock you inside every night.' Every morning, I woke up at five a.m. and cleaned the shop, scrubbing oil stains and food waste from the ground. I cleaned my hands and started cutting tomatoes and cucumbers while waiting for the man to open the shop doors. I then helped him prepare sandwiches and meals all day. I became famous among his customers for the omelette sandwich I make. I always added an extra spoon of flour to it to make it fluffy.

'I want to travel,' I told him after a year of working there. 'I want to fly away from here and never come back.' He looked me up and down and suggested that I go to Egypt. 'You can work at a restaurant or something,' he added. 'They love Syrian cooks there.' I finally gathered enough money to leave the whole country and move to Egypt, thinking that by escaping the whole country, I could leave the past behind. I shared my first apartment in Cairo with eight nineteen-year-old boys studying at al-Azhar University. We argued a lot about whose turn it was to wash the dishes. I found myself a job at a small newspaper and wrote stories for a living. A year later, I could afford to live on my own. My first apartment was haunted by a ghost that liked to smash dishes at night, which explains why the rent was so cheap.

I met Santa Claus at a book fair; he was buying a book about the role of Islam in expanding the knowledge of humanity, while I was buying a Mohammed Al-Mansi Qandil novel. I honestly thought he was gay, and invited him back to my apartment. I realized midway through our travels that he was straight due to his endless references to football matches, and decided to just drink coffee with him and send him on his way. Six hours later, we were eating kushari and drinking heavy tea while roaring with laughter.

He invited some of his friends, and they brought a shisha. One of them had a piece of hash that he was willing to share. It was the first time I'd ever smoked up; I dozed off into a land of colour unmatched by anything I'd ever seen. I guess I got too high for my own good: the wall of my apartment broke in front of my eyes, collapsing brick by brick, while the boys' talk became the background noise to the loud destruction of my apartment wall, revealing behind it a cartoonish land of happy toys and mermaids flying across a sky made of water.

I tilted my head, examining the world of wonder in front of me. I lifted my hand and asked everyone to shut up. They fell into silence. I started telling them stories about the world I saw. They listened with amusement, adding details of their own to the stories. We harmoniously built that world together, then escaped to it.

In the morning, I woke up to find myself sleeping on my couch, snuggling against Fady's shoulder, while Santa Claus was passed out on the floor.

A few weeks after I left the hospital, broken and friendless, I moved in with a man named Ayman. Our house was large, with three bedrooms, two dogs and a balcony. He felt safe. I needed safe.

Ayman was a bit older than me. His mother, a short-haired French-speaking woman, had known that her son was gay since his early childhood. She must have accepted his sexuality long before he was aware of it. She embraced him with a tender hug when he came out to her. He came crying from university into her house, knocked on her door, and collapsed at her feet. He explained how rejected he felt. He described how disconnected from everyone he was. She told him that all he needed was her and she never let him go. She opened up her house to me, and welcomed me to Christmas dinners. For two years, Ayman and I were lovers. Ayman was just as afraid of the world outside as I was. We spent days upon days wandering the apartment without any connection with the outside world. He made enough money through his financial practice for us to survive without ever leaving the house. At first, that felt safe, and I welcomed this disconnection from everyone. After two years, I couldn't stand it any more. I felt like a prisoner who was in love with his gatekeeper. I asked him to let me go, and he refused.

'You have to stay with me,' he whispered. 'You're mine.'

'I'm no one's,' I replied, and I walked out with one suitcase.

In 2009, weeks after I departed Ayman's home, I decided that I was done with Egypt. I walked the streets of Cairo, afraid of the shadows of people walking behind me. I felt alone and forgotten by the world.

I moved to Istanbul for six months before I returned to Syria. I had a bed in Istanbul's cheapest motel. It was a small four-storey building on the outskirts of Istiklal Street. The room was small; I shared it with random strangers who slept in the other bed for a night or two and never exchanged words with me. I lived there for six months, drinking whisky in cheap side bars hidden between old buildings and skyscrapers, meeting people on the ferries as I randomly jumped onto them in the early morning hours, growing my beard and marching in every protest I saw, repeating Turkish words I didn't understand.

While I was living in Istanbul, Jawad asked me to move in with him and I said no. I had met the Turkish rent boy when he was being roughed up in a back alley as I left a gay bar drunk. I'm not a fighter but I knew how to escape a beating. I shouldered one of his attackers and grabbed the hot Kurdish twink out of their circle, running toward the main street.

That night I slept in Jawad's house. He had black curtains on every window. 'You don't want the neighbours to see my type of work,' he said jokingly. To show his gratitude, he offered to let me sleep in his bed. 'We can share it,' he whispered. 'I won't charge.' I didn't sleep with Jawad, not that night anyway. We shared a bed. At three-thirty in the morning he turned to me, rested his head on my shoulder and smiled. I slipped my fingers into his thick black hair. I felt responsible for him.

Jawad and I talked for hours every day. He used to come to the back alley where we first met. We stood there drinking coffee and tea and smoking cigarettes. The first time he kissed me, we were walking in Istiklal Street. I knew my way in that street: take the left turn after the first Starbucks and you will find yourself in a gay nightclub; slip into the old, abandoned streets, following the rainbow flags raised high, and you will find yourself in the gay alley. He grabbed my arm on a late-afternoon walk we were taking, going from nowhere to anywhere, and he kissed me. It was my first kiss in public. It was delicious, sweet, horny and wet. I heard my friends cheering behind us, but I was lost for a second in the kiss. Weeks later, he asked me to move in, and I said no. I wanted to be on my own; I couldn't bear the idea of another person in my life.

When I returned to Syria in 2010, I rented a small house in Damascus. The house became the party hub for all the dykes in the city, invited by Maryam to join us. In 2013, a year after I left that house, clashes took place in the same Damascene suburb. A tank destroyed the house and sat on the pile where it used to be.

When I finally left Damascus, a little under a year after Khaled was arrested and I stopped buying white T-shirts, I asked you to come with me. You hesitated; you were worried about your family, and you didn't want to leave your secure job doing nothing in an office that sold things that no one bought any more. You shivered whenever you heard an explosion and you worried about snipers even in the relatively safe downtown area of Damascus. You told me that you didn't want to come with me. 'I love you,' you whispered, 'but I don't want to go.'

You called me two days before my trip and asked me to meet you. We met in Pages Café and you sat there, with the angelic light from the door coming in behind you. The café was deserted by then, and people rarely came in to drink coffee or play tawlieh. The smell of freshly baked petit fours had abandoned the place as well. 'I will come with you,' you told me, as soon as you sat down, 'but you have to promise that you won't ever leave me alone. You have to promise me that you'll always be there with me, every step of the way.'

I made that promise, not knowing that for three years in our future, we wouldn't even pick up the phone to say a quick hello.

Our house in Beirut had high ceilings; it was built in the late-nineteenth century and it felt the pressure of being over a hundred years old. The house, cold and cranky like an old sailor, played practical jokes on us. The trio of needs never came together. In that house, we either had power, water or internet, never the three together. We did not know what the future held for us in Beirut. We were tired of climbing to the rooftop looking for our water tank, carrying a long hose that stretched all the way to a truck downstairs carrying salty sea water. We had to buy water because the government didn't deliver water to our house.

I could see that broken soul of yours, peeking from behind your eyes, after you spent a day at the General Security of Beirut District, trying to renew your visa to stay in the country. You and the other Syrian refugees were treated like animals. The police officer carried a power cable in his hand, and he lashed you on your back, where that bird-shaped burn rests, when you walked into the building without asking for permission you didn't know was required. He called you a terrorist and you screamed in his face, asking him to treat you like a human.

The stories coming out of Syria made our lives a living hell. We saw our faces in the faces of dead men from our country who had died in yet another massacre. People shared those on social media, thinking that they are doing well by the world by bringing awareness to a war that no one wanted to deal with. We started to see the signs being hung in the neighbourhoods around Beirut, instructing Syrians to a curfew, asking them to remain in their houses after sundown.

One morning, without telling you, so as not to build your hopes up, I went online and I searched for a friend who lived in Canada. I typed the words into Facebook Messenger: 'Yes, we want to immigrate to Canada. How can we do that?'

I remember when you woke me up in the middle of the night in that house. 'Hakawati.' Power was out, and it was a hot night. We both were sweaty. 'Habibi, would you wake up?' I reached for a glass of water next to the bed, and it fell to the floor and shattered. My leg was resting on yours; our dog rested her head on my back.

I opened my eyes, my heavy eyelashes barely apart, as I asked you what was the matter.

'The dog pushed you, and you pushed me. You're almost dropping me off the bed.' I took a minute to understand, then I pushed the dog back. She woke up, growled softly and went down to sleep by our legs. I moved around a bit, allowing you more space.

'Is this better?' I asked, and you turned around, resting your head on my chest, your black hair brushing on my lips. 'Yup, it's much better.'

'I hate Beirut,' you mumbled. The sounds of cars passing by our window were keeping both of us up. 'It's okay, we will leave soon.' I sighed; I could hear your thoughts. 'I love you' – you murmured it.

'I love you too.'

10

THE TALE OF THECLA WHO
PRAYED TO GOD THREE TIMES

Yesterday was my birthday. Happy birthday. You're too drugged to remember, and I don't mind it any more. I used to hold a big space in my heart for my birthday celebrations; I used to count the days to my birthday weeks before it arrived, planning parties and getaways, inviting friends and acquaintances and expecting a gift or two. I think it's partly a childhood abandonment issue. No one ever celebrated my birthday when I was in my family's home. My mother was busy with her transformation, like Medusa who was once a joy to the eye of the beholder, before she was cursed to turn those around her to stone under her gaze. My father was busy escaping our makeshift castle, as if he were Ali Baba sneaking into the cave of wonders, staying for greedy moments to steal another jewel, trying not to forget the magical phrase that opened the doors.

As I got older, my birthday stopped being a reminder that I had survived another year, and became an omen for the arrival of death.

You haven't left your bed in a couple of days, and I worry about you. I wake up in the morning, trying to avoid the gloom filling our bedroom. I push the clouds of sadness around as I head to the bathroom for a long shower, turning the hot water to its max, hoping to skin the layer of mourning off my body. I return to you, aching, my skin red. I pull the curtains of our bedroom open. You squeeze your eyes and moan in agony. 'C'mon, hop on,' I tell you, extending my arm to you. 'You need to leave this bed.' You complain that I'm too old to carry you, and you worry that I might break a bone or snap my spine. I insist. 'You have to move,' I repeat. 'You have to leave this bed.'

You finally give in, and you start to uncover your tired body. You pull yourself out of the bed slowly, and you leave a mark of sweat and crumpled sheets behind you. I support you as you walk toward the door. We place our palms on the side of the wall, and they touch as we try to make it to the stairs. We walk down the stairs together, one step at a time, rhythmically touching the stairs with our feet. Here is that squeaky step. I need to find the time to fix it.

We reach our seating area, and I help you slip to the floor cushions. They are red, green and blue, with beautiful mandalas drawn upon them. You grab your favourite and you hug it. I leave you there, as I notice Death in the side of my eye, slipping into the seating area. I give him a dirty look as I head to the kitchen. I walk to the fridge and empty everything we have that can be considered a breakfast into bowls. I bring you a full tray of food and a teapot filled with hot tea. The three of us sit together on the floor, and we start eating slowly.

'Did you know that yesterday was his birthday?' Death whispers, eating a piece of halawa dipped in butter.

'No. Yesterday was not his . . .' I say, but I get interrupted.

'Oh, shit. I forgot,' you say, talking directly to Death for the first time. 'Was it really, love? I'm sorry, I forgot,' you add, speaking in a matter-of-fact tone, while I'm still stunned by the interaction.

It's soon then. It's coming. The moment when you give up on life; the moment your soul abandons this world for the next. The moment you give up on me and leave me alone to navigate a life I don't want to experience without you. Death has always been my friend. He came to me in a moment of a final breath, and allowed me a second chance to meet you. Now, it's your turn to befriend him, to tell him stories and to hold his icy fingertips. I mumble something about my birthday and leave the gathering while holding onto my tears.

I stand in the corner, holding a cold cup of coffee that I pretend to sip on for the tenth time as the two of you have your first conversation. It isn't a shy one. It isn't timid. You lightheartedly tell stories to Death, and Death pays attention and listens without hesitation. I witness the casual exchange from afar. You laugh and Death laughs with you; the echo of your laughter squeezes my soul. I drink another cup of imaginary cold coffee and I eavesdrop on your conversation. 'What are we talking about?' I whisper as I enter your space with Death, which now feels sacred and holy. 'We're talking about our immigration,' you say.

Your mood has shifted from the morning; you're cheerful and sweet. You welcome Death into our seating area, allowing him to snuggle with our red and green pillows, as if he were an old friend. You open up to him like you never open up to me. You tell him things that are new to me. I suddenly cannot gaze into my own fantasies as you talk to me; my fantasies are gazing back at me now, and I need to focus on what you say.

I wish you'd see what I see. I wish you'd realize the situation I'm in. I'm standing there, suddenly hopeless, losing my grip on the rope in the tug-of-war Death and I have been playing with your soul. You're the blue scarf in the middle of our rope, and I pull with all of my might, anchoring my feet into our reality while my head is swimming in the sea of my illusions. His fingers are stronger on the rope, and he is winning. I'm out of breath, and I exhale deeply as I lose more ground to him. Your blue scarf is withering in the wind. It's almost within his reach.

'We contemplated the idea of immigrating to Canada for weeks,' you tell him, and Death listens closely. 'It meant that we would have to face the reality of being refugees.' In Lebanon, they didn't call us refugees – they preferred to call us 'displaced persons'. The last time Lebanon had taken in refugees was right after the wave of Palestinians escaping as the Israeli state started to take shape in 1948. They moved to Lebanon and started to build camps and take over villages. The Lebanese thought the Palestinian refugees were temporary visitors who would return to their homes in a couple of months, carrying olive oil and lemons and forgetting all about Lebanon. The situation in Israel continued to escalate, and seventy years later, Palestinians in Lebanon are still considered refugees; their children are raised with a spoonful of the 'right of return' salt that they had to swallow. The land of Palestine became a distant memory; difficult to gather. Some of them won't even believe in this memory any more. They want to become citizens of Lebanon, but the Lebanese government still does not give them proper status or the right to work.

A whole generation of Palestinians grew up without status or a home; they grew up inheriting the keys to homes long destroyed in their grandfathers' land, a final reminder that they belong somewhere else that they might never know.

We were called 'displaced Syrian persons' so that we could be returned to our rightful owner when the time came. We felt as if we were someone's keychain, and that person had displaced us. They looked for us on the coffee table and under the kitchen sink; they searched for us in the pockets of jackets and pants. We were never found. We lost our faith in our owners, and we lost our faith in the gods who put us in this place to begin with.

'That reminds me of the story of Thecla, the virgin saint,' Death says. Thecla was a woman who heard the stories of Saint Paul, as he told them after the death of Christ almighty. She was converted to Christianity by St. Paul. She wanted to give her soul to the God of all, who would only take her into his love if she was a virgin. She abandoned her fiancé and her mother in Konya, a city in Turkey, and tried to escape the infidel kingdom she was born and raised in. 'They captured her in the dead of night and pulled her by her hair to the judges,' Death says. You're listening closely, and I'm holding my tears back. 'They ordered her to be burned at the stake like a witch.'

On the column, with ropes tightened around her body until they broke her skin and crushed her bones, she cried out to her newfound God. She prayed as they brought fire to the wood around her, and demanded God's protection. 'God in his skies heard her songs,' Death says. A storm unlike any storm before it came upon the city; it rained upon the flames surrounding Thecla. Its winds carried her column away until it reached the outskirts of the city.

'She knew she had to continue her escape,' Death adds. 'She stood up, freed herself from the ropes, cried for her mother, and started running.'

'Jake was our storm,' you point out. I remain silent, remembering Jake. I can't tell any more, since Death is not by my side to explain my fantasies to me, but I think I can see his ghost standing now in the corner of our seating area, eavesdropping on our conversation.

Jake, who lived in Vancouver, added me randomly on Facebook years before our immigration. He flirted with me for a bit, before realizing the depth of my love for you. 'Vancouver is a beautiful, rainy, open city filled with love,' he explained, sending us YouTube videos with aerial footage of the city. He explained that Canada had a programme called the Private Sponsorship of Refugees, and suggested we apply for it. 'You'll be sponsored to come to Canada by a group of Canadians who will take care of all of your needs for a year,' he said, glowing at the privilege his country had given its citizens. 'You'll be able to live here out of the closet, openly, and celebrate your love.'

His came from a Jewish Syrian family that immigrated to the US in the 1940s before resettling in Canada. Jake's grandfather owned a small shop in the old souk in central Aleppo where he sold and repaired backgammon sets. The small shop, cornered between Aleppo's old citadel and the civilization of the new city outside, had a wooden door that rang a soft singing bell when opened.

One day in the late 1940s Jake's grandfather waited in his shop for a customer, but no one came. He had spent most of his day working on one of the backgammon sets he was entrusted to repair. It was a beautiful historical piece that had been built seventy years before; it had rough edges and had seen dark days. He wore his little working glasses and used a hair-thin clip to place pieces of coloured wood and seashells to fill the gaps in the table's design. He took breaks multiple times throughout the day, making himself some tea on the smelly gasoline fire gun in the corner of his shop, which he sometimes used to give the wood an aged, burnt touch that makes it shine. He also left his operation table, as he liked to call it, a couple of times a day to change the radio channel, trying to find a station that played his favourite Asmahan song.

At that time, while Palestinians were escaping their homes carrying only their house keys, Syrians were protesting. France had left Syria months before and the country, shaken after years of imperialism and colonialism, could barely survive another political earthquake. Syrians heard the rumble of war drums and their hatred for whoever was different increased.

The grandfather sat there in the warm red V-neck his wife had made him the previous winter and waited for his customer to come as agreed. The bell never rang until he stepped outside himself and decided to close shop for the day. He felt the eyes of people around him and didn't completely understand what was going on. He had suddenly become the negative side of a magnet pushing away everyone around him. His own presence repelled everyone around him; wherever he walked, everyone avoided him.

In the cold, windy, snowy Aleppo night, as Jake's grandfather slipped through the night returning home, he couldn't hear the steps coming behind him. He didn't see the familiar faces. He too was attacked for who he was. He too lay motionless, taking sharp breaths and watching his spirit wandering about his body, while the two people who attacked him searched for his Jewish gold.

'Where do you hide your gold, you profane pig?' the men asked him, when they barely found a couple of lire in his pocket. 'You must have some hiding place!' They pulled his pants down and searched his underwear. He felt violated and wished he hadn't taken his usual shortcut through an abandoned street in the back alleys of central Aleppo.

When the men found nothing in his underwear, they decided to flee the scene. One of them turned around and returned to him. He grabbed him by the hair and smashed his face on the uneven floor. 'This is for Palestine,' the man said, possibly without even being able to point out where Palestine was on a map.

Thecla started running fast toward the Mediterranean Sea. She hoped to find a boat to take her away from the country where she was rejected for who she was. She was lost for days; she ran endlessly and hid between trees at night. God, who became her only companion, directed wolves away from her road and planted fig trees for her to eat. She thanked him at every corner and accepted his gifts with an open heart.

She knew that her city wouldn't forget about her, and she saw knights coming after her from afar. She heard their horses. She was in an open field and she knew they would see her no matter where she hid. She was standing on the same spot where, 1,950 years later, Jake's father would be beaten to within an inch of his life, and she fell to her knees like him. She cried and asked for an escape.

God, her protector and benefactor, heard her again. He instructed the wheat around her to grow faster, with the heads aching to reach the skies. The wheat ears grew stronger and filled the open field with a long, endless green cover. The knights lost her among the bushes and she managed to escape them once again.

Jake helped us fill out the application forms and paid the fees. He found a group of Canadians to sign the papers with him, and worked with a local organization to support our application to move to Vancouver.

'They Skyped every day,' you tell Death, with a side smile on your face. 'I thought they were in love.'

I never loved Jake. I thought of the older man as the father figure I'd never had. I respected his world, and he tried to understand mine. 'It was Tiffany's! Yes!' Jake said while carrying his iPad around his office, showing me his glorious treasures and collection of photos. 'Oh, I have a story for you,' he said. I smiled; I was soaking in the early October sun on our balcony in Beirut while listening to him telling me stories. In the mid-eighties, he and his then-partner lived in New York for a while. They had registered a crystal pattern when they moved in together. 'We threw a bunch of housewarming parties, friends wanted to buy gifts,' he explained. The employees at Tiffany's said some colourful things, little rude jokes, about the gay couple to their guests who were buying gifts. 'One of those guests happened to be Larry Kramer,' Jake added. Jake got the company to apologize and institute a diversity-training programme for all of their sales staff.

New York, I nostalgically tell Death, was the ultimate city of dreams for me. I was introduced to New York in my childhood, watching sitcoms like *Mad About You* and *Friends*. Somehow, my young brain thought that this is how people react, this is how they tell jokes and how they live happily ever after. New York seemed like a city of beautiful buildings and funny friends and married couples with dogs. In New York, Jake enjoyed his mid-twenties. 'I saw Chris Reeves naked,' Jake said. It was the mid-eighties, everyone was naked at some point or another. Jake and Reeves worked out at the same Powerhouse Gym on Broadway, on the Upper West Side of Manhattan.

After we applied to immigrate, we only had to wait a year or so until our application was processed. We stayed. We froze in time and we held our breath for a year. We slept through the nights, with our white dog resting her head on our legs, and with closed curtains to hide our forbidden kisses. We waited, and we had nothing else to do but wait.

You excuse yourself from the conversation. 'All this talking has tired me,' you say, and you walk to bed unassisted. I look at your back as you slip away from the light of the seating area, and I feel a shiver in my heart.

The next night and the night after you sleep faster, quicker; you don't ask me for stories any more. I feel worried, I stay up all night. I hold you here with me and I will never let go. I won't let the story end here. It's too early for our story to end; it's still untold. I feel untold. Stay with me just one more night. You mumble something that I don't understand, but Death, on the other side of the room, mumbles something back and you smile.

'I will tell you stories forever if I have to,' I whisper to Death. 'I will be your slave until eternity. Just leave him be. Don't talk to him.' Death, with a friendly, understanding smile, rejects my pleas.

'I have no control over how he sees me and when,' Death tells me. I look him in the hollow eye and I tell him our immigration story anyway.

It was four a.m. when we finally got on the plane heading out of Beirut. Hariri International Airport was a long drive from our house, and two checkpoints were in the way, but both of them let us slip through easily. 'You're leaving the country for good?' one of the soldiers asked us. 'Never come back. We don't want any more Syrians here,' he demanded, as he signalled us to continue. When we arrived at the airport, friends were waiting for us there. They carried flowers and Canadian flags. We were surrounded by hugs, kisses and promises of see-you-soon. We glided through the gates waving endless goodbyes, turning on our heels and looking back with teary eyes. The glass wall separated us from our friends. We couldn't hear them any more. They had longing eyes and big smiles. We met some of them again, while others slipped out of touch and out of memory. We sat in the airport and waited, surrounded by seven big bags that carried all of our lives with us. 'We are leaving everything we know behind,' I told you, and you squeezed my shoulder with your palm. You were equally nervous; it was your first trip on a plane.

'We will be fine,' you said. Your voice didn't even convince you. We both knew our kind of luck, so we kept our thoughts to ourselves. I knew you were thinking that with your luck, the plane would fall into the Atlantic Ocean and we would never make it. I worried that a police officer might stop us from going on the plane. We had been in a drought for so many years that the touch of rain broke our dry skin, and the feeling that safety might come, and with it a sense of belonging, a sense of home, made our heads crawl with anxiety. We heard the call for the plane and we headed to the gates, shivering.

Jake gave us a phone call as we entered the plane. 'You'll be fine. I've prepared everything for you, don't worry,' he told us, then we heard the call from the captain to turn off our phones.

As for Thecla, she heard that Damascus might be a safe place for her to go. The city was a young four-hundred-year-old haven of culture and religion. It was there that the miraculous conversion of St Paul took place. Travelling circuses and merchants came to Damascus from the Far East, starting their journey in Mumbai, walking across the Silk Road, passing by Isfahan, rushing through Baghdad, touring Palmyra and resting their horses in Damascus. They brought elephants and Indian spices with them, and they bought swords and gold from the Assyrians who built that city and ruled it like kings.

Thecla reached a mountainside that stood in her face like a wall. She was on the outskirts of Ma'loula, a small town near Damascus. She saw the knights coming, carrying black flags and heading for her head. She knew if they caught her they would tie her arms together and drag her along the rocks of the road, behind their running horses. She cried for her guiding light, for her God.

God reached out with both of his hands and cracked the mountain open, opening the road for her to escape through. She ran in, while the knights kneeled in front of the miracle and decided not to rush after her any further.

'Everything is ready for you,' God whispered, as Thecla walked into the tunnel that devoted Christians and tourists would walk into for thousands of years after. 'You'll be fine.'

Jake's grandfather woke up in the hospital two days later into a world that had changed completely. The noise outside was ear-shattering. His sixteen-year-old son, Adnan, and his young wife gathered around his hospital bed. In that relative safety, they witnessed the 1947 anti-Jewish riots in Aleppo.

The grandfather's leg was broken in multiple places and he was forced to stay in bed and let his son navigate the streets back to their house to get some of their clothes. 'The country has gone insane,' Adnan said as he walked back with dark features. 'The UN vote in favour of partitioning Palestine has driven everyone mad.'

He told his father that their street had been burned down. They called that street 'al-Yahood Street' – the Jews' street. The fire had started when a group of boys found some old children's books in Hebrew and decided to burn them. The fire grew and spread. Many from neighbouring streets came to help put it out, but it wasn't enough. 'We're leaving Syria,' Jake's grandfather said, demanding that his wife and son start packing so they could leave the minute he was discharged from the hospital. He didn't want to go to Israel, so he took his family and what was left of his small savings and slipped over to Beirut. There, they booked a small cabin on a boat to London. Three years later, they found themselves on another boat to New York.

Adnan, who would eventually become Jake's father, was old enough to remember Aleppo and hold it dear in his heart. After Adnan finished high school in New York, he decided to study finance at the University of Toronto. He fell in love with a Canadian woman and planted his tree there with her, but Adnan's father was angry with him. He called him and asked him to return to New York. 'Why would you want to live so far away from your family?' Jake's grandfather insisted, but Adnan had already grown up in a nomadic life, so he never felt that pull toward one city. He was pulled toward people he loved, and he found his lover in Toronto.

As a child, Jake would wear his favourite V-neck sweater - kept only for fancy dinners and visits - and go visit Uncle Altman in his coffee shop on Church Street. Altman wasn't really his uncle, he was a close friend of his father's from university. Altman was gay - Jake and his father knew that well. Adnan had grown up in London and New York, and was open to the world around him. He refused to take on his father's rigid views, and was supportive of his gay friend. Altman welcomed the young boy into his coffee shop every other day; he gave him books to read, made him a cup of tea and sat him next to the street windows. The young Jake read books about Marxism that he didn't understand.

He preferred easier books, and developed a love for James Bond novels. His father and his uncle tried to convince him to read other novels that might give him a better look at the world around him, but he wasn't interested.

Altman was arrested with many others during Operation Soap in Toronto. He was visiting a bathhouse, which is something he rarely did, when the police stormed the place. They forced the men out into the street in the cold early-February night with only towels to cover their privates. Jake didn't know, but his father and mother went out and helped spread flyers about a protest on Church Street.

Adnan stood in the face of policemen threatening people with metal wands and glass shields. He screamed in their faces, 'Out of sheets, out on the streets,' and demanded the release of his friend. Jake's mother stood on top of a car, watching the three thousand protesters storming Church Street and screaming her lungs out when her husband was elbowed by one of the police officers when he got too close to the police line.

They never got arrested; they returned home that night to find Jake asleep, without a care in the world. They walked toward the bathroom and spent an hour there making love in the shower.

Now that God had ensured the safety of his beloved Thecla, he found her a cave and asked her to pray for him until eternity.

'Thecla happily obliged for the next year of her life,' Death says. 'She prayed every day to her God, and praised his glory. She kissed the stones she imagined he had touched, and poured water on his cross and cleaned it with the remains of her clothes.' After a year, Thecla started to see the world differently. 'How long will I be praying for you? How long do I dedicate my life to thanking you for saving me?' she asked, and she didn't hear an answer. She knew that this would be her fate forever. Did she regret her decision to cross the world for her God? Did she get bored of praising him endlessly? She might have. She might have asked God to release her from her servitude, but he refused to let her go. 'I saved your life. I grew wheat ears and cracked mountains for you,' he said. 'You've got to love me forever.'

You cracked those mountains because you can and I can't, she might have thought. *You grew the wheat ears to show your glory, not to save my life. They will remain green and strong forever, while my soul withers in this cave glorifying you.*

'Legend says she lived in that cave until she died,' Death finally adds. 'She died a lonely old virgin hag. The mountains remained cracked, Damascus remained glorious and Aleppo remained green until the war burned those cities down.'

Jake introduced us to his friends as his refugees. 'I saved their lives,' he said repeatedly, with a glowing look in his eyes. He elbowed me in the side and whispered, 'Tell them. Tell them how I saved your life.' At first I happily obliged. I told them glorifying details about Jake's hard work and his generosity. After six months, I felt like I was performing for his amusement. He was addicted to the sense of importance our cause had given him, and he wanted to devour it endlessly.

He accompanied us everywhere. He decided who should be our

friends and who should be our enemies. He insisted that we only trust him, because no one else was worthy of trust.

'You felt like a monkey jumping to his command,' you tell me, and Death nods in agreement.

He asked for attention all the time, and called us a billion times a day. 'Do you want me to come over?' he said on the phone. If I refused, he would start to whine endlessly. 'I saved your lives, is this your payment for doing that?' he would say, and I sighed, aching for the freedom I came to Vancouver to find.

Six months later, I had a huge fight with Jake. 'You only helped us come here for your personal glory. You wanted to feel that you had a cause to support,' I told him. 'You wanted two birds in a cage to sing for you.' Jake had a saviour complex. He was addicted to his success. He had never faced a challenge in his life, and he felt small in front of his father's and grandfather's accomplishments.

Jake told his father and mother that he was gay when he was fifteen. They were having lunch, and he had prepared a whole speech. He asked if he could tell them something, and they both looked up at him. 'I'm gay,' he said, with tears in his eyes. His father looked at him, and then at his mother. 'All right, thank you for telling us,' the father said. 'Can you pass the salt?'

'On many occasions,' I add, 'I couldn't help feeling a bit jealous.' Jake didn't struggle to reveal his sexuality to his parents. His father, understanding, loving and supportive, stood by his son. His family took the right turn after every crisis. He reached a place where he could explore himself, and I couldn't. I felt, at times, limited. My challenges were heavy cuffs placed on my wrists; they dragged me to the bottom of the sea so many times. I grew up without that support, without that love, and I felt the pain of loneliness. I remember. I remember sitting in the schoolyard, surrounded by a hundred children like me and thinking to myself that I was the loneliest child in the world. Jake never felt that way; he never had the chance to be challenged. He lived a life where he witnessed the challenges of others, but they never affected him. 'It made you the man who you are now,' you say as you prepare for bed. 'Those challenges made you the person you wanted to be. That sheltered upbringing of Jake's took away his agency, twisted love in his mind. It made him unaware of his privileges, and he abused you.'

'Maybe he did,' I reply.

The silence fills the room for a while. On the ceiling, an image is painted with colours of beauty: Aleppo roads zoom in and zoom out, beautiful and dark, with a small backgammon shop on one corner, its bell ringing, its only lantern lit.

11

THE TRUTH-TELLER AND HIS TALE

There are some impenetrable memories inside my head. Things that I only tell myself in the darkness, in the moments when my naked mind is stretched until it's ripped in half. My broken pieces cry for completion; those old memories feel like the waves of an angry sea, carrying me deeper into the black waters of depth and sorrow. The waves are silent, like skulking monsters, hitting me in the face as I attempt to hide behind metaphors and fantastical beings.

Those memories vary. One of them is bitter, like a rotten squeezed lemon, as it contains my feelings of loneliness when I woke up in the hospital in Egypt, surrounded by white walls and nurses. It took me a moment to realize where I was, and another moment to hear my own heavy breathing as I struggled to pull air into my bruised lung. I waited in that room alone, one eye open, mouth shut, for anyone to notice me, to come to my rescue and fill me in on the details of my body's marks. I wondered if I would be able to walk, as I saw my leg stretched in front of me with a cast surrounding it from the knee down. I wondered if I would be able to see again with my left eye, as I felt the heavy eyelid closing on it like a prison gate, and I wondered if I would ever be able to trust a friend again as I remembered the heavy boot smashing my nose.

Wave after wave. Wave after wave.

I see myself roaming my grandmother's room, trying to hold myself so I wouldn't pee in my clothes. My body was twitching, hoping to release the flood of water inside of it, but the door was closed and I didn't dare to knock. I waited for hours, trying to overlook the growing pain in my lower stomach. I tried to ignore it, I held it in and tried to think of dry deserts and scalding sun. Finally, when my grandmother opened the door at midnight, I rushed to the bathroom. I stood there, peeing and seeing blood staining the pee, colouring the water orange. I didn't tell anyone about that.

I remember the first time I spent a night away from you in Vancouver. I climbed into my new twin bed, too small for a couple to share. I tried to sleep on the left side of the bed, but couldn't feel comfort. I felt your eyes staring at me from the other side, and I turned my back on your ghost. I couldn't sleep, I just kept my eyes open, looking into the darkness of my bachelor studio and wondering where you were. Your warmth was filling out someone else's bed, your hands were touching someone else's back and your lips were printing kisses on someone else's face. I turned around and slid myself to the right side of the bed, and I felt the cold of the sheets squeezing my muscles and forcing me into a fetal position. I suffered with losing you as if you were my phantom limb. You ached me, and no painkillers would calm my agony. I finally found myself slipping to the middle of the bed, extending both hands to touch the sides and crying like a lost child until I fell asleep.

I offer you souvenirs: my stories, the pieces of my soul, to help you sleep. I pick the memories that I dare not share, and I twist them and burn them. I turn them into an unrecognizable fable to amuse you. You catch me in the middle of my sentences, you see the truth behind my tales, and you pull it through the lines of my stories, like pulling a charred photograph from the ashes of a fire. My memories wear my stories like the skins of dead animals, but you undress them and place them in my view. I feel their truth mocking me, knowing that I can't hide from it. It eats me from within. My stories are my own Limos, my Greek monster of hunger. Limos infected Erysichthon with a hunger so strong that the king ate himself; I wonder what my stories would do to me. Then again, I might be insane. My mother was before me.

Her mother was before her. By the time I was old enough to remember, but not old enough to understand, her story was over; she had enough energy to survive her first thirty years before she gave up on life and retreated within herself.

The world has played its games with me before. I might be imagining all of this around me. Maybe, like my mother, I lost my mind at the age of thirty and this whole house – this whole life – is an elaborate vision of happiness I'm experiencing while drooling in a mental hospital bed. I mean, look at me, sharing stories with Death and his ghosts. Wouldn't you, my possibly imaginary lover, question my sanity too?

I slip away from our bed, tiptoeing around the robes of Death, who is napping on the rocking chair, using the wood of his scythe to rest his skull and his hooded cloak as a blanket. I feel deserted, alone. I'm saddened to realize that even if I am imagining this world around me, my imagination limits me to an ending where you, my dear, leave me behind.

In my darkest hour, I find myself in my office; I ignore my stash of hash. Today is not a day for fantasy and escape. I surrender to the waves of memories washing over me. My wounds are opened, my fears are running free and the world inside my head is chaotic and slippery. My mother used to have a photo, a beautiful photo from when she was twenty-two. Her hair, brownish and wavy, had a beautiful red flower in it. At the time, *Kassandra*, a Venezuelan telenovela that was broadcast in Arabic on national Syrian TV, had become a hit among many Syrian women; in 1994, every woman in Syria had in her closet a red fake flower, a pair of gypsy earrings and a long, colourful skirt. In the photo, my mother smiles a shy smile, avoiding the camera, looking into the sea in the background. In her ears rest a pair of gypsy earrings.

The photo was resting between the wood of my mother's vanity and the layer of glass on top of it. There, after endless spills of water and coffee, the photo was stuck to the glass. My mother, using a sharp knife and lots of water, finally managed to add that photo to the pile she had gathered, waiting to be burned on our balcony.

It took her three years to switch personalities, to become something she never intended to be. Maybe I'm as mentally unstable as her. I'm a mental bomb: I might explode into a wreckage of disorders and social anxieties at any second. I might have exploded long ago.

I'm spent. My veins are all open and the tree of life within me has grown without love: it has been years since I cared for myself, and now that tree is warped and unrecognizable. I still have stories to tell you; some of them you know, others are tangled within the worlds I create. What have I done to myself? In my mind, I examine our life together as I see it now. Death rocking on his chair by our bed as our battle for your survival continues. On the kitchen counter, there are bills to pay and mail to sort. I interrupt a fight with Death to answer a telemarketer or pay our electricity bill. I tell you stories as I witness ghosts from the past roaming our home, like lost souls carrying lanterns hoping to wake people up. My mind is like a factory that mixes our reality with epic elements of heroism, and my tongue is the end of the production line. The stories come out and I can't untangle them, I can't tell the reality from the dream.

I relax back in my office chair, rest my feet on my desk and close my eyes for a second. In my dreams, there are two versions of me: the screaming, agonized, insane version and the calm, understanding and capable version. The two are playing chess with my body, taking turns winning control over my mind. Crowds of faceless nurses hold the insane one as he tells truths, while the sane one sips on his scalding-hot coffee: it burns his insides but he keeps his poker face.

Battalions upon battalions of spoken words curve around me and they slowly tattoo themselves onto my skin. A billion singing voices tell my stories and a million flutes play. My heart slides over the side of the letter meem; like a rollercoaster, it uses the kaf as a parachute and jumps away from my body. I wake up.

'What are you doing in your office?' I hear you saying from the stairs. 'Come back to bed.' I remember walking with my mother in al-Hamidiyah covered market in old Damascus. The historical market was built back when Damascus was the end of the line for those travelling on camels across the deserts on the first international trade route in history:

the Silk Road. The souk feels like a tunnel that takes you from the heart of the old city to the skin of the new one. It runs five hundred metres from east to west and ends with a Roman archway overlooking the Umayyad Mosque. Most of the souk is arched over with high iron ribs of corrugated metal. The ancient Roman fortress that the souk was built upon can still be seen, like the blurry background of a colourful new image. As we walked in the souk, among people walking in the middle of the street where no cars are allowed, I was lost in my daydreams. The loud exchange between men and women buying chessboards, jewelry and gallabiehs filled the air with an endless glee.

As a child, even with a limited knowledge of history, I could imagine the ancient market evolving throughout history. From the days of selling swords and slaves to the days of selling locally made superhero T-shirts and knockoff Armani bags, the market remained beautiful, a never-ending centre of civilization that lasted there despite five thousand years of storms around it.

I walked hand-in-hand with my mother, who was trying to avoid passersby with her big pregnant belly moving ahead of her. I was jumping from one pool of light to the next. The market roof, made of iron and copper boards, had little holes in it, so that the wind couldn't fly it away. Sun would shine through the holes in the high ceiling, creating a grid of dots on the wet ground. In my child-mind, I imagined that those were the holes of bullets. 'The men of my country fought to liberate us from France,' I would tell myself, too shy to share.

My source of information was a TV series called *Ayam Shamiya*. The popular TV show depicted life in the old days of Damascus. Its creators chose bits and pieces from Syrian history and mashed them all together into one unrecognizable pile of overrated drama. It was stereotyping Syrians to Syrians, mingling history, extending that period somehow until the arrival of the Assad regime.

My mother, busy in her thoughts, had been quiet for a while; I was too young to tell, but she hadn't been happy lately. She was ending the final chapter of her life, preparing herself to let go of reality and slip into the unknown. In that time, she knew there was something wrong with her. She hung up the phone after the long hours she spent speaking to no one, suddenly realizing the illusion she was living. She tried to ignore those recurring illusions and focus on her life with my father. Syrian women believe that when they have pregnancy cravings, say a certain fruit, those should be answered immediately. 'Or else the fruit will replace the boy's eye,' she would tell my father, who smiled to her. At the time, he wanted to fix things. He was trying. He showed up to birthdays carrying gifts and he bought me a Superman T-shirt once. Life, at the age of eleven, seemed beautiful and promising.

Then my mother began struggling more with her illusions.

'We need to go buy those spices,' she said to me, her belly opening the crowd around us; the city was clean, fresh after a soft rain. The white government buildings around old Damascus stood clear and breathed; their windows shone. 'I need to cook waraq enab today,' she explained, holding my hand, her eyes looking everywhere. Earlier that day I had questioned why she had a big bag with her; when I got no answer, I decided to come up with an answer on my own. *Maybe we are buying a lot of stuff.* The bag seemed heavy; it clicked on the old bricks of the road. We stood outside the bakdash and I asked if I could buy myself some ice cream. She said no.

We waited there until the street was empty, and the red lights they turned on at night were aflame. 'She is not coming,' she whispered to me, holding my hand tighter. 'She will never come.' The voice on the phone she heard wasn't going to meet us at the souk. We stood there and the laughter of the old market was gone. Silence filled up the space, and she looked in each direction before pulling the bag, and pulling my hand, and taking me home.

That night, we didn't eat waraq enab. When we returned home my father was there, as usual. My mother emptied the bag and prepared a simple dinner. 'You need to know how to make eggs,' she told me, her hair covering her eyes. 'You add a spoon full of flour to the mix,' she taught me. 'It makes them fluffy and delicious.' It was her final act of parenting; her child needed to survive hunger, and he needed to know how to make the simplest of food items. She miscarried a daughter that night. As she screamed for the loss of her unborn child, she dipped her face into the dark water of her fantasies, and never came back.

The first cracks of dawn break into my office; my eyes adjust to the light. My nose is cold. I decide to attempt a couple of hours' sleep. The light glances at me from last night's darkness. I feel better. My brain is calming down. I walk past a mirror and I look at myself. I'm a reflection of my own choices. Sigh. I walk up the steps, uninterested in being quiet. 'Hakawati,' I finally hear you say, 'will you tell me a story?' I smile.

'Have I told you about Adam?' I whisper in a tired voice as I enter the bedroom. 'The guy I used to date, who made up for what he lacked in human intelligence by being aesthetically pleasing.'

You laugh, turn around and clumsily smash into me. I laugh. For a second, we're our young selves again. We kiss. 'I see your face, I can read it,' you tell me, mid-kiss. 'You were lost in your own thoughts again, were you not?'

I try to avoid your eyes. They can read the truth between the lines of my stories. You explore each memory with ease. For me, my memories are glass jars I squeeze endlessly but can't open. You take them from me, and suddenly they pour their goods out for us to taste. 'I don't want to hear about this Adam,' you whisper. 'I want you to tell me what's going on in your mind.'

I will tell you a story, I will tell you two stories, I will tell you a million stories. 'Just stay with me for one more night,' I whisper. 'I need to cleanse my soul to you.'

They call her insane, but she takes it as a compliment. Through the cracks of her old, tilted house's walls, she can hear them talking about her. Some are wondering where she came from, others are just speculating about her past. According to one story, her father abandoned her as a baby on the doorsteps of the old church; the nuns cried, but took her in among them. As the story goes, she ran away at the age of seventeen, lured into an abyss of drugs and love affairs with older men who fed on her daddy issues, until she went crazy when she was gang-raped at a private party.

Another story tells of her career as a high-end prostitute, known among her customers for controlling the fates of political figures and businessmen, until she rejected the advances of a minister – or even a president, according to another version of the story – who kidnapped her and drove her mad, locked deep in the basement of his summer house. She laughs as she eavesdrops on these stories, told by lonely women abandoned by their husbands throughout the day and well into the night. She sits on her makeshift patio overlooking the old, dirty street, shooing the chickens away and enjoying her well-made cup of coffee on her own.

She hears the voices of her past in her head sometimes. They whisper to her, as if they were calling her on a shaky landline and leaving encrypted messages about rendezvous and futures together. She doesn't care to listen to them any more.

One thing stands between her and her ultimate contentment: the shadow of the bridge passing over, blocking the sun from reaching her old, one-floor house. Like a flower breaking through the layers of winter snow, she needs the sun to guide her through her mind's maze of railways, where her trains of thought pass by one another, creating loud, vivid music, but never crashing. Her mind is a map of supernatural lines, twisting and turning, knotting and untying one another. The peace she feels, as she allowed her soul to slide along these roads, is overshadowed by the muffled sounds of cars crossing the bridge over her head, and the dark shadow, a long and cumbersome block denying her rightful demand for warmth and light.

There is no problem without a solution – she knows that well.

He calls her a whore, slams her on the glass coffee table, which smashes underneath her. He mounts her as she tries in vain to get her body off the floor, pinning her deeper into the shards of glass that enter her body in countless places. He grabs her wrists, holding them down together with his heavy hand, and with his knees he pushes her legs apart. Her underwear is still stained with the blood from his attack this morning, but with his other hand, he snatches it away and the silk slices through her buttocks before it tears to pieces.

She figures that there is no escape, so she allows her soul to wander away. Her mind drops into a sweet and happy memory. All her happy memories involve him – their wedding day, or their honeymoon on a beach in Malaysia. He stabs her with his penis, she feels him inside her as if he was bashing a knife edge into her most sensitive self; she blocks her nose from smelling his alcohol-tainted breath. His invading touch is transformed into the soft first touch he ever gave her, before everything, before all.

She returns to his world as he drops his weight on her body, panting. She gently tries to squeeze herself from underneath him, calmly at first, and then more viciously, trying to push him away. His heavy body is trapping her breasts against her heart (*the breasts I paid for*, she says in her head, mimicking him). When she finally manages to get from underneath him, he slides in his sleep over the shreds of glass; she doesn't mind, and neither does he. Her bathroom mirror reminds her that she should allow herself to feel the pain again; lines of blood across her back and arms create an abstract painting of sorrow. For the first time in years, she can read the message clearly: she needs to finish this.

Her mind is full of surprises, and today she is building a tower. She thought about it long and hard, and her idea continues to sink in deeper. She will build a tower, a tall beast of wood and nails, to allow her a moment of peace, all the way up by her lonesome. She will be away from gossiping women and she will welcome the sun on her face every morning. She needs a ladder and lots of wood, but her quest to reach the highest heights, to create her own Tower of Babel, has given her energy to move mountains.

She starts by gathering a layer of mud and then she raises four long pieces of wood as columns for her next floor. Then, using ropes and belts, she climbs up, creating a layer of wood as a new floor, pasted together with mud. Mud. Columns. Floor. Repeat. Her plan is flawless; she can feel the sun tanning her dirty face and giving strength to her bare arms as her tower grows taller.

The kids in the street now help her. They don't know why, but for some reason her quest to reach the sky seems so exciting to them. They point her to where she can find abandoned wood and they gather mud for her in little baskets they stole from their mothers' kitchens. The gossiping women continue to gossip, she assumes; she sees their lips moving faster and faster, and she sees their gazes aiming at her, but she is too far into her project to actually hear them.

She can't surrender to her fate any more. She feels like a whale that was abandoned by its pod. Each of her heartbeats feels like it is her last; her body aches as if her skin were dry and calling for a drop of water to revive her. She feels helpless like a whale in shallow water, deep to her knees in her pain, planted with his hateful sperm, and no one has found her yet, no one gathers around to push her back into deep water. In her fantasy, he is a pack of wolves roaming the sands, metres away, waiting for her beating heart to weaken before taking her life once and for all.

She feels like the lights are weakening around her, as if her face were reflected in the light of life inside her body, and it's fading away, her bones are misshapen and her face has forgotten its own details. She looks around her and sees the smashed glass table. She is used to his attacks, coming through the house like a hurricane, destroying her favourite vase, smashing the TV set and waking up concerned neighbours. By the time he returns the next day, she will have cleaned the house, replaced the TV and had a hasty conversation with a neighbour. She is used to cleaning up his messes. She searches in her soul for an escape, but all her happy memories have been burnt out, all of his sweet touches are now painful stabs.

She can't handle the squeezing walls closing in on her body, cracking her ribs. Changing the laws of nature, she runs, she steps on his body as it rests among the glass of the shattered table, she steps on the glass, she can't care, she runs to the door, jumps to the elevator, leaves the door open behind her. She presses the buttons. She flees, she runs.

In her car, the road feels dark and monstrous. The torchlight of her soul opens the road and she feels like a child on an amusement park ride. She stamps on the gas pedal and the car roars, jumps out of the building, into the street, onto the bridge.

There, by her lonesome, in that early morning hour, she wonders: where to go now? Should she go back to her family's house? Should she take a tour around the city and return before he wakes up? She is not sure. She calls for a miracle.

Next to the bridge, she sees a woman standing in an impossible space, floating in the air like an angel. Then she realizes that the woman is standing on a tall, makeshift wooden tower. She sees her, and in her, she sees her future self.

She feels like she can fly, on the top of her castle, at the end of her tower; she is Rapunzel with short, fuzzy hair, a beautiful dame with love for the sun. She is on top of her mud tower and she is capable of anything. She hears the sound of cars behind her and she remembers: a vision, a tale, a premonition. She cracks a smile and looks back toward the bridge for the very first time.

On the other side of the bridge, a woman is driving her car, lost in her own thoughts; she sees her, and in her, she sees her past self. Time laps, turns around, creates a circle; and at her feet, deep in the fresh mud of her tower, time rests like a purring cat.

I'm curling within your body, crying like a child. You're sitting there, touching my hair softly with your fingers. 'Here, here,' you whisper, 'everything will be fine.' I can't talk, I can't break the cycle of endless crying. It feels like the river of pain I held within me for so long has finally reached the point of flooding. It feels heavy, unstoppable, painful.

But for some reason, it also feels comforting, as if the pressure of my own tears were filling my skull with an endless headache, and suddenly, as the tears spring from my eyes, I feel relieved.

For the first time in months, I fall asleep while you stay awake.

12

THE TALE OF THOSE WHO LEFT

For a while, we live happily. We invite friends, old and new, and they join us in and around the house. You're less clumsy and more dynamic. I feel better about our lives. Everyone asks where we were. 'We were hibernating,' you say, holding a glass of orange juice. 'All Arabs do that.'

We laugh. They laugh. The house lightens up with the late light of summer. Even Death stands in the corner, surrounded by the dogs, waving hellos around, trying not to spill his drink. The summer continues, painted with your smiles, warm and fuzzy, like a morning snuggle. It could continue endlessly, but it doesn't. By Halloween, Death's favourite holiday, fall returns and cold winds squeeze your body; you cough a bit, but you keep the smiling face on.

'I will do a theme party,' Death explains, and we both agree. 'Let's call it *The Survival Night!*' On that night, Death will tell the stories that scare him the most: the tales of those who survived him, and how they managed to survive. We both laugh and we agree to the silly game.

At night, you still sleep soundly without a story. Your eyelids slip slowly, closing your eyes, while we lie face to face, smiling, on our bed. You sit on the balcony, carrying a glass of water in your hand, on your favourite chair with its red pillow. One of the dogs stretches and comes to sit next to you. 'It's a beautiful city,' I tell you as I sit next to you. I carry my glass of whisky. You smile. Your skin looks shiny and new. Your eyes sparkle with love and you look at me.

In the afternoons, when we used to fight, you, Death and I now gather around a table to share stories and plan events. Sometimes Death and I take a joint in a corner while you listen to your favourite Syrian diva, Assala.

'He looks better,' Death tells me, pulling the last purple breaths from the joint. *Yeah*, I never add. I look at you from afar. My fears grow inside me and I'm tempted to face them, but I hesitate to voice them out loud. At night we gather in the warm living room. Death tells us one of his stories. He speaks about kings and fools and once again tells his old and favourite tales.

'I'm so bored of those stories; stop telling them,' you tell Death, aware of my growing fears.

'My stories are now boring?' Death looks at you, trying to calm himself.

'Oh, don't be such a queen. I'm kidding.'

That night the fight escalated in bed. 'I wasn't saying that his stories are boring,' you tell me while pulling the covers. 'I cannot believe we're still talking about this.' My face is yellow; my eyes are glowing in the dark. The dogs are worried, they whimper.

'It's not about the stories,' I explain. 'Just please don't get on his bad side.'

'Here we go again.' You say it from under your tongue. I hear it loudly. 'You cannot live without the drama,' you whisper from the other side of the bed. 'Now can you let me sleep?' I silently agree.

In my dreams you're my ghost and I'm your shadow. We slip together on the surface of clean, murmuring rivers, then slide over the curves of a waterfall. I write you stories and you sing them; we playfully make love. In my dreams we continue to live happily ever after. We slip into a land I create underwater; the two of us sing and a tree of life grows from the bottom of the ocean, there so completely. Underneath the two of us rest in a small world of our own until forever.

The next morning you apologize. 'I didn't mean to hurt him so badly,' you explain. I shake my head and agree. These are the final moments, I have agreed to it; those are the final lines of our stories and these are the moments that I will forever remember. Today I accept that this is your final glimpse of life before the end.

'He is coming to terms with you,' I whisper to Death. 'Those are the final signs.'

'You just need to accept it,' Death says, pulling another purple breath from yet another stolen joint of mine. 'He is enjoying it himself. He doesn't want to be reminded of the end.' I need to keep a strong face. I need to enjoy it too; those are the moments that will count.

We silently gather around the dinner table. The pumpkin head is in the middle. 'No one knocks at the door any more,' I say. The three of us agree, humming. A moment of silence later, we break into laughter. The fire of the warm house feels stronger again. We feel like a family of insane characters and we accept one another. The evening feels happy; it feels like it will continue to be pleasant for a while.

'Who will tell the first story?' Death asks.

'George,' I explain, 'wanted to escape Turkey to Europe. Dozens upon dozens of people managed to do it, but he just couldn't.' Neither of us had met George, although we heard about him repeatedly. He was a Syrian legend.

'The last I heard of George, thirty years ago, he was planning another trip to Europe,' I say over dinner. 'Do you remember George?' You shake your head; you don't recall George at all.

George used to be a library clerk in an elementary school. The Christian man, with his green eyes and his friendly smile, wasn't the brightest of his generation, but he loved his work and the children cared for him. George escaped the war in Syria with a large scar on his face, right under his eye. The scar drastically changed the sweet, goofy-looking man-child. He looked like a molester-murderer.

With his new appearance, along with his old personality and the lack of any caring relatives, George left his town on the outskirts of Homs for Turkey. He was told that someone could help him there. In the refugee camp on the border of Turkey, George sat in a tent while it was pouring rain outside, and a doctor took a look at his eye. 'No, I'm sorry to tell you,' the friendly doctor said, 'the scar is an old, minor injury, and we would rather spend our resources somewhere else.' The doctor advised George, however, to go to Europe – 'Maybe to Greece?' – where they would help him with his scar.

George, being one who never passes up good advice, decided to go to Europe. Maybe Greece. Some told him that his eye could be fixed elsewhere, but he never listened.

'Every now and then, someone told him to get on an illegal boat,' I say, 'or pay some money to get the border guards to let him pass.' His scar, goofy personality and love for yellow hats made him recognizable – almost famous – among Turkish officials and border guards.

'He was returned a thousand times,' I giggle. Finally he managed to get on a boat, illegally travelling the seas at night, and landed in his dream country. The boat people dropped him five hundred metres away from the shore of Greece and told him to swim. By God, he swam. A friend had paid someone a handsome sum of money to fake an Italian identification card for him. 'That night he was stopped at a checkpoint. At first, they really thought he was an Italian touring Greece,' I explain, 'then they found his Syrian passport, in the sole of his shoe.'

George was illegally deported that night. The officers poked fun at the weak, scared man-child, treating him like a joke. 'They placed him in a boat, told him that they would beat him up if he made a sound, then deported him back to Turkish shores,' I say. George's story continues but we never heard of him again.

You rest your head on my shoulder. 'Oh, Hakawati,' you whisper. 'Even when you tell stories of survival, the ending is never a happy one.' In my head, George is happy. For him, escape is a puzzle that needs to be solved. The joy he felt, albeit momentarily, when he reached Greece was overwhelming, but it was the beauty of his plan, which he calculated and readjusted according to each attempt and failure, that gave purpose to his life. In my eyes, George celebrated both raw feelings: the journey he took and the goal he would reach.

'I can tell you a story of survival,' you say, looking at the silver clock on the wall. 'I know a man who knows a man.' That man of yours, you explain, is a Syrian man who travelled the world looking for a home. In his early twenties, he was gay-bashed by a group of people he used to call friends in Egypt. 'Years passed,' you add, after a pause, while my face is turning red. 'That man was on a Beiruti beach with his lover.' The beach, rocky and dirty, was famous for its large waves. The two slipped through the broken gate and reached the open space facing the American University of Beirut. In the summer, with the calm sea waves and tanning sun, the beach was kept private for the AUB students.

It was a sunny April morning when the couple wore their swimming costumes under their jeans and went to the still-public beach. They dared one another to jump in the wavy sea. 'The water was cold and salty,' you say. I remember. 'The level of toxic waste in the water might be blinding, so the couple naturally got themselves some goggles.' Death smiles.

The couple, out far enough to escape the break, floated on their backs, the sun in their eyes charming them into relaxing into the waves, wave after wave carrying them to the unknown. They realized a moment too late that they had drifted too far. 'The world traveller could barely swim any more by the time they reached the rocks,' you explain. 'A wave carried him and slapped him, like a painful insult, against a rock. He lost consciousness.'

Freaked out, his lover looked for any sign of him above water, before he placed the goggles on and went back beneath the water. There he saw the traveller slowly sinking to the bottom of the deep sea. He swam to his aid, caught him by the ankle and pulled him up.

'When the world traveller was finally lying on his back on the dirty shore,' you say, slowly, emphasizing each word, 'he was already dead.'

Death held onto his rocking chair. He was captured by the words floating out of your mouth. 'His lover tried to give him CPR, which he had learned on TV,' you say. 'They never say on TV that you need to break the sternum; his lover couldn't save his life with soft pushes.' The weak ribs, broken the day that man was gay-bashed, gave in too easily. His lover heard a soft crack followed by a deep gasp of air. 'The traveller lived,' you finish. From within the cloaks of Death, the man that used to be me smiles.

'This is spooky,' Death says, pulling an old jar from within his cloak. 'But not spooky enough for me.' Death drops his jar and it breaks into a thousand pieces. The world around us is drawn aside; we're all sitting on a couch floating on a stormy sea. The rain hits us. My clothes are suddenly wet. I scream. My heart jumps. You hold onto the couch.

'She is over there,' Death shows us and we see. 'Inside that huge cooking pot she rests, unaware of the world around her.'

Shaza, a five-month-old Syrian girl, unknowingly accompanied her family on an illegal boat trip from Alexandria, hoping to reach Italy overnight. 'The truth is,' Death adds, 'I welcomed many of them into the depth of the sea.' The war at home forced them out, the host countries wanted them out. There were millions of them and the world was giving refuge to hundreds. A huge wave hits our faces: we both gasp for air. Our eyes burn with the salt of the sea. Shaza is asleep in her pot, protected from the waves by the lid, tight enough to keep the water out and loose enough to allow a small amount of air for the baby to survive. 'The pot, with its large, flat bottom and tiny mouth, kept its head above water at all times, acting as a makeshift submarine that kept the baby alive.'

Her mother was the one who came up with the idea. She knew that it was possible that everyone would drown on the journey. She wasn't thinking of herself any more. The mother just wanted her baby to survive. When her husband questioned the insane way she carried her baby into the boat inside a cooking pot, she screamed at him, 'It's none of your business.'

The last time he had seen her this angry was when he was disappointed she gave birth to a girl. 'This girl is your daughter. She is your doing,' she told him. She had seen an obstetrician on the first national channel in Syria once, explaining how the genes of the father determine the gender of the baby. 'Accept what God gave you with love. Call her something beautiful.'

They called her Shaza, meaning a sweet lingering fragrance.

The rain slows down. It stops. The pot waves goodbye to the storm while the sun shines upon the sea. Our couch continues to float; small

172 • AHMAD DANNY RAMADAN

fish are swimming around us. A small boat appears from afar, carrying the Italian flag. The boat stops by the pot. When they open it, they hear the little baby's cries. 'She was dehydrated,' Death says, softly touching the forehead of the little girl, carried gently by an Italian officer with a sweet, wrinkly, worried look on her face. 'She could barely breathe. But she survived. She made it across the sea.' He looks at the Italian woman as her face breaks into a smile, brightened by the sweet morning sun. The baby calms. 'She made it,' he says.

We're back in our living room. Our clothes are dry. My skin is warm; it feels the same way my bed feels after I return from a cold visit to the bathroom in the middle of the night. Morning, cloudy and filled with possible rain, comes upon us while we are still telling stories. With tipsy steps, the three of us collect the glasses of wine. We clean the living room. We brush our teeth while we watch half an episode of *Family Guy*. We laugh with foamy mouths. I drip some on my Batman T-shirt.

You hold my hand closer to your body in bed and I slide my body next to yours. We look each other in the eyes for a second. We smile. We sleep.

In my dreams, we live happily ever after in a small Damascene-style house that we build ourselves in a town we call home. We care nothing for fancy matters or elaborate designs. We build it with love and with devotion to our journeys and ourselves. Together we wake up every morning, play Mary Lambert or Julia Boutros music, drink our Turkish coffee in the ard diar, enjoy the afternoon roaming the tiny, spacious house or the small, loving towns and cities that we build around it. Our friends and all those we love join us in this eternal cycle of creation and destruction. We build beauty upon beauty and we become our own gods.

In my dreams, we return from our busy, godly afternoons to our home, where we sit while the art of others is presented to us, beautiful works of art that were never completed. Art, you tell me, is better left incomplete. That allows it to appeal differently as different people see it. We give to art as much as it gives to us, you explain; we complete the missing pieces left by true artists with pieces of ourselves. They leave it for the readers, the viewers, the watchers to finish up and give it its true value. Without that forbidden touch between minds, art is pointless.

In my dreams, we entertain our friends sometimes. They come visiting from their own worlds. We laugh, we tell meaningless stories of past, present and future. We smile and we hug with tears in our eyes.

On rare days when my sleep is deep and my day isn't tiring, I dream of you and me at the end of a long, happy day touring worlds and creating others. We lie together in our bed, the dogs curl and rest their heads on our feet and we, young forever, make love. Then sleep, dreaming of even better worlds.

13

THE TWO KINGS

The beauty of Arabic is that it has kept its steady roots back into the first glimpses of human intelligence.

When the Quran was written fourteen hundred years ago, it served as a protector of the Arabic spoken at the time. Much like Latin, Arabic continued to serve as the origin of all the different dialects and languages across the region. The spread of Islam also spread Arabic. The religion and the language expanded in a circle of waves heading away from the Persian Gulf. The language and religion left their mark on local far Asian languages and religions, before settling in the Middle East. Arabic faced some losses as local dialects strayed away from their mother. However its old friend, the Quran, kept its roots deep in the minds and hearts of Muslims worldwide.

According to the stories of the Quran, Arabic was born in the aftermath of the destruction of Babel. The people of Babel challenged God and wanted to build a tower so high it would reach the skies, the same way I challenge Death to keep you alive. Sindbad met them on one of his trips, as they feverishly continued to build their tower. He pitied them; he saw God in his seven travels, he saw God in the eyes of beautiful mermaids he met and in the mountains he climbed and the whales he battled. They saw God as an unknown entity and they wanted to reach him in the skies. He knew God well without searching, and they did not know God at all. Eventually God punished them by toying with the speaking part of their brains until they lost their ability to communicate. They couldn't tell each other how they felt or what to build, and the tower fell upon them.

Arabic has twenty-eight letters, and like many other languages, when you place those letters together you describe a word. But each letter carries with it an emotional representation, as if it's a language that tried to transcribe feelings into words. I wonder if the letters of Arabic represent the emotions of the people of Babel. They couldn't communicate, but their pain is one; they couldn't describe beauty, but their happiness is one; they couldn't reach God, but their disappointment is one.

'You're being philosophical,' Death jokes, sneaking into my inner thoughts. You laugh, and your laugh echoes through the kitchen. I have finished preparing breakfast for the three of us, and the table is full of the most delicious of all Syrian dishes: makdoos, halawa and fluffy omelettes.

'These letters are the first words created to describe an urgent need to communicate their feelings,' I tell the two of you. 'Think of it like a tree.' When al-ain, al-meem and al-dall come together, they produce one root in the ancient tree of Arabic. These three letters carry strong sounds: dependable, hard-to-crack sounds.

Many sister-words come from that root, like leaves spreading across a tree: umdah is a man in power, amoud is the column in a house that keeps the roof up, ameed is the head of the army, omdan is a long tower. All of these words describe strong and powerful concepts; they all stretch back in a single line to the dawn of civilization and community. The sounds that make these words have meanings that come from the origin of humanity.

You laugh at me. You look me at me and decide to imitate me. 'You're full of shit,' you say, laughing, preparing a joke. Your laugh is interrupted by a cough. 'Al-meem is the sound of a longing to kiss,' you say, imitating my philosophical tone. I notice your face is turning yellow. 'Al-ha'a is a breath of air you give away for free, and al-baa opens your lips . . .' You struggle. I reach your side. '. . . for a kiss.' You slip slowly from the kitchen chair to the floor. I catch you before you hit the ground. One of the dogs howls.

I rest your head on the cold kitchen floor; I see a teardrop hitting your face. Your eyes are dry. I run outside. I feel like I'm dreaming. I'm running through an endless doorless tunnel. I reach for every door, looking for a way to fix things, and every door refuses to give in and open. Minutes later an ambulance arrives. They carry you out and I run with them, slipping on a warm jacket, mumbling undetectable words, my mumbling sounds like the loud drums at the end of a dramatic song, used to build a grand finale for a mediocre tune.

Khaa is a letter of fear: khouf. It's a letter of loss: khasara. It's a letter of destruction: kharab. It's a letter of shit: khara. It's a letter of the sound of pain and sorrow: akh! They carry you inside the ambulance and I jump in the back with you. Death, gathering his robes, attempts to climb inside the car.

Seconds later, Death is flat on his back in our front yard, looking at me, disbelieving. 'No!' I scream, standing at the back door of the vehicle, tears gathering in my eyes. 'You're not taking him. He is mine. I'm not done yet. I'm not giving up on him.'

The medics look at me, wary. 'You can take him later, but not today. You can't take him like this.' I stand, tall and resilient. I refuse to let go of the doors of the ambulance. 'Stay away from him,' I shout again. 'Please,' this time, realizing my limits, I add with a broken voice.

'Okay. Okay.' Death stands up, dusting off his robes. 'It's not his time yet. Relax.'

Al-ha'a is a letter of love: houb. It's a letter of freedom and relief, houriyah, comfort and sweetness, rahaa. It's also a letter of sadness: hozn.

In the well-lit halls of the hospital, they attempt to separate us at every corner. I accept the doctor's orders while murmuring insults under my tongue. I feel like my hand is holding onto your hand, but my fingers are slippery and they are pulling us apart. But, like the tangled taa at the end of that word you were joking about before you passed out, we endlessly hold on to one another, like an Arabian yin and yang. We're the two unbreakable dots, witnessing the circle of life beneath us.

Ma, ha'a, baa, taa: mah'aba, an endearing endless love, but we don't really pronounce the taa at the end.

The door to your room opens and I glimpse you for a short, impossible moment. I see you, surrounded by nurses and doctors. I see within you. Your face, filled with emotion foreign to you, struggles with thoughts of endings and finales. You look at me, worried and unable to produce a word of comfort for yourself or for me. I know you, my love. I understand you. You feel that you have been good to the world, but the world hasn't been good to you. I slip down in my uncomfortable plastic chair. I rest my head on the wall behind me.

'Did you know he took photos?' I tell Death, realizing that he had just joined me.

'Sorry?' Death asks, distracted by the doors of the emergency room waving around like the wings of bats.

'He took photos of the protests in Syria,' I explain. 'That's what got him that scar.'

Our world is slowly dying. We're slowly slipping into the final days of our lives together. I realize that, I admit it. Reality starts to crumble. The faraway places that we cannot name or pronounce – the ones we wanted to visit but never could – start to disappear first. Those places we used to see on the endless sets of TVs we owned will start to decay and will disappear. They will fade to void. Like an eternal wave on a shoreless planet, a tsunami of blackness hits the world from afar and it moves toward us, closing in on us.

We're in the centre of a tightening circle of fire and goodbyes. You're in your bed and I'm outside in the hallway. The street outside is calm and normal; Vancouver around us is completely in sync. Our little heaven of sorts is holding on to itself, while the world is slowly destroyed. The crumbles of reality gather like pieces of glass. These little pieces form ugly black birds that roam the darkness outside this circle of destruction. Within it, the world rotates, life is normal; outside it, there is emptiness.

'I'm scared,' Death says, able to see the world ending as I see it.

'Don't worry,' I say to him. 'We have time. We will be able to tell our stories.'

We extend our sight and see the wave to come. It's coming from beyond the known, beyond the oceans around us. The outskirts of our worlds, filled with dark corners we couldn't see before, are taken over by a desert made of impossibly tiny black grains of sand.

Unaware of all the nonsense outside, you sleep tightly in your bed. I can imagine you, lost, lonely, but not alone. I can see you there. On your back, I see that bird tattoo.

'Like a migrating bird,' you told me once as you bit your lower lip, enduring the pain. 'This will always remind me of home.' The tattoo artist on Seymour Street dried a bit more blood before adding some more ink to your half-finished tattoo. The artist tried to get your mind off the pain. She asked about the scar and you explained in a matter-of-fact tone.

You were foolish and young, fresh out of your military service. You wanted to see everything your own way. 'I got some money and bought myself an old camera,' you explained. 'I started to take photos of everything that I saw.' Slowly you developed that hobby of yours.

When the revolution started in Syria, before I met you, you were fascinated with the faces of the protesters. You sneaked out in the early hours every Friday, despite your mother's calls and your father's insistence, and you went to the suburbs of Damascus. At night you returned carrying your old camera. Sometimes you returned with a cut on your face or an angry-looking blue bump, growing larger in size, on your side. You were fine. 'I was fine,' you explained. 'The joy of developing those photos was otherworldly.' You used to carry that camera, full of photos you took throughout the day, up to your rooftop, where you had turned a small, abandoned room into a photography studio. You closed the black curtains and worked in your studio until the early hours of Saturday morning.

The faces of those protesters appeared slowly on the large prints you developed. You noticed that the first facial feature to be tangible is always the mouth. It's always large, with sweet lips circling it, as it screams anti-regime slogans. At first glimpse, under the red light, teeth looked like bloody words coming out of the angry mouths.

Fearing for their safety if your work was ever discovered by the regime, you decided to mangle the faces of all the people in these photos. The eyes were the hardest part; they were full of hopes and dreams. They had demands and aspirations. While developing the photos, you used a small brush to mute the eyes, the noses and the significant facial features from your photos.

'By the time I was done,' you added, your eyes cloudy with a tear, 'the photos looked like a sea of screaming mouths, demanding rights.'

I remember the tattoo artist. She was a Malaysian woman with tribal tattoos across her chest and on the side of her neck. 'You know,' the woman said, 'my mother used to tell me that every soul looks like an animal.' The artist's eyes never escaped your skin as she worked on the tattoo. She told a story about Mother Earth, who gave birth to two sons. 'She worshipped them,' the woman said, the sound of the tattoo gun making her words hard to hear. 'She never even cut the umbilical cords connecting her to her boys.' The family lived for a while, until the boys decided to rebel. 'They wanted to see the world, they wanted to know what was beyond the trees.'

You were still half-asleep when they broke down your rooftop door and entered your studio. You didn't move your body as they searched the small room, exposing the incriminating photos to the destructive light. You sat on the small bed there, scratching your head with your fingernails, trying to understand what exactly was going on around you. You didn't resist them until they grabbed you and started to pull you down the stairs, outside. Your mother cried.

When you returned home, two months later, you had lost the wanderlust sparkle in your eyes and gained a V-shaped burn scar on your back.

Your back was acting up again, so you went to your parents' room, knocked softly on the door and opened it. From the small crack you managed to see your sleeping father and your mother sitting on a chair, giving you her back, gazing out of a wooden window with her hands touching softly in her lap.

You murmured her name and she woke up and followed you to your room, where you took off your shirt and she grabbed the ointment.

Your mother stops crying. The artist stops working on your tattoo. Death stops listening to my story. The world stops decaying away. The door to your room opens; I can see you. Your eyes are open; you look at me. A doctor is heading toward me.

'Seen' is a funny letter. It begins the words of illusion: 'sarab' is a mirage, sir is a secret, 'sokout' is silence and 'soum' is poison. It's also a letter of highs: 'sorour' is joy, 'salam' is peace, 'sahab' is clouds.

Like this crumbling world around us, with its sharp edges breaking down, turning into birds and flying away, the country that you loved for so long, since you got lost that morning in the graveyard, was disappearing as well. It was becoming a black hole that sucked in the life of its suns. The circle of destruction expanded around Damascus, the geographical borders became confusing and outdated.

After that miraculous return from the dungeons of the mukhabarat secret police offices, you never felt the same. You felt as if something had been stolen from you between the lashes of the ropes and the electric shocks. There was a door between your inner soul and your outer self that was suddenly closed. You retreated within yourself and pushed furniture and boards around, blocking that door for what you assumed would be an eternity. Syria was the battlefield, but your body became the ruins. Your stories were muted and your pride was broken. You rejected your own tales and your own beliefs. You refused to believe in dead grandfathers coming back to life, you forgot about the jasmine in the streets.

To survive, you allowed your stories to commit suicide. They hanged themselves on a clothesline. To survive, I allowed my stories to consume me: my body will continue this insane swing, regardless of how many times I feel like throwing up.

The doctor tells me that it's a matter of weeks. The two boys in the artist's Malaysian story used rocks to cut the cords to their mother. 'She felt the betrayal,' the woman said. 'She was angry.' Wherever the two sons went, a river would appear to block their way. Like us, they obsessed about finding an escape from their motherland. Like us, they lost. 'They finally decided to jump over the river,' the artist said while putting the final touches on your tattoo. 'One wasn't strong enough. He slipped into the river and turned into a crocodile. The other managed to reach the other side, but he was turned into a tiger.

'When you jumped your river, you turned into a bird and flew away,' the artist added. She asked you to look at your tattoo in the mirror. In your eyes, I saw flags of freedom and wings of wind.

B ack in your room, I'm lonely. I sit by your bed waiting for you to open your eyes again. I was told that they gave you a sedative. Your face looks peaceful. Your hair slips on your forehead. I smile to you. 'Tell me a story,' you say, opening your eyes, or I dream that you do. 'Tell me some more stories.'

'Boy, do I have a story to tell you!' I say, smiling.

Outside, between the borders of reality and the realms of insanity, I look. I see the world as it loses its integrity; it dissolves and I'm the only one who can see it. The edges break and streets fall off into an abyss of the unknown. People walking in these streets continue their journeys, unaware of their pending doom.

I look back toward you. I suddenly realize that all along there were two versions of you at every moment. The one I speak to, a person filled with light, love and life. That person needs lots of digging until he is reached, as he hides behind his closed door. He shines with hope and tenderness and talent. Then there is the one who is slipping away into the robes of Death himself, a man who is imprisoned inside his pain. One man is hidden but full of love, another is present but full of pain.

I smile back at you, and both versions of you smile back, before you merge back together, becoming one person one more time.

'I love you,' I tell you. I kiss your forehead. 'I love you too,' your voice echoes. Twice.

14

THE GENEROUS DEALING

OF A LONELY MAN

The sounds of night coo in the streets outside. I hear the distant sounds of cars and the echo of silences and apologies. The cloudy skies of Vancouver in the deep months of winter hide the sun away. 'I realized long ago why polar bears hibernate,' I whisper, watching the departing sun from our bedroom's balcony. The shortest day of the year is upon us. Like every year, I feel suffocated, lonely, and I question my mental stability and my ability to find a place for myself in the lives of others. 'What's a storyteller without a listener?' I ask Death, sitting in a rocking chair. 'Who will listen to my stories without him?'

I imagine Scheherazade and her life; without her unruly king demanding stories or threatening to send his bride to the swordsman to cut off her head, where would she be? She would have lived a short, pleasant life and married a decent loving man, and got herself dozens of children before dying a forgotten beauty, holding on to thoughts of her past. She needed to tell the king her stories as much as he needed her to mend his broken heart with fairy tales.

You're my listener. Your face is my map to better places, and I rebel at the thought of stagnation. I was lost until I found it. Like a pirate, broken deep within, searching for an impossible treasure, complaining about the sea water in my eyes, I looked for you. I was lost until I found you. In Damascus, I remember I rented a house of my own. The house became the party hub for all the dykes in the city, after Maryam introduced me to the lesbian community. 'I passed by it once,' one of my old visitors said when she met me in Vancouver years later. 'A tank destroyed the small house and sat on the pile of rubble where it used to be.'

'It was your own personal orphanage,' Death whispers. 'The land of dysfunctional toys.' It was my house and it was beautiful. The windows were high in the ceiling, showing only the sky. The moment we walked into that house, we felt that we had transported ourselves into a new world far away from what was happening outside. It was our tiny shield in the face of an upcoming war.

Our final years in Damascus were marked by the looks in the eyes of those around us. At first, we heard about the war in the news; it felt distant and unrealistic, as if it would never make it to our doorsteps. Then we started to see it in the eyes of men and women walking in the street, dizzy with the sounds of bullets and shelling coming from the outskirts of Damascus. Then it slipped into our every conversation, even the mundane ones. We planned our grocery shopping with the war in the back of our minds, picking places to buy our supplies with an imaginary map in our heads. We stayed away from places that were most likely to be hit by a car bomb: marketplaces, homes of known political and military figures, and mosques.

On Fridays, fruit and vegetable merchants used to travel from the countryside to sell their products outside the mosques for people leaving the Friday noon prayers. The cheap fruits used to be our favourite thing to buy for us to eat at night as we drank cheap vodka and beer. I used to sleep past the noon prayers on Friday and then go to the gathering just to pick up fruits. Maryam accompanied me sometimes, and together we would negotiate the prices with the merchants. One day, we were buying bananas and berries when a car exploded on the street metres away from us. We both flew in the air, landing on our backs. A sharp piece of metal had pierced the arm of the fruit merchant, and he was screaming in agony. Maryam and I looked at each other, searching for any wounds; when we found none, we decided to flee the area. 'Wait,' she told me, and she ran back to the merchant. She asked if he needed help. He had a scar on the side of his face, and another on his left arm, from earlier explosions. He told her he would be fine, 'but will you buy those bananas now?' He pointed to his fruits, with his blood dripping on some of them. 'I will give you a good price.'

We both stood there stunned. 'I need to feed my children, ma'am,' he said, almost out of breath as the metal shrapnel was digging deeper in his flesh. 'Just pay me whatever you can.' We left him money and we walked away. Our clothes were covered in his blood, our noses filled with the smoke.

At the time, my future was also scattered all over the remaining pieces of Syria. In my eyes, Syria was a fragile thing, like a glass ballerina. This ballerina fell and broke into thousands of pieces, some so sharp they would cut your fingers as you tried to pick them up. The glass shone like blood diamonds. The damage is done; the ballerina will never dance again. She will never revolve around herself one more time, with one leg stretched in a forever pose. Her head, removed by the fall, stares at me, asking me to fix her. Her arms, dismembered from her beautiful body, are hopelessly waiting on the floor.

There is no way of putting this ballerina together the same as it used to be. No matter how great the craftsman, trying to replace the pieces of broken things only creates monstrous things.

'Syrians are nationless people.' As we wait for news of your recovery, I explain to Death that our part of the world is destroyed; our modern history revolves around our joined misery. Our collective pride in identity is limited to our individual pride in ourselves.

The moments of waiting linger; I'm glued to the phone. Death asks if we should go for a walk. I look outside at the dark skies, I feel suffocated. 'I cannot leave the house,' I explain. 'The hospital might call, or they might bring him back.' I used to be afraid of the dark when I was little; I felt paralyzed in darkness. Now, unanswered phone calls are what scare me the most.

Since I slipped into loving you, I am fearful deep within. I fear calling you at the hospital, but finding no answer. The phone will ring, and it will linger, until I hear the warm sound of a nurse asking me to come and pick up your body. I fear waking up in the middle of the night and not finding you right next to me. The unfamiliarity of my empty bed shakes me to the core. While you sleep – deep within your dreams when we were young, or deep within my stories as of late – the night becomes impossible. I hear all my sleepless nights chit-chatting, and it scares me. 'Maybe you should take a pill,' Death whispers. I smirk.

I managed to survive in Damascus before you. I tried; I could see the abyss opening its mouth up to swallow my city. It started to nip pieces off my ballerina, to eat away at her headless body and her dismembered, stretched leg. Like sand in the wind, my memories of Damascus, Aleppo, Latakia and Homs are dispersed into the unknown and replaced with videos of destruction, memories of dead faces with open eyes that always stare at you at night, right before you fall asleep.

That house was our refuge. It was dark, covered with childish drawings on the walls that we had drawn while drunk. Every night, they would come. We gathered around a bottle of vodka and a stash of weed. We started to break our humanity down in that house; the stronger the flames of war around us, the less human we became. The girls, who used to be shy as they entered the house, politely exchanging smiles and whispers of gossip, became braver in their interactions, laughing louder, kissing each other deeper, drinking more and getting stoned. We used to play a drinking game. 'We drink a shot every time we hear an explosion,' Maryam explained. 'And we make out to the sounds of bullets.' Everyone cheered for the new game, and found it ironic. I sat there among half a dozen lesbians and three gay men, and we made out, and we drank, and we touched and sensually played with each other's bodies, to the rhythm of war. We turned off the news and attached the cables to my old PlayStation to play *Mortal Kombat*. 'It numbed the bloody war for us,' I tell Death. 'It allowed us to survive a violent interaction over and over.' We survived our mock fights while laughing at the size of the female fighters' bosoms. We died on the screen, but we hit restart. Outside my home, clashes between regime forces and rebels took place sometimes, and we would mute the fight on the TV, relying on the sounds of battle coming from outside.

We sat on the dirty mattresses and shushed our laughter as we played MK. 'I'm a regime solider,' one of the gay men whispered as he picked a heavily armed Jax as his counterpart in the game. 'And I'm a helpless rebel,' one of the lesbians said, picking Melina, the princess. They fought on the screen while we ignored the sound of bullets and cries of pain coming from outside. We slowly abandoned the world around us and accepted that life can revolve around casual sex, funny Margaret Cho and Bassem Feghali YouTube videos, vodka shots and *Mortal Kombat*. We put on a civilized face for the world around us whenever we were outside and then laughed like demons when we were in our own personal hell. We accepted that we were collateral damage; we celebrated it. We negotiated within ourselves how uninvolved we were in our country's war; we came to terms with it. 'You wondered if that was it for you,' Death adds, understanding.

I remember – I enjoyed the company of laid-back lesbians and the occasional boy. Every Friday morning, I used to wake up, leave my room and navigate my way through the bodies of rebel lesbian girls and my British roommate who shared my name. I escaped the boy I was dating that week to the bathroom; they were all sleeping in my living room. I knew some of them, others I did not recognize. Ten, sometimes twelve people would be asleep.

I woke them up every Friday morning, the start of our weekend, pushing the bottles of vodka away and emptying the ashtrays. One day, one of the boys I brought home suggested that we go for breakfast in the old city of Damascus; we did. He departed my life that same week and I never saw him again. I don't even remember his name. But the tradition of going to the old city for a Syrian breakfast remained; it became ours.

Your pictures on the wall haunt me as I await the phone call from the hospital, forced to stay away by chatty nurses insisting that I need my own rest. I see your face escaping the frames into reality. Our images re-enact the moments those photos were taken. I rush through the halls of our empty house, looking for the real you. I hear you recite words of abandonment and fear from all the corners, some in your young husky voice, others in your soft, well-spoken older voice. Death swiftly catches up with me; he covers me with his dark cloak. 'Tell me about that breakfast,' he whispers. 'We had foul, tis'eh, fried eggs, makdoos, labneh and Arabian bread,' I told Death, as I lay in the fetal position in his cold, bony arms. The faces of the people joining me at the table would change, but the breakfast remained the same. We gathered around a table in that tiny old street where cars cannot go any more. They call it al-Qamariah Street. Before the war, the street's tiny shops sold silly gadgets, fake tattoos, pirated movies and TV series, Arabian shawarma and the most delicious croissants. In the cold mornings of Damascus winters, you would look up to the clear skies through a bed of jasmine leaves and flowers. The flowers were threading the electric lines and the illegal internet cables crossing between the tiny buildings in that narrow street. Lonely people came here, imitating the happiness they felt before. The shops weren't selling as much. Even our faces were pale, as if the sun never touched us.

I wander into that house's corners in my head. It's warm, filled with love. I see myself mirrored in the eyes of Death, and the man in the mirror is still back there in Damascus, in the heart of the storm of war. I let the old me lead the memory. It's ten p.m. and it's raining outside. Maryam is trying to get the fireplace to work, giving us some needed warmth. Five friends of ours are roaming the house; Fahed, who is originally from Raqqa, is sitting in the arms of his boyfriend. I never liked the boyfriend and I always thought that Fahed deserved better. Who am I to judge? I've dated the worst losers in Damascus you can imagine. They say don't cast a stone if your house is made of glass.

(That house is broken now. One wall is down and the furniture is covered in dust and rocks. The fireplace? I'm not sure if it's still there. Fahed broke up with that boyfriend of his. He went back to his hometown, weeks before the Islamic State announced it as its own capital; I assume he is alive. I can't tell for sure. Phone lines died that day, and no one was to leave that city ever again.)

B ella is sitting next to me. We tuck ourselves closer under the reddish cover with a painting of a tiger on it, as we try to figure out how much we want love and how badly we are willing to put an effort into it. Bella has this smile; you won't believe it until you see it. She smiles and her whole face glints with lights. She is innocent and sweet. She holds me closer as we feel the cold breeze from some cracked window somewhere. We talk about love and hopes; she tells me that she loves me like a brother. No one ever loved me like a brother. Maryam, in her naughty ways, is trying to lift up the atmosphere, telling dirty jokes and calling me a sister of hers. I laugh as hard as I can. Then I light the candle next to me as the power turns off; it's the third time the power has gone off today. It goes away for long hours. It's cold. But Bella pulls the covers and asks us if we want to play another round of cards.

(That was the last time I saw Bella without the ugly scars on her legs, after she was shot twice. One bullet went through her left leg and landed in her upper right leg. The other? It destroyed her knee. When I saw her after months of operations, physical therapy and pain, she managed to visit the house for my birthday. She was still smiling that smile of hers; however something small, unmatchable, unnoticeable was gone. Maybe forever.)

Sama shows up, late as usual, carrying cheap drinks; we cheer him, Bella, Fahed and I, and we start to toss the drinks around. I ask anyone if they are hungry and suddenly everyone remembers that they are. We think of cooking, we think of killing our hunger with some fruits or maybe some tea. But then we decide that the hell with it, we want to eat shawarma. Sama and I walk down to the shawarma place, avoiding the checkpoint with the soldiers carrying their big guns and walking around lazily. We order food enough for everyone; we laugh as the little kittens in the streets suddenly decide to fall in love with us. We look at a hottie passing by and we start to push each other to go talk to him. 'You talk to him,' Sama says, pushing me toward the oblivious guy. 'You're the one with the brave heart.' I look the guy up and down, and I never dare to speak. We pick up the shawarma and start our ascent up the hill toward the house. He tells me that he is in a relationship. Sama is always in a relationship. Sometimes I feel that his heart is so tired of looking it's just settling down to the available. I tell him so sometimes and other times I let him live his life as he pleases. We talk about his mother, coming to visit from Aleppo in a couple of days, and we reach the house where the hungry squad is waiting for us.

(Sama was stuck in Tadamon for over a week under shelling. He couldn't leave his office. He went to work one morning and lost track of time. By the evening, the clashes had started in the street outside and he was stuck inside his office. He turned the lights off and hoped to wait for an hour or two then leave, but the clashes never stopped. A week later the office had no drinkable water, no food and sometimes no power. When the power was on he'd talk to me on Facebook, telling me that he was eating the last pieces of bread he had. I never heard from Sama again. His Facebook Messenger said he was last seen online weeks ago. Slowly, the questioning eyes of the gang hanging out in the house were hushed by answers we never dared to hear.)

'We queers were the loneliest people in Damascus,' I tell Death as I see glimpses of Sama hiding in his robes; he smiles. We looked around the city for people like us. We found many. More people gathered in the tiny house. 'A weekly card tournament was also introduced.' I smile, eyes closed, while telling Death, 'My lucky card was the jack of hearts. I must have won *trex* a million times because of it.'

On one Friday night, I changed my mind about my life.

In those days I felt drawn into an abyss, like a sailor lured by the songs of the sirens. I didn't know you yet, but while you were taking pictures of screaming protesters, I was locking myself from the world in fear. 'We are the safest people in Syria,' Maryam told me one night as she was driving us back home from a Halloween party. Her face was covered in zombie makeup; I was dressed up like the jack of hearts. For that party, we had to drive to the airport highway, and found ourselves in an airport hotel lobby. Syrians had a sense of humour back then, and many of them came dressed up as regime fighters or rebels, with fake blood and body parts flying around. We didn't want to party downtown; we knew an explosion or two would take place around the parties there.

Indeed, two explosions had already killed men and women dressed up as ghosts and zombies in downtown Damascus that night.

As we drove, Maryam explained how navigating Damascus had turned into a balance, a maze for the clever to crack. 'We balance our trips to be close enough to the military checkpoints to be protected by the regime's army, but not too close, so we won't get caught in the crossfire with the rebels,' she said, explaining the tactics like an expert. 'We're a group of drunk, stoned and loud partying adults,' she finally whispered. 'The world structure loves nothing more than cooperative mindless citizens.'

That night, I decided to leave. 'There are two voices inside the minds of humans,' I tell Death, as he strokes my hair. 'One of them is the impulsive, animalistic voice that wants me to party more, to lose my senses and abandon the truth around me.' Death smiles. 'The other is your sensible logical self, telling you to face your pain and your fears.'

That morning, my sensible self woke up and looked around. We were the victims of this war, we were the walking dead celebrating the apocalypse as we aimlessly drove around. We might not have died yet, but our souls were smothered within our drunken, stoned bodies. I navigated the bodies sleeping in my living room to reach the metal front door; the early-morning sun shone upon me from the cracks as I opened it and closed it softly behind me. I didn't want to wake anyone up.

I walked out into the street and noticed a pool of blood from yesterday's battle on one of the corners. I stood there, and I felt dirty, ugly and undeserving of my own ability to breathe. I picked up my phone and I tweeted a picture of the blood pool.

That night, as you carried your brush and tangled the faces of protesters from that day's photos, you used your brush on the picture you took of my face – still unfamiliar to you back then.

With the first ring of the phone, silence comes over our home. The whispering ghosts of our past selves take a break from their Shakespearian performances, returning to their frames. I open my eyes with the second ring. I stand up. I hear the phone ringing from all corners of the house; I reach for it. Death, following me around, looks me in the eyes. I lift up the phone and I whisper a hello.

15

THE RUNAWAY PRINCESS
TELLS HER TALE

E sme asks me to open my eyes wide. 'I don't trust you,' I tell her.
'Sit down, old man.' She pushes me into my office chair and slips
my eyelids open, telling me that she will count to three before dropping
the eye-cleaning liquid in my eyes. She doesn't. She squeezes the bottle
at the count of two. I feel the aching burn in my eyes. 'You're such a
baby,' she says.

People in our childhood street used to call her father 'the Doctor',
despite his lack of medical education. He was capable of telling
the futures of local, regional and international football games. He knew
all the players by heart; his ability to pronounce their names, however,
was questionable. During certain weeks of the year, the Doctor used
to wake my father up at four a.m.; together they sat in the living room,
watching a football match on an illegal satellite connection. They
both shouted unrepeatable words at the TV whenever their favourite
football team lost in the Brazilian tournament. When his wife gave
birth to a girl, the Doctor decided to call her Esmeralda, thinking that
the name sounded Brazilian; that country had given him his favourite
World Cup team. Her family struggled with the huge Brazilian flag
hung over the balcony. They also struggled with finding a nickname

for her to suit the Arabian ear; they came up with Zozo. I called her Esme.

With experienced hands, Esme pulls my secret drawer open, pulls out my rolling kit, and in a matter of seconds, the well-dressed hag comes up with two joints. 'Let's go for a walk,' she insists. We end up on a bench on the outskirts of Stanley Park. Vancouver's reflection on the cool ocean is glittery with the city lights. 'I have a prescription,' she says, smiling as she pulls the first puff. I take the joint from her fingers.

'So do I,' I respond. We laugh. She was in town for a wedding, she explains, when she heard what happened to you.

'I think you should take him back home,' she whispers, counting her words. 'I think he wants to go home.' I know you must have called her.

The Doctor owned a wedding hall in a small neighbourhood in Damascus. The hall was designed with traditional weddings in mind. It was large, with a high ceiling and lots of expensive-looking chandeliers. The hall was crowned with a well-lit corner stage featuring two chairs where the bride and groom could sit and take the obligatory photos with overbearing and over-eating family members while attempting to have a conversation. In the centre of the hall, a larger stage was built for the dancing young women. 'These girls were over-dressed by their mothers as soon as they reached the appropriate age,' Esme told me. In her eyes, I could see the young girls covering their faces with makeup, trying to impress old and possibly senile women in hopes of scoring a husband. 'Other mothers, looking for brides for their sons, sat there in the wedding hall with hawk eyes; they were ready for their young prey.'

You must be lonely now, in the wee hours of the morning, waiting for a glimpse of sleep, waiting for my story. I feel untold, imprisoned and locked away from you. My stories are boiling inside of me, and the hot mess forms a shape inside my head. I'm a prisoner of the decisions of the doctors who insist that you shouldn't be disturbed. 'He can't sleep without my stories,' I protested, but they told me that there is no scientific evidence for storytelling.

'What are you going to do?' Esme asks me. We are both gazing at the city ahead of us. I look at her, my only childhood friend. I sigh. She knows that I feel so small. I'm my own demon. I'm the memory that haunts me the most and there is no escaping me other than to you.

You're so far away, deep under the covers of your hospital bed. I'm denied spending the long winter solstice by your side, taking warmth from your embrace. 'I'm going to do the best I can,' I tell Esme. She switches the conversation around. She reminds me of Damascus. I allow the conversation to drift.

Esme's father and my father were best friends. They hung out at each other's homes all the time. Since we were three, Esme and I were allowed to sit in the living room and watch cartoons on TV. This habit grew with us, and at the age of thirteen we sat together watching *Mad About You* and *Friends*. She is the one who found us Jim Carrey's *The Mask*. I learned to calculate time zones to figure out when *Buffy the Vampire Slayer* aired on Egyptian and Emirati channels. The two of us found something to talk about in a world where no one wanted to discuss anything in depth. We watched every TV show we could and spent days discussing them. In our teens, she loved *Bewitched*. I adored *Angel*. In our twenties, I introduced her to *Hannibal*; she introduced me to *True Blood*. We spent days theorizing about the future of the Marvel Cinematic Universe. I told her that I wanted to be as awesome as Clark Gregg.

I also remember the last time I saw her in Damascus. I took her to watch *The Avengers*, then to the sushi place inside the hall of the only good cinema in town. While struggling with our chopsticks, we discussed my new, blossoming relationship with you. I told her that you had passed by my office the other day; you brought me flowers. She told me about her plans to abandon Syria. 'The world is closing in on us here, Hakawati,' she whispered. I barely heard her over the overjoyed screams of teenagers heading to watch a flick. I inspected her beautiful features. She had the same look I saw in the eyes of everyone leaving the country. We were all children of this dying nation; although our mother's steady march toward death brought us destruction, we didn't want to abandon her.

I can see you sitting there alone in your cold, colourless hospital room. 'He must feel abandoned,' I tell Esme. I feel that my face is cracking. 'I'm lost without him, Esme,' I say. She passes me a joint. She touches my arm. I rest my head on her shoulder. The sun – late, cold and deep in the horizon – reminds us of the time.

Esme and I were in charge of the camera for all of our families' joint trips across the Damascus countryside. We would start our journey on Friday evening, heading to the Barada Valley or Bloudan. Esme and I would argue over who took better videos on the video recorder. The Doctor wasn't pleased about handing his precious new toy to teenagers, but after many rounds of negotiation, he finally parted with his camera. He watched us from afar as we played with the new toy, saying something to my father while they prepared the backgammon table for another round. 'Yeah,' my father responded. 'When they are older.'

Esme told me ages ago about things I didn't know. My father first met the Doctor back in the eighties when he booked the hall for his wedding. Esme found my parents' wedding tape in her father's collection. The Doctor had a big wall covered with black VCR cassettes from weddings that had taken place in his hall. He would sometimes sneak into the living room late at night, pick some of his favourite cassettes and watch the young girls dancing while masturbating in the dark.

Among these forgotten cassettes, Esme found a video of my mother, a surviving piece of time that my mother wasn't able to destroy. In the video, I saw her walking slowly in her wedding dress. My father, a young man in an oversized black suit, sits on his chair looking confused. I saw my grandmother sitting in the corner, smiling at the newlyweds. She examined the room with her eyes, presumably searching for possible brides for her other sons. My grandfather, grumpy and unamused, was twirling his moustache repeatedly in an anxious tic. The cassette's music was jammed and almost unrecognizable; it was a wedding song that everyone knows back in Syria, Walid Toufic asking the beautiful one to come to the dance floor, and sway with the other dancers in ease. 'I haven't been to many weddings in my life,' I tell Esme. The skies are filled with clouds; they reflect on the glass buildings of Vancouver.

'I must have been to a million weddings,' she says.

After I departed Syria for Egypt, Esme felt lonely. She continued helping her father in the wedding hall business. Her father was content with the fact that he only had female offspring. Traditional Syrian weddings are gender segregated; women take over the hall while the girls dance and the older women make eye contact with their future daughters-in-law. The Doctor knew that having two daughters was good for business. No men were allowed inside the hall, and he needed women to act as servants and organizers. His two daughters were his eyes and ears in the hall, taking care of the wedding as he taught them. Esme worked during the first half of the night, when the wedding hall was dedicated to the women and their quest for more weddings. The Doctor joined her and her sister in the wedding hall later, when a handful of men were allowed in, following a long traditional male-only wedding dance and song at the hall gate. 'They can work in the hall until they get married,' the Doctor used to say. 'After that, they will be someone else's problem.'

One night the wedding hall filled up with women and their makeup and dresses. Esme finished her shift and started to relax as the gender-segregated phase of the night ended. She announced that the men were about to enter the hall, then sat on a faraway table watching the female guests putting on their long jackets and headscarves. She sighed, trying to relax after the long night, but an old overweight lady came searching with sleepy eyes. The lady, an aunt of a friend of the bride, sat nearby and instantly rested her head on Esme's shoulder, slipping into an immediate sleep. 'It was a typical sitcom situation,' Esme said the first time she told me the story.

Esme - cursing her sister for switching work shifts the day before - tried to push the heavy head of the sleeping woman away from her shoulder. From afar, the Doctor finally walked into the wedding hall, carrying his beloved camera. He saw her struggling, then pulled out his video recorder and decided to take a film.

After she lost hope of freeing herself without waking up the lady, Esme - trained all her life to be silent and polite - stayed motionless, transformed into a pillow for the old lady. After a good half-hour, Esme's tears began to drop down her face. She felt suffocated as the heavy head of the old lady pressed on her chest, crushing her ribcage. She felt a growing anger deep within her. It was a fire growing stronger; it was crawling under her skin. Her heart started beating fast, pumping her boiling blood across her body. She pushed the old lady's head off her shoulder, waking up the overdecorated hag. She walked out of the hall. She took a final look at her room, with its single bed, blue mattress, her wooden windows, her shelves of CDs, some broken, some intact. She said her goodbyes and she never saw them again.

N ow visiting hours are upon us and Esme asks me to walk with her. 'I am seeing the end of the world in front of me, Esme,' I whisper. The black birds still haunt me everywhere. 'Our world is in a constant state of ending,' she says.

She stops me as we walk up to the hospital elevator. 'I know you're hurting too, Hakawati,' she says. Her eyes are glowing with tears.

Your smile cracks when you see me. 'I can't sleep without you,' you whisper in my ear.

'I told the doctors but they didn't believe me,' I reply with a smile. We exchange words of love untold by anyone before us. I feel that my soul is recharging as I touch your neck. I feel the sorrows of the long winter nights leaving my body, as if a wave of warmth had crashed upon me. Esme hugs you; she pulls you closer to her embrace.

Time loses track of us. We age backwards, like a curious case for medicine. We return to an old moment. That memory is always locked away and forgotten, awaiting until the three of us meet.

We were sitting on the shore of a tiny lake in Lebanon on the last weekend before we abandoned the Arab world for Canada. We weren't prepared to swim, but we stripped down to our undies and jumped in the icy-cold water pouring from a small spring. On the shore of that magical place, the three of us sit now. We carry our young faces. We laugh our old laughs. I play music on my mobile. We jump in the water. We dance.

When we're tired, we retreat to the shore. 'I miss your voice,' you whisper in my ear as we sit on the sandy shores of the lake. 'Tell me a story.' I lie back on the warm, soft sand. I look up to the sun through the cracks of the mountains. The sun reflects on my face, writing stories of happiness and sadness there. You pull me closer. You kiss me.

'Tell us a story,' Esme adds.

'I cannot,' I whisper. I hide my face in your shoulder. I cry. 'I cannot lose you,' I whisper. I pull you closer to me. I cannot lose you after all of our stories. My life is tangled into yours and I fear that pieces of me will die with you. I cannot see you lying in a bed that is not big enough for the two of us. We found each other in an abandoned world. You pull me closer and place a kiss on my forehead. You ask me again if I will tell you a story.

'Tell me something sweet in Portuguese,' I ask Esme, knowing that she learned Portuguese at some point in honour of her father. 'I want to learn something new.'

'Well, I have love for one word that only Brazilians say,' she tells me as I inspect her beautiful features. She has the same look I had once seen in the eyes of everyone who was leaving our country. 'Saudade is the enjoyment of remembering, a feeling that comes to you when you remember things from your past and feel good about them.'

'That's nostalgia, right?' I say, trying to think of a similar word in Arabic.

'No! Nostalgia is not always a good feeling. We are talking about a genuine feeling of happiness that comes from remembering things that are long past.' I let my mind drift as I climb next to you in your hospital bed.

I'm not born yet. My mother is in her wedding dress. I see the video years later and she looks amazingly content. She has long brown hair, which is softly decorated with white little pearls. She is smiling at the camera and smiling at my father. They feed each other little pieces of chocolate cake.

She twirls around herself, like a bird flying in circles. Her dress flies around her, floating like a beautiful, endless river of sparkles.

I steal the video from the Doctor's collection; I keep it in a drawer where I've hidden the remains of my books and the poster of Kate Winslet rushing through a sinking Titanic. The drawer is in the closet where I keep my sheets in my grandmother's home. My grandmother is sick; she couldn't wake up for the prayer. 'God will forgive me for missing his commands for one day,' she whispers and coughs. 'Go back to sleep.'

I slip out of my grandmother's bedroom. I walk to the balcony and

I look upon Damascus. My fifteen-year-old eyes are adjusting to the darkness of the wee hours of the night, and I see the cracks of sunlight across the mountains. The cold breeze hits my chest, and I feel a need for warmth. I sneak into the living room and insert the cassette into the VCR. I sit down, covered in a warm blanket with a tiger printed on it, and I watch, on mute, my mother twirling on TV. The image replaces her angry features in my head for a few seconds, and suddenly I feel loved.

I'm five years old. My father is building a clothesline swing on our balcony. My mother is carrying me on her shoulder, taking me to the kitchen. She sits me down on the kitchen table, then turns around and starts making some Turkish coffee. 'You should always leave the coffee on the fire until it's well cooked,' she says, watching the coffee bubbling in the small pot. 'You wait until it's ready, then you pour it in the glasses.'

She makes me my first cup of coffee. She fills half of it with milk and then pours the dark coffee into it. 'Let's go see what your father is doing.' She walks me outside; we are carrying the cups of coffee. He is outside, pulling on the clothesline, making sure it's steady. 'It's ready for you, love,' he says, and pulls her toward him. They sit together on the swing. She is in his lap; he is in her arms. 'I built it just for your eyes,' he says.

'I would build a tower for you,' she replies.

I look at them with wide eyes, sipping on my first cup of coffee.

I'm in my late twenties. You and I are sleeping in bed. You wake up to me tossing and turning. I have a fever. You jump off the bed. I see your naked body as you dress up fast and call someone. I see your body glowing in red due to the fever and my blurred vision. I go into a trance. I wake up after what seems like minutes, but it's not. I have been in a semi-coma for eight hours. I see your face. You look tired and worried. I reach out to you and try to sit up but you force me to go back to sleep. I point to my throat and you bring me a bottle of water. I cough. Your eyes are tearing. I cough again and you produce this voice, like you're in agony yourself due to my pain. You reach with your lips toward me, you kiss my forehead and whisper that I should go back to sleep. I wake up the next morning to find myself sleeping on your chest. You're sitting in bed, asleep, and you're hugging me with both arms. I'm wide awake but I don't want to move. I just want to stay in your safe arms forever. I smile, and I go back to sleep.

We both look at you as you fall asleep. Esme asks me, whispering, if I'm ready to leave, and I whisper that I'm not. We leave your room, filling out the papers to discharge you and take you home. We wait in the hospital's waiting room. She rests her head on my shoulder; for a moment, I look at her silently. Suddenly I pull my shoulder away and she slips, losing her balance. I grab her before she falls and we both end up on the floor in a hilarious, harmless fall.

We hear laughter coming from the far side of the room. Nurses, doctors and patients passing by break into spontaneous laughter at our mischief. We laugh too.

16

THE SANDSTORM AND
THE WITCH

We rarely leave the past behind and completely let go. Sometimes we even forget the past, but its residue remains within us. One of our dogs once saw a raccoon escaping into the bushes across the street from our house. Throughout that winter, she continued to growl every time she passed by those bushes at a raccoon that was long gone.

'Are you comfortable?' I ask. You are sitting, reading, in bed right next to me. You nod your head. You smile. Your glassy eyes reflect the nearing end. I shiver.

The painkillers have reduced the pain to a manageable afterthought; they do nothing to the hole growing within your soul, eating you altogether. They do nothing to the universe's destruction around us, as it falls apart and breaks away while people go on within their preset races that have no finish lines.

I see that hole: it's growing in front of me. It's moving around your face, eating pieces of it. It scares me beyond belief. I snap. 'I'm very happy you're fine,' I say sharply. 'I'm glad that I can be of service.' It's nothing you did. It's not the automatic smile, not the extra room you take for yourself in our bed or your lousy understanding of personal space. It's my reaction to fears and disappointments that I have long forgotten but cannot let go of.

I don't want to drift into one of my hurt monologues. I slip into bed, giving you my back. I turn off the light on my side of the bed. I explain that I'm tired. It takes you the usual moment; your hand slides under the covers, climbs my side and pulls me toward you. Like the dog, I whimper. I'm restless for reasons that I refuse to admit. We waste the night debating the small incident.

Death joins our little meaningless lingering debate about the depths of gestures that we didn't really give to one another. Like children, we refuse to acknowledge our differences or even the shallowness of the fight itself. Death places his bony fingers on my shoulders; he spreads my life with you in front of me. Like the pages of a gigantic pop-up book, our fights are gathered in front of me, while Death stands by idly. I open the pages one after the other; each page contains a motionless moment from one of our fights. As I push through to the older pages, our cardboard cut-outs become younger. The edges of their shapes become softer. We fight closer to one another; we fight as if we're about to hug one another. We fight with the passion of lovers.

'I feel emotionally dry,' my cut-out whispers to yours on one of the pages. Your cut-out's eyes cry paper tears. Moments later, we pour love upon one another, like children, unaware of how rare those emotions are. 'You are duelling with demons of your own creation,' your cut-out tells mine on another page. Its words appear in a comic balloon next to its head. I turn my head away. I flip the page. I hide the pain. Most of our fights are endless rounds of rants about unintentional mistakes. We dramatically leave rooms, but we come back. We refuse to negotiate and then we negotiate to agree to negotiate. Days after our silly fights, we wonder what drove us to the edge of insanity. We let go. We let things slip and disappear. We find new, meaningless things to fight about days later.

I flip the book to another page. That's a fight I remember. 'It was a silly fight. I was pouring out my anxieties,' I whisper to Death, looking at the arguing versions of us. You'd remember this fight too. I know you would. It all started with a silly little thing. Some days I wanted love and attention, some days I wanted space. I pushed you away with one hand while pulling you back with the other. I reacted to every motion you made. We clashed; we fought. We loved each other; we clashed. It was a nightmare. 'I can't do this any more,' you whispered. I closed my eyes. We were in bed, late at night, listening to the silence of Vancouver. 'You're fighting demons of your own creation,' you added. That was the day we broke up for those three unmentionable years.

During those years, I had to deal with the demons of my childhood. I had to struggle with the ghost of my mother haunting my house. She carried me in her lap, sitting on that clothesline swing. The city of Damascus, the sunny country with its yellow buildings and endless sky, was ahead of me. I saw it for the very first time. The warmth of the sun hitting our faces shone through. She rested her feet on the ground, playfully pushing the swing back and forth. She smiled.

I held her hand when I was six years old as we descended into a dark tunnel during our tour of the Crac des Chevaliers. As darkness took over, I told her, 'Don't be afraid, Mother,' my voice echoing in the empty citadel. 'I'm here with you,' I said, tightening my grip, afraid. 'I'm here with you too,' she whispered, smiling. The light from one of the closed windows escaped a bit into the dark tunnel.

I feel small. I shrink as I lie down next to you in bed. You pull me closer to you, and tingle my ears with a whisper. 'She accused my grandmother of witchcraft,' I tell you. 'She bagged our stuff and took us on an imaginary date with the singer Ragheb Alama after midnight.' I shiver. 'I feel that I'm still caught up in her fantasies,' I whisper to you. 'Maybe I'm insane. Maybe I'm imagining all of this while sitting in the corner of a dusty living room in Damascus, endlessly watching TV.'

You shush me, kissing my back, 'But does this feel real to you?' The kiss sends warm beats of music down my spine. 'That's exactly what a fake version of reality would say to me,' I whisper.

With little hesitation, Death pulls my mother's ghost from within his cloak. She appears among us. She sits down and asks me to tell her a story. 'Tell me my story, Hakawati,' she says, smiling. Next to her, a tree grows. It starts small, only asking for the littlest attention, then it grows bigger, wider, endless. On one of its branches, a clothesline swing slips, ready for her. She pushes the swing. I tell her a story.

I.

He gazes at her with questioning eyes. He sees her put her hand in her small bag, which she clutches with both hands near her chest. She pulls out a number of small bills, blue, red and yellow, and places them in a pile on the table in front of him, before she balances her thick glasses on her nose.

He places his hand on top of the money, fearing that the sea breeze might carry it away. In the shattered glass of his office table, he can see the old woman's reflection. Her thick glasses are projecting small white spots of sunlight onto the broken glass.

'This amount of money is only enough to rent the boat for an hour, maybe an hour and a half,' he says loudly, so she can hear him. 'You have to return to shore before your time is up!'

She nods her head in agreement and reaches for a small plastic bag on the ground, absent-mindedly rearranging her white hair back under the simple veil around her head.

He stands on the beach, watching anxiously as she drifts further away, heading toward a distant ship. He looks at his wristwatch and wonders how she convinced him to rent her the boat. He will charge her extra for the delay in returning the boat, he thinks. That calms his nerves a bit.

A cold wind blows and he gazes into the darkened horizon, seeing the lights of the ship glowing in the sunset. He doesn't notice, deep in the horizon, a tiny black cloud, spreading ambitiously, promising a coming storm.

II.

She hears the voices coming from the phone again. It's ringing in the back of her mind, and she has to pick up. Sometimes the voices promise her sweet escapes, other times they demand sacrifices. She goes into her son's bedroom, carrying a knife. The voices told her to cleanse his soul of the demons that live in his eyes.

'Don't touch me,' he says to her. 'Just stay away from me.'

He isn't her baby boy any more. He is taller, older, with longer hair and his beard unshaven for days. But she can't understand: why is he calling her crazy? Why does he refuse to allow her to take away his demons, to prevent him from falling into the land of nightmares when asleep? She has done nothing wrong; all she cares about is protecting him. She will make sure he does his homework and lives a happy life, and gets married to a woman who will tie his leg to the bed, preventing the land of nightmares from conquering his happy home, cleansing his soul of demons and devils.

The following morning haunts her for four years. She can't tell where to categorize it in her mind. She comes home to find a broken key in the lock. She knocks on the door repeatedly, but no one answers. She cries silent tears at first, followed by howls of pain that gather neighbours around her. He didn't even say goodbye.

Despite how unattached he becomes, she keeps following him around during his years at college. She appears out of nowhere at the doors of his university with a big inauthentic smile, carrying her small bag near her chest and balancing her thick glasses on her nose. Usually he leaves his friends to take her home without exchanging a word with her.

She has tried to talk to him on many of these trips, but he steps up his speed until she can only ask him to slow down so she can catch her breath and balance her thick glasses on her nose.

She follows him around until she figures out the location of the apartment he is renting. She waits until he is away and spends hours chit-chatting with his landlady. The two old women become friends and the landlady allows her to visit her son's apartment.

She enters the small apartment, comfortably knowing that she has time before he finishes school. She cleans it up, places flowers next to his bed, prints kisses on every page of his books and of course, to keep away the Monster of Shadows, she leaves a candle on his desk. She leaves.

She doesn't know about the fire until she tries to visit again two weeks later.

One night in October he tells her about his plans to immigrate to Canada. She asks him to start visiting her every night and to join her for dinner at her house. He smiles and explains that Canada is a faraway place, making it hard for him to visit her every day. She looks away in sorrow and she keeps her mouth shut.

He used to come and visit many times, she thinks, while he was in college. College is far from home as well! Why can't he do the same when he is in Canada?

On the day of his promised departure, she wakes up early, prepares him a big bag of food and heads directly to the harbour. There he hugs her one last time, kissing her three times on her shoulders and once on her forehead, asking her to take good care of herself. She places the bag of food in his arms. He smiles politely, apologizing that he can't take the food, informing her that travel regulations forbid him from carrying any food on the ship. She insists again and he finally agrees to carry the food.

From afar, she can see him entering the gate of the harbour, but before he does, he places the bag near a trashcan while he taps his many pockets searching for his passport. He doesn't look back, not even once, toward her or the bag, before disappearing inside the harbour building.

He must have forgotten about the bag, she thinks as she rushes toward the trashcan. She picks the bag up and runs as fast as she can toward the harbour gate, where she spends long minutes begging one of the guards to allow her in.

After failing to enter the harbour, she stands on the sand, holding the bag in her hand, gazing at the departing ship. Then she decides to do something.

III.

The morning after the storm, little Alice is playing in the cold, wet sand. She is investigating the small prizes thrown onto shore by the waves of the storm when she finds a pair of glasses; one of the lenses is shattered, while the other is thick, suitable for old people.

She puts them on and runs to her father with a big smile on her face. The father smiles, lifting the glasses off her eyes, and throws them back into the sea. The glasses shine for a second before drowning in the waves once more.

Years after we abandoned Damascus for Vancouver, my mother remained. Her roots were tangled within the land where they were planted. She sat in her living room, in a corner, watching TV. She went for walks. She waited for things to calm down again. Her hair was a nightly waterfall: it was decorated with grey meteors, slipping through her hair in the past years without permission. She dreamed every night that she was building towers that would take her higher than the war around her. Her hair grew longer and the people who remembered her grew smaller in number. One day she closed all the windows and doors in her house and was never seen again. The last anyone saw of her was when she threw the TV out the window onto the street, then closed the window for good.

That night, sands came upon Syria. A sandstorm unlike any other swamped everything in its way; many died in the first night, mostly fighters from all sides who were out in the open killing one another anyway. Citizens and officials alike seemed unable to find an explanation for the strange event. Many believed that it was the wrath of Allah for all of the bloodshed in the cities of Syria. The sandstorm intensified the next night, carrying Islamic State terrorists, who exploded in the air like fireworks. It also carried the regime's tanks and stopped the air force from shelling any cities. People begged the current immortal president for a solution, but he couldn't come up with anything. He told everyone to stay calm and trust his wise decision-making process. By the third night, many people left Syria, which had turned into a sandy desert. The farmers who would have kept it green were either killed or fighting. The president's people begged him to leave too, but he refused. He too closed all the windows of his castle, tightened all the doors, kept his fridge filled and stayed. The castle was covered with sand by the fourth night.

You whisper that love is what makes worlds real. 'I have no way to comfort you about your reality,' you tell me. In your world, sand never came, war never stopped and castles never drowned in quicksand.

'This is the real world,' you tell me, while Death holds his laughter.

'You're not going insane,' you say to me. I want to end all fights with a sandstorm. I smash into myself and I smash into you. In our bed, I kiss you and I whisper that I love you. We kiss. I hold you closer to my heart. 'I'm here with you,' I say. On our balcony, a jasmine flower opens, whispering an old tale of spring. In the heart of Damascus, the sand starts to give way to the jasmine flowers underneath it, growing stronger by the second. The spring flowers break the hot sand away, opening their blossoms up into white flowers. The branches keep some buildings locked up, while opening others, moving the sand away down the surprisingly strong stream of the Barada.

As we kiss, the hole breaking down our universe shrinks back slowly; the birds return, flocking back together into dark pieces of the universe. People, unaware of how broken they remain within, return to their daily races. Death, with a final wave, allows us our final moments together. 'It's almost time,' he murmurs as he exits the room. We're alone in our bedroom in Vancouver, lying in bed, looking into each other's eyes.

We kiss. I hide my tears. We kiss.

17

THE LISTENER'S TALE

You ask me to tell you a story. 'I will tell you a story,' I whisper, tears in my eyes, 'but all I ask of you is to suspend your disbelief.' You ask me how to start telling a fairy tale. I tell you that it just starts.

'How does it end?' you ask.

'No one knows how any story ends,' I explain. 'We only write the beginning.'

I tell you a story: the little mermaid wears shells upon her breasts, to hide the beauty of her sea-flowers from a sailor who hasn't dreamed of seeing such a wonder before. He asks her to let him kiss those unreachable flowers. He tries to lure the mythical creature with smiles of sadness in a face that knows nothing but tears. She denies him love. She rejects his adorations. She flips her tail, she escapes into the water, slipping back into the land of her grandfather the king, the lord of the Seven Seas. She saved the sailor. He will survive. The mermaid accepts her fate as a creature of the sea. She refuses to trade her voice for legs to walk freely on the land. The lovers sleep the night apart. The sea witch stays alive, haunting the dreams of the two lovers forever.

'Stop it,' you hush me, like a demanding sultan. 'This is the story of Beirut.' The Lebanese capital is a city of unavailability; it's a city of crushed dreams, broken promises and farewells. The city, a beautiful mermaid guarded by her warlords, waves a slow goodbye. She stands on the shore by the abandoned lighthouse. She stands among the university students sunbathing while war intensifies in the suburbs. The mermaid disappears and the people gather around her, watching; she is lost in the crowd. You ask me to retell the story. I whisper to myself, 'What difference would that make?'

In Beirut, we walked fearfully, as if we were stepping on the sharp edge of a knife. When we arrived, we were wide-eyed fools falling in love with a city we thought would welcome us. We took the téléphérique up the mountains of Jounieh to the temple of Harissa. We took photos right next to the statue of the Virgin Mary, and we asked her to protect us the same way she has protected the city for years before us. We felt the light breeze on our faces, standing on the edge of the mountain. I wanted to hold your hand but I couldn't, fearing the eyes of people around us.

But Mary had never been able to protect those who cared for her. The war has left its scars on the city, in buildings that remain standing despite the many bullet holes in their sides, and in the faces of people who cannot accept any more foreigners coming to add to their misery. You came home one day from work and found me crying my eyes out. 'What's wrong?' you said, as you rushed to my side. You sat by me and caressed my hair. 'Is everyone all right?'

I explained that I had seen a face on the news. The face of a Syrian man was haunting me. He was walking around Bourj Hammoud in downtown Beirut and was attacked by four men, who accused the refugee of sexually assaulting their sister. 'I don't know if he actually did it or not,' I whispered between my tears. They carried stones with them, and they smashed the side of his face repeatedly. His gruesome photo was spread across social media, and the comments on every page were praising the boys for protecting their sister's honour. 'He is a nobody. His murder will go unnoticed, his death will not be mentioned,' I told you. 'Worst of it all is that he looks just like me.'

In his shattered face, I could see my own: my large nose, my brown eyes and my brown hair. The beard I trimmed so carefully was replicated on his face; the little mole on the side of my cheek was planted on his as well. You held me closer and you insisted that I should leave the house.

We went clubbing that night with Maryam and Esme. Maryam had changed since last I saw her; her hair was longer, her eyes were shifty. She was visiting Beirut on one of her sudden appearances before she disappeared completely. Esme lived in Beirut, near Achrafieh, for a year or two before she found her way to Brazil. The four of us decided to go to B 018, the fanciest club in Beirut. It was extremely exclusive, but Esme worked her magic and got us inside. If you passed by the club, in the heart of Karantina, you wouldn't even know it was there. The door is located the middle of a parking lot, leading down a flight of stairs through a tunnel. The parking lot is large and empty, but the club is lively and full of beautiful people dancing to the beats of the best DJs in the world and drinking overpriced mixers.'Did you know,' Maryam told me as we stood outside, smoking a cigarette, 'why they call this area the Karantina?' She explained that it's the slang word for 'container'. 'When the Palestinian refugees took over the city, the government decided to bring them here and contain them in this area.' I looked around the empty neighbourhood. 'One day a massacre took place here during the Israeli invasion of Lebanon and all the Palestinians were killed,' she added, taking another puff of her cigarette. 'The government sold the area to the club owners, who turned it into the hottest spot in town.'

The club, with its black walls and seats shaped like coffins, was purposely designed to imitate a mass grave. Its stairs take you underground and leave your spirit strangled by the mashed faces of those who died here before. Then the music sets you free, breaking your chains from a humanity that never cared for your freedom. It was a joke made by the club's designer, wasted on a generation that refuses to remember its own past.

We walked back into the club, and I saw the ghosts of the dead dancing with us inside. Beautiful people wearing label clothes are laughing and drinking; they sway to the beats of the music, while the ghosts of past refugees are swaying with them and dancing to the beats of their dead hearts. Their faces are shattered; their bodies are dismembered.

'That city loved no one,' I tell you while we lie in bed. 'It loved people for so long before us, but as you get broken so many times by love, you harden, you become resilient to falling in love again,' you tell me. 'I wish you could have lived with me in the land of the living, away from your monsters and your demons.' You hold my arm.

You plant your face into my chest. Your pulse is weak, your breath is shallow and your eyes are dancing around a final dance. Stay with me, I beg of you, I will tell you more stories, I will keep you among the living.

I tell you a story: the little mermaid wears shells upon her breasts, to hide the beauty of her sea-flowers from a sailor who hasn't dreamed of seeing such a wonder before. The sailor ignores the mermaid. He thinks she is a dream whispering sinful thoughts into his mind. He abandons the quest for her love; the mermaid was just the dream of a man walking along the beach next to a sea that he loves without knowing why he loves it so much. The sailor gives up on life upon the waves; he returns to his car and drives home.

On his way home, his life streams in front of him on the silver glass of his windshield. Boring, lonely and loveless, he feels broken within, unaware of how to reach a safe shore. Slowly, the rain covers the glass until nothing can be seen. The only reflection is the beauty of the mermaid, who followed the sailor back to the car. She is hiding in the back seat. Through the front mirror, he takes a look back at her, beautiful, magnificent and unbelievable to see in his back seat. The lights of the street glow upon her and she shines like a creature of light. She attempts to communicate with the sailor using gestures and signs; she gave up her voice to a heartless sea witch. The sailor whistles a song of love and lust. He doesn't know that the words he sings are also words of blue lovers and broken dreams. The sailor sings songs about the rain, about the life that awaits the mermaid on the face of the earth.

Mud, clay and dirt can be seen through the windows of the car; they break the mermaid's heart. The tear streams left behind by rain on the window make her miss home. She doesn't want to sit idly awaiting a lover on a rock by the shore, singing songs of warmth for the mud of a cold world. She wants to return to the sea and wait for yet another wave that will wash away her old shells.

The mermaid, then, will wear new shells upon her breasts, to hide the beauty of her sea-flowers from a sailor who hasn't dreamed of seeing such a wonder before.

'This is a story I do not like.' You wave your hands. Death, standing outside the door, peeks in to see what all the fuss is about. He returns outside, respecting the private moment. 'This is not the end of our story,' you whisper, holding my hand. 'Leave Cairo alone.' The mermaid chants songs of loneliness and abandonment in the streets of Cairo. People wearing black and green grab her; she disappears into the unknown. History repeats itself endlessly in Cairo, the heartbreaks return anew. The pain is in knowing what will happen to a city older that its own memories, watching history unfold as the people within the city scream at one another.

In the January 2011 revolution, Egypt tried to change its own story. It abandoned its endless cycles around a circular path determined by the gods that ruled it; it wanted a new path. I left the city, but it didn't leave me. It came with me to Damascus as I sneaked onto websites, away from the eyes of the dykes in my home, to read its news.

People walked in the streets and carried flags. They prayed on the Qasr al-Nil Bridge leading to Tahrir Square, while government goons sprayed them with high-pressure water and tear gas. Santa Claus, with his big belly and his heavy boots, marched with the protesters. He walked screaming, demanding fair jobs, bread and social equity. He had a fight with one of the soldiers and pushed him back. 'This is my land, my right of living,' he said, and the soldier lifted his gun in Santa's face and shot him. Santa Claus lost his left eye that day. He woke up in the hospital, surrounded by white walls and nurses. It took him a moment to realize where he was, and another moment to realize that he could only see with one eye, as he struggled to search his body for injuries.

Fady came to terms with his sexuality. He fell in love with an Italian man who was visiting Egypt at the time. When the revolution happened, they fled the country together. The humanitarian organization the Italian man worked for had an evacuation plan, and Fady was the Italian's plus-one. He ended up living in Rome for many years, until he and his partner returned to Egypt and lived there until the end of their days.

The protests continued, and the king was replaced with another, then another, then another, until the end of time.

Cairo feels like a mermaid who gave up her voice for the sake of useless legs. Her choices define her. They make her who she really is. There is no erasing the past, only hiding it away. The dirt is close, always swept under the rug. My choices haunt me; they drag me to a hell far away from your arms. You bring me back.

'All I ever wished for was to know you completely,' I tell you.

'I was always whatever you needed me to be,' you respond.

You saw my pain, and you couldn't describe it. You stood by my side and protected me from my own demons. Without you I unfold, I smash on the shores of my fantasies. I snatch you out of another moment of dying light. You ask me to stop singing songs of pain and sorrow. I ask you if I can retell my tale. You take a moment of silence. 'I wish you wouldn't ask me to tell stories any more,' I tell you.

'You'd have stopped telling them if you didn't want to hear what you would say,' you respond.

I tell you a story: the little mermaid wears shells upon her breasts, to hide the beauty of her sea-flowers from a sailor who hasn't dreamed of seeing such a wonder before. The sailor approaches her; she sees him from afar. She is frightened. He shows her his hands, filled with golden toys and singing birds. She smiles to him. Her hair – blue and long like a summer day – looks like the leaves of river trees our sailor cannot name. Her eyes – carrying the blueness of waves – tear with seawater at all times. She grabs the toys from his fingers fearfully.

Alas, the moment her smile breaks into laughter, her father, King Marduk of the Seven Seas, appears carrying a large trident and three swords; he is riding a magnificent cart pulled by six dolphins. It's rumoured to be a gift from his brother, the Mesopotamian god Ashur, and made from the same tree as Ashur's war cart. The sailor tries to fight as the tsunami hits him. He fails. It breaks his blue dreams of resting within the mermaid's hair. The sailor drowns in the waters of Marduk, the vengeful god. The sailor's hands are frozen in his final gesture, reflecting his wonderment.

'Stop it,' you demand, like a child. 'This is Damascus, the city that disappointed you.' Damascus is a mermaid child with blue hair and red eyes; she cries tears of salt. The girl drowns in the depth of an endless sea. We attempted to save her so many times, only to find her lost body in the waves of the red sea. Like the father of a child lost to the sea, you stood all these years on the shores of Damascus, calling her name.

You speak to your beloved city like a lost child you loved too much. Like a father dropping chocolates into the ocean for his dead child, you drop memories of love and devotion for the city that cradled you. You don't want to forget her, facing the waves of Marduk, the god of the sea, as he floods away the city that slept between the mountains.

You tell me that, like the sailor, you realize the importance of love. You cry for the mermaid like a daughter of yours; you imagine her a woman. You take a seat by the millions of refugees, drinking Arabian coffee together in the café of the forgotten, and complain about the tireless waves of the endless sea. You throw a message in a bottle for her and the sea brings it back to you. The girl with the blue hair stands on the shore of the Mediterranean Sea; her feet are wet, sand sticks to them. She waves to you a sweet goodbye.

You overpower your demons, and you hush your own cries. You have accepted that you will never see your beloved city again. You look at me. You touch my face, and you whisper, 'Have I got a story for you.'

I look at you; darkness is hitting the side of your face, slipping slowly to your eyes. You smile, and your beard, white and shaggy, shines with your teeth. I'm surprised. I lean toward you, and I listen.

'The earliest memory I have,' you tell me, 'I remember I was sitting on the last step of my family's house in Damascus.' You sat there, waiting for your father to return carrying fruits and desserts, when you noticed a little boy kicking a stone away as he walked by you. You felt a strange connection to the boy, and you followed him with your eyes.

You walked up to him, and you asked him if he wanted to play with you. He looked at you and without hesitation accepted your invitation. 'He just wanted to connect, to play,' you whisper. 'We jumped rope together, we played dahal and we laughed endlessly.' You felt that by making him laugh, you would make his day better. You might have not changed his life forever, but you gave his soul a little more room to breathe.

His mother – young, beautiful, with black hair that slipped onto her shoulders – saw the two of you from afar. She rushed toward you, pulled a small camera from her bag and took a quick photo.

With tears in my eyes, I remember a photo burning on the balcony of that dark house, a photo of two boys jumping rope, laughing with open hearts. We stretch across time, from the day we jumped rope together, to the day you lie in my bed with an open heart and a departing soul. I pull you closer; I print a kiss on your lips. I whisper a final 'I love you.'

You smile. 'I know you do,' you whisper. Your voice is pure, like the first drop of rain. You take a final breath. You close your eyes. You sleep.

ACKNOWLEDGEMENTS

First and foremost, I would like to thank Dara Parker for her guidance throughout the past two years. You have been a wonderful mentor, a great support and a loving friend since the day I met you, and I wouldn't be publishing this book if it wasn't for your friendship and mentorship.

A huge thank you to Silas White for believing in me from the very first minute he met me. Thank you, Silas, for taking the time to read this book, and for trusting me to keep my material true to how I wrote it, and opening the door for me to become a published author here in Canada.

Endless appreciation to Nicola Goshulak, who embodies everything a writer needs in an editor. I felt how much love you placed into this book, and I saw your commitment to it. I'm thankful for the hours you spent supporting me, and guiding my writing, and helping me crystallize my ideas. I'm a better writer because of you.

Thank you to Amber McMillan and everyone else at Nightwood Editions and Harbour Publishing for the hard work they put into this book. I felt supported, appreciated and welcomed into your world, and I'm thankful for your dedication.

I would also like to thank Chris Morrissey, David Salter and Kevin Bougher, among my other Canadian friends. These people put a lot of effort and love into guaranteeing my safety and my stability on the journey from being a Syrian refugee in Lebanon to being a published author in Vancouver. Thank you to my fellow author Tash McAdam and my trusted critic Rob Easton. You were my first readers and my reliable friends – I appreciate your input and I celebrate this book with you.

Finally, I come from Syria, a nation of storytellers. I'm surrounded by folks who shared with me so much of their happiness and sorrow, and for that, I'm thankful. I'm forever in debt to all of my friends: Rawan, Cyril, Jiana, Riham, Abd Nova, Dania, Masa, Zdravko and David Munir among others. You poured your stories in my ears and filled me up with so many lived experiences that I mixed, wove and cultivated into this book. This is your story as much as it is mine.

ABOUT THE AUTHOR

Ahmad Danny Ramadan is a Syrian-Canadian author, public speaker, storyteller and an LGBTQ-refugee activist. His debut English-language novel, *The Clothesline Swing*, was published to acclaim in Canada in 2017. It won the Independent Publisher Gold Medal for LGBT Fiction and was shortlisted for the 2018 Lambda Award for Gay Fiction, among numerous other accolades.